SARAH BENNETT has been reading for as long as she can remember. Raised in a family of bookworms, her love affair with books of all genres has culminated in the ultimate Happy Ever After: getting to write her own stories to share with others.

Born and raised in a military family, she is happily married to her own Officer (who is sometimes even A Gentleman). Home is wherever he lays his hat, and life has taught them both that the best family is the one you create from friends as well as relatives.

When not reading or writing, Sarah is a devotee of afternoon naps and sailing the high seas, but only on vessels large enough to accommodate a casino and a choice of restaurants.

You can connect with her via twitter @Sarahlou_writes or on Facebook www.facebook.com/SarahBennettAuthor

Also by Sarah Bennett

The Butterfly Cove Series

Sunrise at Butterfly Cove
Wedding Bells at Butterfly Cove
Christmas at Butterfly Cove

The Lavender Bay Series

Spring at Lavender Bay
Summer at Lavender Bay
Snowflakes at Lavender Bay

Snowflakes at Lavender Bay

SARAH BENNETT

ONE PLACE. MANY STORIES

HQ
An imprint of HarperCollins*Publishers* Ltd
1 London Bridge Street
London SE1 9GF

This edition 2019

First published in Great Britain by
HQ, an imprint of HarperCollins*Publishers* Ltd 2018

ISBN: PB: 978-0-00-832107-9
EB: 978-0-00-828134-2

MIX
Paper from
responsible sources
FSC
www.fsc.org **FSC® C007454**

Typeset by Palimpsest Book Production Ltd, Falkirk, Stirlingshire
Printed and bound in Great Britain by
CPI Group (UK) Ltd, Melksham, SN12 6TR"

This one is for my Aunty Andrea, with fondest love x

Chapter 1

Owen Coburn stared at the bottles lined in neat rows on the mirrored shelves opposite him. He'd never been one to drown his sorrows, but the collection of single malts seemed to whisper a lullaby more seductive than the songs of the mythical siren which the seafront pub had been named after. With more effort than it should've taken, he wrenched his eyes from the array of spirits and studied the rest of the busy bar as he waited to be served. Like his bedroom upstairs, the place was spotlessly clean, if a little worn in places.

Black-and-white photographs studded the pale-blue walls, showing scenes of Lavender Bay from times gone past. Ladies in white dresses clutching parasols in one hand, the fingers of the other tucked into the arms of besuited gentlemen as they strolled the promenade. Fishermen sorting their nets in the old harbour, faces leathered from years of exposure to sea and sun.

On the side of the wooden upright beside him a ragged line of young men dressed in their Sunday best beamed out of the past, their expressions a mixture of shy pride and cocky confidence. With their hair neatly slicked and battered suitcases at their feet, not one of them looked older than he was now. Owen wondered if any of them had understood what awaited them on the bloody fields of Europe and how many—if any—had returned. Faint writing at the bottom of the photo caught his eye. Hating the need inside him, Owen scanned the cramped squiggles on the photo. No Blackmores among them.

With a snort of disgust at himself, he turned away. What the hell was he doing chasing shadows? According to the piece of paper burning a hole in his pocket, Deborah Mary Blackmore had been 17 when she'd given up her son for adoption. She'd listed Lavender Bay as her place of birth, but extensive searches had yielded no trace of her. Either his mother was a ghost, or she'd lied about her name.

Requesting his original birth certificate had seemed like a good way of setting the final pieces of his past to rest. After a childhood in care where the kindest thing anyone had ever done was ignore him, compartmentalisation had become his daily survival technique—what hadn't killed him didn't make him stronger so much as it got stuffed in a mental box and shoved to the furthest reaches of conscious memory. As a result, he'd managed to convince himself that delving into his origins could be an exercise in intellectual curiosity, nothing more.

Unprepared for it, the emotional tsunami caused by the arrival of the innocuous brown envelope had swept him so far off course he wasn't sure who he was anymore. With the words 'father unknown' thwarting half of his search before he could even get started, finding Deborah had become a near-obsession. He'd joined every online genealogy website he could find, and spent hours trawling through scanned images covered in spidery writing to no avail. After those efforts came up blank, he'd switched his focus to the whimsically named Lavender Bay. If he couldn't find his mother, perhaps he could forge a connection with her birthplace instead. And, as the owner of his own building and property development company, if he could turn a profit in the process, so much the better.

When he'd boarded the train from London the previous

morning he'd been full of foolish optimism. Walter Symonds, a local solicitor Owen had been cultivating a relationship with for the previous six months, had called to give him the heads-up on a potential property. Located directly on the seafront at Lavender Bay, it had looked ripe for development from what he'd been able to tell via Google Maps. The previous owner had died, leaving everything to a young woman who, from what Owen had been able to tell, had moved away from the area some years before. Hoping to jump the queue, he'd taken the unusual step of visiting in person to extend an offer to buy.

Expecting her to be grateful for an excuse to offload the place, Owen had been disappointed to find her well ensconced behind the counter of the emporium with zero interest in selling the place. An afternoon touring the local estate agents as well as a good recce on foot had yielded nothing in the way of other empty or struggling properties. In a last-gasp attempt to find any sign of the Blackmore family, he'd spent the past couple of hours tromping around the local churchyards and come back to the pub with nothing to show for his efforts other than a nasty nettle sting on his arm. In other words, his entire weekend was a total bloody bust. Time to put this foolishness behind him—he'd managed thirty years without any family to speak of, he'd manage the next thirty just fine.

'Pint, lovey?'

Startled, Owen blinked at the smiling older woman on the other side of the bar. 'What? Oh, yes. Lager, please, Mrs Barnes.'

'Right you are. How's your room, have you got everything you need?' *Oh great, she was the chatty sort.*

'Yes, it's fine thanks.' In so far as it had a bed and a kettle. Egyptian cotton and designer coffee machines hadn't made it to Lavender Bay, that much had been clear from the moment he'd set foot in The Siren the previous day. Not that it mattered, now he wasn't staying. 'What's the earliest I can check out in the morning?'

3

Mrs Barnes placed his drink before him with a wry laugh. 'I'll try not to take offence at your eagerness to leave. You can settle your bill before you turn in tonight and then you're free to leave as early as you like. You'll be wanting some breakfast before you go, though, surely?'

Owen shook his head. 'Not the time I'm planning on leaving.' He pulled a card out of his wallet, then hesitated. 'Do you need cash?'

Her laughter shook her whole body. 'Oh, you city folks! The magic of contactless payment has made it as far as the south coast, I assure you.' She produced a card reader from beneath the bar. 'Tap away, dear.'

Valiantly fighting a blush, Owen moved his card towards the machine, then hesitated. 'Can I buy you a drink by way of an apology?'

'That's sweet of you, and I'll take a glass of red for later, but not because you owe me an apology. You're not the first to assume we're a bit behind the times here, and you won't be the last.'

Owen watched her tap the keypad a couple of times before offering him the machine once more. Mrs Barnes might not have taken offence over his assumption, but he was annoyed with himself. He'd had enough of people passing judgement when he was younger, and had always thought himself better than that. Being in the bay had thrown him off his stride far more than he could've imagined. Just as well he was going to cut his losses and head back home.

'Didn't you come down on the train?'

Placing his card on the screen, Owen felt a sinking sensation in his gut at the question. 'Yeah, what of it?'

Mrs Barnes gave him the kind of pitying smile that did nothing to ease his increasing bad mood. 'Well if you're hoping for a swift getaway in the morning, I'm afraid you're out of luck. The first train on a Sunday isn't until 9.30—proof we're behind the times on some things, I suppose!'

Bloody marvellous. 'Well in that case, looks like I will be staying for breakfast, after all.' As he was stuck there, he might as well make the best of it. A thought occurred to him. 'Have you lived in Lavender Bay all your life, Mrs Barnes?'

'Please, dear, call me Annie. And in answer to your question, I'm born and bred here, though compared to my husband's family, we're newcomers to the bay. There's been a Barnes behind the bar of The Siren since before Nelson lost his eye, as Pops would say.'

'Pops?'

The smile on Annie's face was full of warmth, with just a touch of wry exasperation. 'My father-in-law. He used to run this place—and interferes often enough for anyone to think he still does.' That warm expression slid into something more considering. 'Is there a reason for you asking?'

Kicking himself for letting his guard down, Owen gave her his best smile. 'Not at all, Annie, just making conversation.'

A raised eyebrow told him she wasn't taken in by his glib response, but she didn't push, thank goodness. 'Of course, dear. Well, I'd better get on. Enjoy the rest of your evening.'

Not filled with any expectation of finding much enjoyment, Owen cast a quick glance around the bar. A few families; a handful of old men playing dominoes; a gaggle of teenagers who, in spite of the thickness of their eyeliner and the shortness of their skirts, barely looked old enough to be drinking the cider they were giggling over.

A couple of the girls caught him staring, and he cursed himself as they nudged each other. Owen turned swiftly back towards the bar, hoping he hadn't drawn their attention. He wasn't ignorant to the way he looked, and the last thing he wanted was to spend the evening fending off the clumsy flirtations of girls using him as target practice. Perhaps an early night might be better after all.

Shoulders braced, he waited with dread for the clip-clop of

high heels on the wooden floor behind him, but when he heard nothing he began to relax. Perhaps the girls had decided not to try and tangle with him. Shaking his head at his own arrogance, Owen took a mouthful of his pint—perhaps they weren't remotely interested in a bloke a dozen or more years older than them. He'd just convinced himself the coast was clear when the hairs on his arm prickled and he felt the presence of someone at his elbow.

'Even if I didn't know everyone who lives in Lavender Bay, I'd know you're not from around here.' The slightly husky voice carried the soft burr of the local accent.

Owen didn't look around. He supposed she meant it as a compliment, but the reminder of his outsider status rankled. Nothing had worked out liked he'd expected it to, but wasn't that the story of his bloody life? It was ridiculous, really, to have supposed he would feel any connection to a place he'd never heard of even six months ago, but the barb struck, bringing a sharper edge to his tongue than he might otherwise have intended. 'The lack of webbed fingers gives it away, no doubt.'

'And the lack of manners. Wow, Beth wasn't kidding about you.'

It was her scathing tone as much as the mention of an unfamiliar name that caused Owen to turn. Expecting to see a giggling teen tottering on a pair of heels, he found himself instead staring down into a pair of bright blue eyes half-hidden by a shock of luridly dyed fringe. A snub of a nose—as though whoever had conjured her had left it unformed with the intention of returning to it later—sat between that vivid stare and a bow-shaped mouth plastered in scarlet lip gloss. A chin bold enough to be labelled stubborn finished off her heart-shaped face.

As if she'd used up every available colour between her hair, eyes and mouth, the rest of her tiny frame was shrouded from neck to toe in unrelenting black. Even the fingernails tipping the slender hand braced against the bar were coated in a glossy black polish. She looked otherworldly, like some pixie, or sprite hellbent on causing mayhem. Attraction punched him in the gut—raw, visceral and entirely unexpected. She was nothing like the women he normally dated. Too small, too scruffy, too *individual*. Owen never made a move without knowing exactly what the end outcome would be. Her impish smile told him all bets would be off if he took her into his bed.

Bed. Just thinking the word sent a kaleidoscope of images through his head and all the blood rushing to his groin. Too busy trying not to do something stupid like throw her over his shoulder and march her up the stairs to his room, Owen's brain lost control of his jaw muscles and allowed it to sag open in disbelief.

The pale skin around her piercing azure gaze tightened. 'What are you staring at?'

'I…I have no idea.' His brain still hadn't caught up, apparently, because there could be no other explanation for allowing those words to escape from his lips. Scarlet stained her pale cheeks, creeping down her throat to disappear beneath the black material of her shirt. His eyes followed the blush as he wondered just how far down it went.

The sharp snap of her fingers mere inches from his nose startled his gaze back to her face. A fierce scowl twisted her rosebud mouth into an ugly pucker. 'What the hell is that supposed to mean?' Shoulders suddenly drooping, she folded her arms across her chest and curled into herself as she turned away. 'I should've listened to Beth; you really are a colossal arse,' she muttered more to herself than him.

Damn, somehow he'd managed to offend her. A panicked feeling rose in his chest; he couldn't let her slip through his fingers. He cast around for something to say. 'You keep mentioning this Beth like I should know who you're talking about.'

Keeping her eyes averted, the pixie gestured with a flick of her fingers to where a pretty brunette cuddled close against the side of a man he recognised. Sam was Mrs Barnes' son and had served him at breakfast that morning, had even gone to the local shop to fetch the papers when he'd requested them. And the woman next to him... '*Ah*'.

He hadn't known her first name, but Beth was the owner of the shop next door who had turned down his offer to buy the place. She'd also turned him down when he'd tried to suggest they negotiate over a drink, which had irked him at the time. With long brown hair curling over the shoulders of a navy Fifties-style tea dress, the well-turned-out woman was much more his usual type.

His eyes strayed to Beth once more but found little to hold his attention compared to his little sprite. He slid a couple of inches closer then leaned against the bar to be sure he was in her eyeline. 'I thought I'd been very charming in my dealings with your friend.'

The pixie sniffed. 'You wouldn't know charming if it bit you on the arse.' She turned her attention to Mrs Barnes as she moved towards them. 'Can I get a bottle of champagne and a couple of glasses for me and Beth please, Annie? We're celebrating her inheriting the emporium.'

Owen suppressed a grin as he watched the pixie try her best to ignore him while she chatted with Mrs Barnes as she served her. She might be only a slip of a thing, but she seemed to contain enough energy for a woman twice her size. If he held his hands towards her, he'd expect to see a current arcing from her towards his fingers, like one of those plasma energy balls. Though she did her best to pretend she was ignoring him, he couldn't miss the way her eyes flicked in his direction every few seconds. This might get interesting, after all.

He let his gaze trace the pixie from the tips of her black boots to the peacock shock of her hair before leaning into her space a touch closer than was strictly polite. 'You were wrong in what you said about arse-biting, you know. I've always found it *very* charming.' That bright red flush mottled her cheeks once more, and he wondered if he'd miscalculated. It had been a harmless bit of flirtation, something that came as easily to him as breathing. Her bold appearance and brash words had given the impression of an experienced woman. The blush told a different story, however.

Clutching the ice bucket holding her bottle of champagne like a shield before her, she started to edge past him before stopping to stare up at him through her thickly mascaraed lashes. 'What did you want with the emporium anyway? I hope you weren't planning to sling up a load of ugly apartments like they did at the other end of the prom. They're a dreadful eyesore, and not the kind of thing we need around here at all.'

The disdain in her tone shattered any sympathy he might have been harbouring towards her—and any other kind of feelings for that matter. The fact she'd hit the nail on the head about the kind of project he was interested in didn't help either. Owen bristled. 'Those flats bring a much-needed touch of class to the prom. People want more than donkey rides and kiss-me-quick hats, these days. This place is dying on its feet. You should be grateful anyone wants to invest in a provincial little backwater like Lavender Bay!'

Shock widened her azure eyes, and in their depths he read a deeper emotion, almost like pain. Expecting her to lash back, he squared his shoulders in preparation. When she spoke, instead of sharp and spikey, her voice was soft and full of disappointment. 'I was right, you're definitely not from around here.' With a shake of her head, the pixie walked across the bar and out of his life.

If she'd slid a knife up under his ribs, she couldn't have scored a more fatal blow. Turning his back, Owen gripped the edge of the bar as her words ricocheted around his brain. *Not from around here.* Myriad insults and accusations from the past swelled up to join them, forming a tortuous chorus. *Bad blood will out. Rotten little bastard. No wonder your mother dumped you. Get back to where you belong.* That last one was ironic to the extreme because Owen didn't belong anywhere. Not in any of the foster homes he'd passed through, and most definitely not in this one-horse excuse for a town.

Bile burned the back of his throat and he swallowed it down with the last dregs of his pint. It was just as well the deal to buy the emporium had gone nowhere. Whatever he'd thought he was doing coming down here—looking for his bloody roots or some such bollocks—it had been a mistake. The only person he had ever been able to rely on was himself and he had the bitter experience to prove it.

Having slammed his empty glass down, Owen marched from the bar. Sod Lavender Bay, and sod big-mouthed pixies who didn't know a good thing when they saw it. The sooner he got away from this godforsaken little town, the better.

Chapter 2

A few weeks after his impulsive visit to Butterfly Cove, Owen was finally starting to feel back on track. Things were running smoothly at CCC—Coburn Construction Contractors—the company he'd built from the ground up. Who needed a grotty old shop in some old-fashioned seaside town when he could be inches away from a securing a client that could propel the business to the next level? After eighteen months of submitting unsuccessful bids to them, one of London's most prestigious property developers was seriously considering CCC for part of their overall conversion package for a huge disused warehouse area. If Owen could get a foot in the door with Taylors, he'd be made for life.

Feeling pretty bloody pleased with himself, he decided an early celebration was on the cards and put in a call to Claire, a woman he'd been seeing. They'd been out for drinks a couple of times and now seemed like the perfect time to up the ante with a date at Fabiano's, one of the most exclusive restaurants in his local area. Taylors wasn't the only deal he was hoping to secure that night.

Placing a hand on Claire's back a few inches below the end of the glossy blonde mane flowing over her shoulders, Owen steered her through the front door. As a server helped his date out of her jacket, Owen let himself appreciate the way her neutral-toned designer dress clung to every curve. Owen wasn't on top of the latest female fashion trends, but he knew quality when he saw it. The logo on the handbag hanging from her arm was large enough to be seen from space. *Good for her*. If you've got it, sweetheart, flaunt it.

A couple waiting at the bar for a table turned at their entrance, the man's eyes lingering on Claire for a few more seconds than was strictly polite. To Owen's satisfaction, Claire made a point of slipping her free arm through his as she leaned into him, making it clear who she was with. There was no hiding the little smile on her face, though, but that was all right. There was nothing wrong with a woman enjoying being admired; if he hadn't already been with her, Owen would've taken a second glance himself.

'You have a reservation, *signore*?' The maître d' asked.

'Coburn. Eight o'clock. I believe you have a corner booth for us?' Owen slipped the man a tip large enough to make his eyes gleam.

'Most certainly, let me escort you to your seats.'

They'd just got settled when Owen's phone vibrated in his pocket. Alex, his second-in-command at CCC had promised to let him know the moment they heard anything from Taylors. Owen glanced across the table to where the maître d' had been replaced by a waiter who was fussing and fluttering over Claire. Figuring he had a couple of minutes' grace, he slipped out his phone and opened his emails.

'Owen? *Owen*?'

'Hmm? Whatever you want to order is fine with me.' He glanced up from the email response he was hesitating over and caught Claire's exasperated glare. His fingers clenched around the phone. Contrary to his expectations, the news from Taylors wasn't good. Far from offering to sign on the dotted line, they were demanding a fifteen per cent reduction on a contract already pared down to the bone. Swallowing down his frustration, Owen gave his companion his most winning smile. 'I'm being rude. Forgive me?'

The ice around her eyes melted a fraction. 'You've not heard a word I've said, have you?' He stared across the corner booth at his dinner date. The perfectly made-up face he'd first admired at a local networking event was currently twisted into a disappointed pout. Owen bit back a sigh. One of the things he'd found attractive about her was that she ran her own business and would therefore—he'd assumed—understand his erratic schedule. Apparently not.

Eyes on the prize, mate. Reaching over, Owen took one of her hands and raised it to his lips in a calculated gesture he'd melted many a frosty heart with in the past. 'I'm sorry, Claire. I just need a couple of minutes to resolve a work problem, and then you'll have my undivided attention, I promise.'

As expected, her pout transformed into a delighted smile. Nails lacquered in the same café au lait shade as her lipstick dug briefly into his palm as she squeezed his hand. 'Don't mind me, I've just been looking forward to this evening ever since you told me you'd booked us a table here.'

Booking Fabiano's gave the right message to a woman like Claire who valued symbols and linked them to her own sense of self. She'd worked hard for those rewards, and he understood the desire to control perceptions and project the right kind of image. As a child, he'd been powerless to do so, and been judged by people who couldn't see past hand-me-downs and bargain basement rubbish. Those days were gone now, and he wouldn't stint himself, or anyone he spent time with. 'Why don't you order us some champagne, while I finish this up?'

Eyes sparkling, Claire waved their waiter over. Owen let her grand production of perusing the wine list amuse him for a moment before turning back to his phone. He'd done enough to seal one deal for the evening, time to put the other one to bed, so to speak. Thumbs poised over the automatic keyboard on his phone, he considered the best way to phrase his response. Taylors had enough money to buy Owen a thousand times over and still wanted to bleed him dry. The fifteen per cent they were demanding would mean less than nothing to a business as large as them, but would cover decent year-end bonuses for Owen's staff or help to replace a couple of their older company vans. And what if all the other companies he was hoping to attract through this new contract were just as tight? Kudos wouldn't pay the bills.

What was he doing risking the company he'd built from scratch? Was his ego so bloody fragile he'd throw away everything he'd worked so hard to build for the chance to link his name to people who wouldn't give him the time of day if they knew his back-ground? There were better jobs to chase than Taylors. Jobs which would bring a decent profit margin and be a damn sight less stressful for all concerned.

Mind made up, Owen tapped a quick reply. *Tell them, thanks but no thanks. We've offered a damned good package and if they can't see that there are plenty of others who will. Send the email then GO HOME! Debrief at 8 a.m.*

The waiter returned just as he was putting his phone away. 'Your champagne, sir. An excellent vintage, and if I may suggest the perfect accompaniment to the chef's dish of the day. The salmon is truly exquisite.'

Owen's eyes travelled from the distinctive shield-shaped label on the bottle to the slight smirk on the waiter's face. He might well look pleased with himself considering Claire had ordered the most expensive offering on the menu. The commission on a bottle like that would be a nice boost in the waiter's pocket. Well, it served Owen right for being an arse and ignoring her, he supposed. Some days, being the boss sucked, but he'd take the hit to his wallet. 'Ladies first.' He gestured the waiter towards Claire and watched her simper and fuss over tasting the straw-coloured wine like she knew the difference between a two-hundred-pound bottle of Dom Perignon and a supermarket prosecco. The champagne matched her hair, nails and dress to perfection. *Fifty shades of beige.*

Out of nowhere, the image of the black-clad, wild-haired pixie from Lavender Bay popped into his head. He bet she'd never set foot in a place like Fabiano's, and likely wouldn't give two hoots about it. No sexy high heels and skin-tight dresses for her. He couldn't imagine her sulking over his need to deal with a work problem if they'd been out on a date. She'd have either understood and let it go or turned on her heel and walked away. A wry grin teased the corner of his mouth. She'd already done the second, so a date with her was never going to get beyond the hypothetical. Not that she was his type.

Resting his chin on the tips of his fingers, Owen studied the woman opposite him. He could admit to a grudging admiration for the audacity she'd shown in ordering the top-priced champagne the waiter was currently pouring with a flourish. It was all just business at the end of the day. Owen had let his guard down and she'd taken advantage. Score one for Claire. It was what people did. What she hadn't realised yet, was that he would only let someone get away with it once.

His gaze roamed around the room, more than half a mind still on the pretty, spiky girl who'd marched away from him clutching an ice bucket. She'd bought champagne that night, too, and likely enjoyed it as much if not more because her eyes hadn't watered at the cost of it. The sleek lines and discreet lighting of Fabiano's were a world away from the cosy, slightly shabby taproom at The Siren, and a deep desire to be standing at the bar with Mrs Barnes smiling up at him filled his heart. A bone-deep weariness crept over him as the disappointment over the failed Taylors deal struck home. Whilst he didn't regret saying no, there was still a big hole in their projected work schedule which needed to be filled. He should be at home with a takeaway, a cold beer and his laptop, not trying to prove his success by being seen at the right place with the right kind of woman.

Owen gave himself a shake. This was why digging around in the past had been a bad idea. He wasn't one for self-doubt and deep introspection. He'd built this life for himself, and it was a damn good one. A night off with a beautiful woman would do him good. *All work and no play makes Owen a dull boy, and all that.* Accepting a crystal flute from the waiter, he raised it in toast to Claire. 'What shall we drink to?'

Mirroring his pose, she fluttered her eyelashes. 'How about to the future?'

'Perfect.' Owen drained the sparkling liquid from his glass and tried to ignore the ping of his phone. Claire's mouth tightened as he reached for it. With a swipe of his thumb he turned it off then tucked it in the inside pocket of his jacket. Work could wait for a couple of hours. He'd been the one to suggest their date, the least he could do was give her a nice evening. Reaching across the table, he took her hand. 'I'm all yours. Why don't you tell me what you've been up to lately?'

The rest of the evening went well. Once she'd got over her initial mood, Claire proved to be as interesting and knowledgeable as he'd originally hoped. Beneath the labels and the perfect spray tan sat a sharp mind and a level of ambition to match his own. As they lingered over coffee, the spectre of the lost deal with Taylors came back to haunt him. Regardless of his gut instinct that turning down the deal was the right thing to do, he hated losing something he'd worked so hard for.

Fingers touched his. 'Earth to Owen.'

Shaking his head, he pushed his work worries to one side and offered Claire a smile. 'Let's get out of here, shall we?'

Her lashes flicked down then up. 'I'd like that.'

The taxi stopped outside a neat block of flats and he ducked his head to study them through the window. Not the best part of the area, but by no means the worst and he knew the local council were working with investors on several regeneration projects. Give it a few more years and the place would be worth considerably more than current market value.

'Are you coming up for coffee?' Ah. The universal code for extending the evening. On autopilot, he paid the cab fare and slid out after Claire. As she fumbled around in her oversized handbag, an image of the two of them a few years down the line formed in his mind. They were sitting at a long dining table in an immaculate flat full of chrome and granite and all the latest gadgets. To his left and right sat two rows of shiny, well-to-do couples in grey suits and neutral body-con dresses chattering about their latest holidays to somewhere exotic. The right place, the right wife, the right friends, it was exactly the kind of thing he'd dreamed of as a kid scuffing along streets like this in a too-thin coat picked up from the local charity shop for a couple of quid. Now, though, it seemed cold and lifeless, more nightmare than fantasy. A shudder rippled down his spine and he took a step backwards.

'There it is!' Claire gave a little laugh of relief as she slid the errant key into the lock and pushed open the door. She'd made it a couple of steps inside before she realised he'd made no move to follow. 'Owen?'

His feet were glued to the pavement. His future was right there in front of him, but all he wanted to do was run. 'I'm sorry, but you'll have to excuse me, Claire. I've got a bit of a headache, so I'm going to pass on that coffee.' And anything else that might come after it.

'Oh.' Uncertainty flickered in her eyes. 'Well, if you're sure?'

If he crossed her threshold, she'd want something more from him than one night and she deserved it—just not from him. Owen nodded. 'Goodnight, Claire.' Tucking his hands in his trouser pockets, he forced himself to stroll down the front steps— rather than sprint as his brain was urging him to—and turned randomly to his left, desperate to get away from the eyes he could feel boring into his back. At least he'd done the right thing and walked away now before things got any further down the road between them. The thought didn't make him feel any better.

He wandered aimlessly for a few streets, trying to get his head around the jumble in his brain. Claire was perfect for him, so why didn't he want her? The blue-haired pixie's face popped into his head and he shoved the image away with a silent curse. He needed to forget about her, and everything else about Lavender Bay in the process. There was nothing there for him. He'd made it through the last thirty years without his mother, hadn't he?

A fine drizzle drifted from the sky adding another layer of misery to his mood. Ducking into an empty shop doorway, he withdrew his phone and switched it back on in order to summon a cab. He'd barely clicked on the app when the phone started ringing. Hoping it wasn't Claire checking up on his non-existent headache, he was relieved to see an unfamiliar dialling code on the screen. *Did he even know anyone who used a landline these days?* He swiped to answer. 'Hello?'

'Oh…umm…hello, is that Mr Coburn?' The deep country burr was about as far from Claire's clipped tones as Owen could imagine. He'd spent a weekend surrounded by that rich accent, and all thoughts of his disastrous date fell away as a sense of anticipation filled him.

'Speaking.'

'Ah, right then. I hope you don't mind the lateness of my call, it's been a very busy day and I've been in two minds over whether I should even be bothering you at all. I want the best for me and my girl, see, and I heard on the grapevine you might be looking to buy a property down here in Lavender Bay, and it seems like too good an opportunity to pass up. I was thinking about retiring next year, so I think we could help each other out. You'd have to promise not to breathe a word about it until after Christmas as I need to get a few things in order and I haven't talked to my girl about it. I know she'll be on board though, once I explain it all to her properly. She's had no life here, you see, and I've not been able to give her the chance she deserves to get out and see the world for herself. Well, not until now, that is…' The stream of consciousness pouring into Owen's ear trailed off leaving him not much the wiser.

'I'm not quite sure what you're saying, Mr…?'

'Stone. Mick Stone. I heard you were looking for a business to buy in Lavender Bay and I've got one to sell, but maybe I got that wrong? Beth was talking about it in the emporium, see, and there was your business card sitting on her counter so I popped it in my pocket.'

All those good intentions of forgetting about Lavender Bay fell away in an instant as his heart began to pound. If he believed in providence, he'd take this as a sign. Getting himself established in the community might be the key to finding some answers about his family. It didn't have to be forever, but people might open up to him if they got used to seeing him around the place. Worst case scenario, he could spend a couple of months doing up the place, turn it around for a profit and walk away again. Hope bloomed inside, and he had to fight to keep the excitement out of his voice. 'No, Mr Stone, you didn't get it wrong. Please tell me more…'

19

Chapter 3

'Now you're sure you don't mind me popping out for a bit, Libby-girl?'

Libby bit back an exasperated sigh and turned instead towards her father with a smile. 'Of course not, Dad.' Taking in the whiteness of the collar of his shirt half-trapped beneath the lapel of his best jacket, she cocked her head. 'You look smart, got yourself a hot date?' She'd meant it as a tease—though nothing would please her more than if her long-widowed father found a companion to share his life with—but regretted the words as an ugly flush mottled Mick Stone's cheeks.

Gaze dropping to the cap clutched between his fingers, Mick shook his head. 'Nothing like that, lovey, just a bit of business. The accountant wants to discuss last quarter, the usual stuff.' Libby relaxed. The books were all in order, but their accountant still liked to keep in regular contact. It was a personal touch she knew her dad appreciated. *And just maybe the conversation would work its way around to plans for the future.*

Stepping forward, she eased the wayward point of his shirt collar free and straightened it before letting her hand drop to smooth over the rough tweed covering the big heart which had given her all the love a girl could ever have needed growing up.

'Ignore me, Dad. It's nice to see you looking smart, that's all. Take as much time as you need. Eliza's still at a loose end, so she's going to give me a hand with lunch club.'

Friday lunch club was a tradition her parents had started when they'd first opened their fish and chip shop on the seafront promenade at Lavender Bay. The tradition of eating fish on a Friday might have waned in popularity, but the pensioners still flocked through the doors for a bargain meal. Rain or shine, through the high heat of summer and the cold depths of winter, they turned up like clockwork and went away smiling with a small cod and chips, and a pot of mushy peas for those so inclined. What they lost in profits through the discounted price was more than covered by the return in numbers—and community goodwill.

It was not lost on either Libby or her dad that for some of their customers, lunch club was a highlight of the week. Nobody was rushed through their order, and on warmer days such as that morning they put a handful of folding tables and chairs outside the front door for those who wished to linger and share their meal.

Her father paled. 'Oh, lovey, I forgot all about blooming lunch club when I made my appointment. I…I could put it off.'

This time she didn't hide her sigh. 'Give it a rest, will you? I can manage the shop with my eyes shut. It'll do Eliza good to do something other than mope about the place.' Libby scrunched her nose. 'That sounds awful. I don't mean it like that, I'm just really worried about her. Nothing's been the same since she came home.' Eliza, one of Libby's two best friends, had recently split from her husband and returned to live with her parents who ran The Siren, the main pub a few doors along the promenade from the fish and chip shop. Her other best friend, Beth, lived next door in a flat over the shop she'd inherited earlier in the year.

Since leaving Martin, Eliza had been at something of a loose end and Libby worried that if she didn't find her way soon she might think about leaving Lavender Bay again. Both she and Beth

21

had moved away permanently following their university courses, leaving Libby alone. University had never been on the cards for her, not that she'd ever been that academically inclined to begin with. From the first moment the careers advisor had called her in to talk about the future, Libby had had only one answer: she would work alongside her dad in the chippy.

Though the loss of her friends' physical presence had sat on her heart like a stone, she'd never felt jealous of them. Lavender Bay was her home, and she couldn't imagine herself anywhere else. This was where her mum was: in every grain of sand upon the beach; in the cry of the wheeling gulls high over the rolling waves; in the weft and warp of Libby's daily routines.

There was no denying her relief that both Beth and Eliza had returned to the bay, nor that she'd been completely lost without them. Oh, they'd each done their best to keep in touch with regular Skype chats and not-so-regular visits home, but it had only served to emphasise the difference between their lives. While they grew and expanded their life experiences through both successes and failures, like a fly suspended in amber, Libby's life had remained resolutely the same.

And then there was her dad. Mick Stone had always hung the moon and stars for Libby, and his quiet strength had been the rock she clung to through the maelstrom resulting from her mother's painful illness and eventual death when Libby had been barely 13 years old. Her resultant teenage rebellions as she struggled to adjust to their new status quo had bounced off Mick's solid frame without seeming to make a single dent at the time. It was only as she grew older that Libby had begun to come to terms with just how difficult she'd made things for him.

Mick's weathered face softened. 'Poor Eliza, she's been through the mill, hasn't she? Let me get this business out of the way, and then I'll pick up the slack here.'

She snorted. He wouldn't know slack if it pinched his nose. No one worked harder than her dad. Though she did her best to ensure they split the work as evenly as possible, he was forever looking for an excuse to give her a break. She adored him for it, even as it drove her crazy. They were partners in crime, a team through thick and thin, though she didn't plan on selling fish and chips for the rest of her life. The future she'd mapped out for herself lay under this roof, and her dream was to turn the chippy into a café and bakery. But those plans were for other days, and she was happy to bide her time until her dad decided he'd had enough and was ready to hand over the reins.

In spite of it being the hottest day of the year so far, lunch club had proven as popular as ever, and without Eliza's help, Libby would've been rushed off her feet. With the fryers on, the heat inside the shop had been punishing, even with the little air-con unit on the back wall running at full blast. With the last customer served, she clicked off the power to the fryers and the heating cabinet then moved to stand beneath the air-con and let the cold air wash over her. Eyes closed, she stood there until the combination of the frigid air and her sweat-soaked T-shirt sent a shiver through her entire body.

'Oh, that looks good.' Opening one eye was almost too much effort, but Libby cracked a lid and watched as Eliza propped the folding chairs she'd been carrying against the wall then came to stand beside her. 'Okay, I'm never moving from this spot.' Eliza dragged the hygiene covering from her hair and gathered the mass of curls spilling loose in one hand to expose the nape of her neck to the chilly blast.

Since they'd been little girls, Libby had always envied Eliza for her hair. The curls always seemed full of life and vitality, not like the limp, brown mop her own hair would be without all the dye and gel. Picturing the horror show lurking beneath her hat, Libby shook her head. 'How is it possible for you to work non-stop for two hours in Lavender Bay's own version of Dante's *Inferno* and still look like some pre-Raphaelite goddess at the end of it?'

Eliza laughed. 'You must be joking. I caught sight of myself in that mirrored sign over there as I walked past, and my face is glowing like a neon sign.'

Libby didn't agree but was too hot and tired to argue the point. With a healthy flush on her cheeks and a bit of life back in her eyes, Eliza looked better than she had since returning home. 'Have you thought any more about what you want to do?'

Laughter fading, Eliza scrunched up her face. 'Not a clue, but I'll have to find something soon before Mum and Dad get too used to the idea of me being behind the bar again. It's great to be home, don't get me wrong, but I don't fancy the idea of pulling pints for the rest of my days. Do you know what I mean?'

Not really. With the death of her mum, it had been only natural for Libby to step into her shoes and help her dad with the business. At first it had been a case of pitching in around their two-storey home above the shop, keeping the place clean so her dad didn't stay up half the night doing chores after being on his feet all day. It had progressed to prepping the batter, stocking the cold drinks fridge and taking orders whilst Mick manned the fryers. The day he'd deemed her old enough to work them herself was still one of the proudest moments of her life. Not a grand achievement to most, but it had been a milestone on her path from adolescence to adulthood. She loved the shop, loved the ebb and flow of people's lives through the door. Shared their triumphs and commiserated their disasters as she shook, and salted, and wrapped the food which kept them going at the end of a long day.

It was the people she loved the most. *Her* people. They came through that front door in good times and bad. If someone was having a hard time, it showed in the way their orders changed. When a regular customer reduced their order, her dad would often slip them an extra piece of fish or add another scoop of chips to their standard portion size. He greeted each and every customer with the same 'What'll it be then?', even those whose order never deviated in the dozen years she'd been helping him out. She'd asked him about it once, and his answer stuck with her.

'When we started out, your mum and I made a point of learning what people liked, thinking it added a personal touch when we asked someone if they'd like their usual order. Then one Thursday Bill Curtis came in, same as he always does, and when I said "the usual?" he burst into tears. Poor sod had just been laid off and he didn't know how he was going to pay for supper, never mind tell his wife when he got home. Your mum took him out the back and told him in no uncertain terms that until he was back on his feet, Thursday supper was on the house. Wouldn't take no for an answer, and I agreed with her. Took him four months to get a new job, another year after that to catch up on overdue bills and the like. The moment he was square again, he insisted on paying us back for those free suppers, not that we expected him to, but his pride had taken enough blows so we didn't argue.' Mick wiped his hands on his apron then put an arm around her shoulders. 'This place is more than a chippy. We're a community centre, a safe haven for people in trouble. I don't have a lot, but what I have got I'll share with anyone that needs it. Asking people what they want rather than assuming I know gives them the space to change their order without any sense of embarrassment, do you see?'

She did, and her heart swelled with love for his big, generous soul. Libby leaned into the reassuring bulk of his body. 'I see what you do, Dad, and I think it's brilliant.'

With that memory warm in her heart, Libby took a deep breath, then opened her heart. 'I've found my place in the world, Eliza, and it's right here.' She gestured around the shop. 'I love what my parents built here, and I want to keep playing my part at the heart of our community, but I want to do it *my* way. Ignore the smell of hot fat and vinegar and picture little wooden tables painted in pastel shades laden with pretty plates full of cakes and sandwiches, sparkling cutlery and real cotton napkins. Replace the fryers with a glass-fronted refrigeration counter holding fresh-baked quiches, flaky sausage rolls and glass bowls full of salad. Shelves along the back wall full of specialty teas and coffees and a fridge full of traditional bottles of lemonade, ginger beer and elderflower water. I'll paint the walls soft lemon and buttermilk with watercolour paintings of scenes from around the bay, and hang frothy lace curtains at the windows.'

A long silence followed the tumble of words and butterflies began to chase each other around Libby's stomach. It was the first time she'd let anyone else in on her plans for the future, and she could hardly bear to meet Eliza's gaze. Her best friend had the kindest heart and would say all the right things, but would she mean it? If she looked into Eliza's eyes and saw pity, it might break her heart. Needing to keep busy, she took a cloth to the already spotless counter and began to clean it.

'Libs?' Soft fingers touched her arm, stilling her hand mid-sweep. She couldn't bring herself to turn around. It mattered too damn much. Eliza released her only to slip her arms around Libby's waist and prop her chin on Libby's shoulder. 'God, Libs, it sounds wonderful. Just perfect.'

The husky warmth in those words eased the tension holding Libby's frame rigid. 'You really think so?'

Eliza gave her a squeeze. 'I *know* so. Watching you today was a revelation. Feeding people, taking care of them, it's in your blood.'

Blushing, Libby stared down at the cloth now wound between her fingers. 'I'm not exactly in Sam's league. A few sarnies and cakes won't hold a candle to the Cordon Bleu experience he'll be offering.'

A finger jabbed in her ribs, making her turn with a yelp to meet a soft scowl from Eliza. 'Don't do that,' she admonished. 'Don't talk yourself out of it before you've even started. Sam's restaurant will be for people wanting a one-off experience, some-where to celebrate a special occasion. What you're talking about is a place people will return to time and again for everyday comforts.'

Everyday comforts. Libby liked the sound of that. She'd never seen herself as in competition with Sam, that was just her insecurity digging in its claws. Deep down, she knew her plan was a sound one. The café would fill a gap in the current market, offering healthier alternatives alongside luscious cream teas. Friday lunch club would continue, but she'd offer salmon quiche or tuna melts and salad in the summer, and thick bowls of hearty chowder or fish pie in the winter. She also had plans for a pensioners' afternoon tea special once a fortnight. Lavender Bay had plenty of takeaways and pubs serving hearty meals and one or other of them would likely expand their menu and add fish and chips—and good luck to them. The day she never had to wash the smell of the chippy out of her hair again couldn't come too soon, not that she'd ever admit that to anyone other than Eliza or Beth—and they'd never say a word.

'You know I'll make the curtains and whatever for you when it's time. I'm making all the soft furnishings for Sam's restaurant, and I'd love to help you in whatever way you need.' And there it was, the reason why Libby had told Eliza before anybody else. In the same way they'd pitched in to help Beth fulfil her dreams with the emporium, Libby knew they'd throw their all behind her.

Eliza had always been a whizz with her sewing machine, whereas Libby could barely manage to sew on a button. Stick her in the kitchen, though, and that was another story. She'd learned to bake at her mother's hip and the café was a way of honouring those precious moments and keeping them fresh in her mind. Beth was the organised one, who would help her sort out the business side of things. Libby had experience helping her dad keep the books for the chip shop, but it would still take a lot of work to adapt to a more extensive menu. Work that would be much easier with Beth to guide her through it.

Eliza removed the apron she'd been wearing over a mint green shirt and matching capri pants and hung it on one of the pegs. 'So, what does your dad think about your plans?' Libby screwed up her face but didn't say anything. Her dad would be 65 next year and the years of hard work were starting to show. He'd dropped a few hints about retiring after his birthday, and that was one of the reasons she was hoping their accountant might be raising the topic at today's meeting.

She hadn't mentioned it herself, because she didn't want her dad to feel like she was pushing him out the door. When he was ready to take that step, she'd sit him down and go through her ideas. 'You're going to have to tell him some time.' Eliza laughed. 'Listen to me, Little Miss Assertive telling you what to do, when I'm just as bad.'

Libby slung an arm around her friend's shoulder and leaned close until their heads were touching. 'We're hopeless. Remember when we were kids how we couldn't wait to be all grown-up and be in control of our lives?' She sighed.

Humming sympathetically, Eliza nodded. 'We thought it would be so exciting, only no one told us how difficult it would be. I can't for the life of me remember why we were in such a hurry.'

'Because we wanted to have all that great sex we kept reading about in those copies of *Cosmopolitan* we used to steal from Beth's mum.'

'Ha! We should sue them for false advertising because we're still bloody waiting.' Eliza pulled back to regard her. 'Well, I am, at least, although you've been very quiet in that regard. Any scorching hot love affairs you want to tell me about?'

As it had far too frequently in the past weeks, the image of Owen Coburn sprang to mind, all cocky smile and hard-bodied perfection. The fluttering that followed dissolved into a deep stab of humiliation. He'd stood out—a bright flame among the usual

28

Saturday night crowd in The Siren, and she'd floated across the bar like a mesmerised moth driven by a fatal combination of bone-deep loneliness and a haze of hormones. And damn, had he burned her with that incredulous look in his eyes.

Men who looked like him probably had women throwing themselves at him all the time. He'd have his pick of gorgeous women with pretty hair and curves in all the right places, so she couldn't really blame him for dismissing her unconventional looks and a figure that barely rippled from shoulder to hip.

And if the way he'd stared at her like she'd escaped from the local freak show hadn't been bad enough, his sneering dismissal of her beloved bay had killed her attraction to him stone dead. Well, apart from when she closed her eyes at night and her treacherous brain wove alternative versions of their disastrous meeting that left her blushing in the dark and aching for something she shouldn't want, and could never be.

Catching a curious glance from Eliza, she realised she'd been quiet for too long. In an effort to distract her, Libby pasted on a grin and waggled her eyebrows. 'Only in my dreams. I keep trying to persuade Beth to dish the dirt on Sam so at least I'd have something to fuel my fantasies, but she just gives me that "cat that got the cream" look and refuses.'

As she'd hoped, one mention of Sam was enough to turn Eliza off the scent. Scrunching up her delicate nose, Eliza grimaced. 'Ugh, and ew, that's my brother you're talking about.' Her expression turned from disgust to something more encouraging. 'Once the summer gets underway there'll be lots of guys around desperate to snap you up. You're just having a dry spell, that's all.'

'More than a spell, parts of my anatomy have been officially declared a desert zone.' As they laughed together, Libby considered what Eliza had said. The influx of visitors over the summer might well increase her chances of finding someone she half-liked the look of. If she could only get a certain arrogant smile out of her head for five minutes. Owen Coburn wasn't her type, and he'd made it crystal clear that she most certainly wasn't his, so why couldn't she forget about him and move on?

Not that there was anything to move on from. Those few cross words they'd exchanged had been the closest she'd come to intimacy with a man for nearly a year, which was embarrassing to the point of being pathetic. There'd been guys in her life before— even one a few years ago who'd got serious enough to start hinting at something more permanent, but he'd been hell bent on leaving the bay and couldn't understand her desire to stay so they'd gone their separate ways—and there'd be guys again. She needed to snap out of it, and Eliza was right. Someone nice was bound to show up at some point over the summer, and Libby intended to be ready to catch him when he did. From this moment onwards, Owen bloody Coburn no longer existed.

Chapter 4

'I can't believe he's back in town. What the hell is he doing here?' Libby muttered as she sank down on the toilet seat in Beth's little bathroom where her friend was putting the final touches to her make-up for the evening. She'd managed little more than a quick shower and a change of clothes after helping her dad with the early evening rush. There wasn't any point in dressing up, it wasn't like she would be seeing anyone worth making an effort for. '*Liar,*' whispered the traitorous voice in her head.

Beth ran a pale-pink lipstick over her lips and pursed them together before she met Libby's eyes in the mirror. 'I don't know why he's here, but it sounds like he might be interested in what Sam's doing with the restaurant, so it looks like we'll be stuck with his company.' Turning her gaze back to her own reflection, Beth ran a brush through her glossy mane of chestnut hair. 'I don't get what the big deal is, Libs. I know he's a bit up himself, but you're acting like we're supping with the devil.'

Libby pulled a face, knowing she was overreacting to the whole business. When she'd walked away from Owen after that first meeting, she'd fully intended to forget him. He might have been the most gorgeous man ever to set foot in the county, but he'd made her feel like a bug under the microscope and been rude about her beloved Lavender Bay to boot! Unfortunately, her subconscious had other ideas and Owen kept popping up in her dreams, the details of which were lurid enough to make a sailor blush. With no prospect of Owen returning, it had seemed harmless enough to distract herself with a daydream or two.

And then Eliza had casually dropped his name into conversation during their recent girls' night and butterflies had been somersaulting in her middle ever since. Not only was the object of several embarrassing fantasies back in the bay and staying at The Siren, he and Sam were somehow considering going into business together! In the hopes of getting him onside, Sam had asked Beth—and by association, Libby— to join them for a drink that evening.

How the hell she would be able to look him in the eye and not burst into flames from sheer embarrassment, she had no idea. 'I don't like him.' It wasn't exactly a lie… Hiding her discomfort behind a scowl, she folded her arms. 'If I remember rightly, you're not exactly his biggest fan, either.'

Beth turned on the stool, and it was all Libby could do not to wilt under the sweet concern in her eyes. 'What's got into you? The main reason for tonight is to meet Jack, and give Eliza a bit of moral support, remember? Owen's arrogant, yes, but I don't remember him being unpleasant. All we have to do is exchange a few pleasantries with him and leave the rest to Sam. It's not like you to let anyone get under your skin like this.' Beth held out her hand. 'If it's going to bother you, then why don't you give tonight a miss? Eliza won't mind.'

Their friend had met a local farmer during a visit to the lavender farm which covered the sprawling hills above the bay and they'd hit it off. Still a bit raw from her separation with Martin, Eliza was feeling a bit uncertain about things, but it was clear from the way she'd glowed when talking about him there was more than a spark of attraction between them.

Libby was delighted for her, of course, but it only served to highlight her own lack of success on the romance front. And now the source of her own personal humiliation was back in town and she'd have to deal with it somehow. It wasn't his lack of interest in her so much as her inability to brush it off and forget him that embarrassed her down to her marrow. That and those ridiculously hot dreams. Libby shuddered, and hoped to hell the man wasn't some kind of mind-reader or else she'd die on the spot.

Squaring her shoulders, she took the hand Beth offered to her and tugged her from the stool into a quick hug. Eliza needed their moral support, and for that Libby could cope with a little discomfort. 'I'm being ridiculous. I know how much the restaurant means to Sam, so I can grin and bear it. Let's go and check out Eliza's gorgeous farmer. I promise to be on my best behaviour.'

Beth made a beeline straight for Sam, who was sitting on his own. A quick glance around showed no sign of Owen's close-cropped dark head. Maybe he'd changed his mind about the drink? Feeling hopeful, Libby scooted over to the bar towards where Eliza was positioned behind it. Head swivelling, Libby scanned the patrons looking for Jack. 'He not here yet then?'

'Not yet, but there's a lot of work to do on the farm so it's not exactly a nine-to-five job.' Libby couldn't miss the hint of uncertainty in her friend's voice as she fished a bottle of white wine out of the fridge behind her, and resolved not to tease her. Eliza held up the wine. 'You having a large one?'

'Does the Pope shit in the woods?' Libby grinned as Eliza shook her head at the deliberately crude comment, but she was laughing too, which was the point.

'Charming as ever, I see.' *Oh, great.* Of course, Owen would choose that moment to pitch up. Bracing herself, Libby turned and gave herself a mental high-five for not fainting dead away. Her fevered memory had done the man a serious misjustice. From the severe crew cut to the tattoo covering his upper arm from the edge of his T-shirt sleeve to his elbow, and the faded jeans clinging to his hips, he looked dangerous and utterly delicious.

Fury at her reaction combined with embarrassment, and all her good intentions flew out of the window. 'You didn't fall under a bus then? That's a pity.' Ignoring the pounding of her heart, she deliberately gave him her back. 'If you're going to let any old riff-raff in here, Eliza, I might have to start drinking somewhere else.'

She could sense him step up beside her, feel the heat of him like a stroke against her skin and it was all she could do to keep her eyes fixed on Eliza. 'A pint of lager, and I'll buy your friend a drink if you slip some arsenic in it for me.'

He was only giving back as good as she'd given, but the dig hurt more than it should've. Eliza giggling like he was the most hilarious man on the planet didn't help. And when she slid the money he'd offered back with a simpering smile, Libby barely restrained a hiss at her friend's traitorous behaviour. 'What the bloody hell is that all about?' Libby demanded the second Owen walked away to join Sam and Beth. '"*It's on the house.*" God, you were practically drooling.'

The moment she'd snapped the words, she regretted them. She'd been the one in danger of needing a napkin whilst Eliza had been nothing more than polite to a man who was not only a paying guest, but who might hold the key to her brother's future prospects. If she carried on projecting like this, she'd end up having to confess her messy feelings to her friends. The too-keen glint in Eliza's eye said Libby's dramatic reaction had already piqued her curiosity.

'What's the problem? You've barely exchanged more than two words with the guy and yet there's all this animosity between you. Has he done something to upset you?'

Libby shrugged, knowing she was acting like a sulky teenager. There was nothing she could say without confessing she'd been dreaming about him like some love-sick schoolgirl. Having no boyfriend when her friends were getting cosy was bad enough without admitting the best she'd been able to do was dream about a bloke she didn't even like! Feeling embarrassed and awkward, she couldn't help but overreact to every mention of him.

It didn't help that he looked better than ever tonight. The black T-shirt he'd teamed with a pair of faded jeans stretched across a set of surprisingly broad shoulders. She'd only ever seen him in a suit before, and the cut of his jacket hadn't done justice to his physique. Libby ripped her gaze away before she did something ridiculous like climb him like a monkey. 'He's a stuck-up git, that's all. Why are you and Sam so chummy with him all of a sudden?'

Eliza frowned. 'I thought Beth would've mentioned it to you. Owen stumbled across Sam going over the plans for the restaurant and he offered to take a look. Having someone with his experience involved in the project can only strengthen Sam's position, and he might even agree to invest because the bank have been dragging their heels apparently. You know how important this is to Sam—to Beth as well. This is their future in the balance. Owen told Sam he was still on the lookout for projects situated here in the bay to invest in.' She took Libby's hand. 'If he's bad news then we need to warn Sam.'

What a hash of things she was making thanks to a bit of singed pride and a ridiculous crush. Sam had been working so hard on his plans for Subterranean and Libby would be damned if she'd throw a spanner in the works. Owen seemed determined to find an investment opportunity in the area, why else would he be back down here after things had fallen through with his plan to buy up the emporium from Beth? And where better for his money to go than supporting her friends? 'Ignore me, he...' It was on the tip of her tongue to confess her embarrassment, but she couldn't face Eliza's sympathy just then. Eliza would be lovely and sympathetic and Libby would feel like even more of a failure on the romantic front. Why couldn't she bump into a gorgeous farmer like Eliza had, or fall in love with the boy next door, like Beth? Libby snorted to herself; the 'boy' who lived next door to the chippy was 70 if he was a day. 'He just winds me up for some reason.' It sounded pathetic, but Libby was determined not to dig the hole she was in any deeper. Taking a sip of her wine to steady herself, she decided to shift the conversation onto more solid ground. 'I wonder why he's so fixated on our little town; you can't get much further from the glamour of London than Lavender Bay.'

Eliza shrugged, her attention now on the small group across the room rather than on Libby, thank goodness. 'Maybe that's the point, who knows? Sam and I thought a friendly drink would help grease the wheels a bit.' Which made perfect sense, much to Libby's chagrin, and Eliza's next words did nothing to make her feel any better about her ridiculous behaviour as she echoed Beth's earlier sentiment. 'If you really don't like him then I don't want to spoil your evening. We can probably just leave him and Sam to chat...'

Darling Eliza, always the mediator, even when she must have been beside herself with nerves over Jack coming to meet everyone. Libby gulped another mouthful of wine. 'If it means that much to Sam then I can put up with Mr Full Of Himself for a few hours. But I'm not going to kiss up to him, so don't expect me to.'

Eliza raised on tiptoe to give her a quick hug across the bar. 'I'm not asking you to, just don't shank him with a wooden spork from the chippy, all right?' They both snorted at the idea and just like that, Libby's bad mood evaporated.

Thankfully, Jack arrived not long afterwards and Libby's conflicting emotions about Owen were pushed to the back of her mind as she did her best to make him feel welcome. It wasn't exactly a chore—Jack went out of his way to be charming, and it was clear from the way they looked at each other that there was the potential for something special between him and Eliza. She could even forgive him for refusing an offer to tour the skittle alley beneath the pub which would be the location for Subterranean in favour of spending a bit of quiet time with Eliza, leaving her without a buffer as she trooped downstairs behind Beth, Sam and Owen.

Sam's enthusiasm for the project was infectious, and Libby couldn't wait to see his vision come to life. Owen seemed to have forgotten their little snit at the bar, and she was only too glad to do the same. She'd chosen a seat beside him, and even managed to shift it further away from him without being too obvious about it. At least this way she could keep her eyes on the others and not stare at him like a complete idiot. They didn't address each other directly, but the conversation flowed easily enough thanks to Beth's subtle efforts. As they worked their way through a second round of drinks, Libby finally found herself relaxing enough to enjoy herself. Owen would be back on the train to London soon enough, and she could get back to pretending he didn't exist.

The men drifted into a discussion over some football competition Jack's nephew was involved in and Libby let the conversation wash over her as she checked the time on her phone. She'd have to make a move in a minute—though her dad had said he'd be fine on his own, Libby wanted to be back in the shop to lend him a hand with the late-evening influx of customers. Five more minutes and then she really needed to be off. Glancing up, she caught the intent look on Owen's face and started to pay more attention. From the way he was talking it sounded like he intended to help Jack out at the football. 'But if it's next weekend, you won't be here!'

All her worst fears were realised when Owen aimed a broad grin at her. 'Now that Sam and I are going into business together, you're going to be seeing a whole lot more of me about the bay.'

Oh. God.

'You're serious?' Sam asked Owen, and for one desperate second

Libby's hopes rose because maybe Owen had just been trying to wind her up.

'Absolutely. We can hammer out the details over the next few days. I'll need to go back to London on Sunday night, but most of my current projects are well in hand so I can be here next weekend. See if you can make an appointment with the bank manager for the Monday or Tuesday afterwards. We should have things sorted between us by then I reckon.'

Monday or Tuesday afterwards? He was talking like he intended to become a permanent resident. And if he was working with Sam and playing football with Jack, then there would be no avoiding him. After her dad, Beth and Eliza meant everything to Libby so she would either have to spend less time with their group or find a way to get over this nonsense with Owen. Hanging around with two couples, how long would it be before the suggestions and teasing about them getting together started? Her stomach churned at the thought. He'd already made it clear he had zero interest in her. How humiliating would it be to have her nose rubbed in it again?

Unable to bear the thought, she stood abruptly. 'I need to get back and give Dad a hand with the late-evening rush. I'll see you later, B.' There was time enough yet, but if she sat there a moment longer, she'd give the game away.

To her absolute horror, Owen stood up. 'I'll walk back with you. Sam was telling me earlier how you make the best fish and chips in the county. I missed dinner, so I'm starving.'

Well, what on earth was she supposed to do now? 'Fine.' Turning on her heel, Libby marched towards the door.

Chapter 5

Tucking his hands in his pockets, Owen affected an air of utter relaxation as he strolled along in the angry wake of the tiny pixie—*Libby*. He couldn't quite get his head around her having such a sweet name. With all her spiky edges, and not just the rainbow-coloured ones radiating from her head, she should have been called something bolder. Libby was for a soft, sweet girl who knitted blankets for stray kittens, or some such nonsense. Maybe she did, it wasn't like he knew the first damn thing about her— other than the fact she clearly couldn't stand to be within five feet of him, and he couldn't stop thinking about her. Oh, and the fact he'd agreed to buy her father's business.

He'd assumed Mick Stone's cloak and dagger act over selling the chip shop to Owen—insisting on meeting him miles away from the bay and then extracting his promise to wait until New Year's Eve to assume final possession of the chip shop—was a bit over the top, but maybe not. If Libby had any idea her dad was selling up, she'd made no indication of it. He'd snooped a time or two during her conversations with her friends, and all talk had been around long-term plans. It was never too early for women to start talking about Christmas, apparently.

Not the kind of thing someone who was preparing to leave

the bay and strike out on her own would be talking about, though her dad had talked more about the freedom the sale of his business would give his daughter than his own plans for retirement. He needed to dig into it, find out what he was getting himself caught up in. 'So, selling fish and chips is your ideal career then?'

Libby stopped so suddenly, like she'd slammed into an invisible wall, that he almost trod on her heels. As a result, when she spun to face him, they were almost nose-to-chest. *Christ, she really is tiny*. A gentleman would stand back so she didn't have to crane her neck to meet his eye. Owen might be a lot of things, but a gentleman had never been one of them, so he stood his ground and waited for the tirade. It didn't take long.

'What the hell is that supposed to mean? Running a chippy might not live up to your lofty standards, but it's good honest work. We help the community and provide a decent meal at a reasonable price. Why is that something to sneer at?'

Well, that didn't sound like someone ready to move on, did it? He was starting to get a really bad feeling about this. Holding his hands up in a gesture of surrender, he sought to smooth her ruffled feathers. 'Sorry. I have a habit of shoving my foot in my mouth every time I talk to you. I just wondered if you were satisfied with what you're doing.'

She fixed a suspicious squint on him, before the tightness in her frame eased. 'I shouldn't have jumped down your throat, you just…' She paused long enough he thought she didn't mean to continue the thought, then muttered, 'you rub me up the wrong way.'

The idea of rubbing her in any kind of way destroyed several brain cells and most of his self-restraint. With effort, Owen forced himself to move until a reasonable amount of space opened up between them. 'We did start off rather badly.'

To his surprise, Libby threw back her head and roared with unrestrained laughter. 'That might be the understatement of the century.'

Her laughter was infectious, and he found himself joining in. 'At least I know I'm safe as long as I stick to the pedestrian promenade.' At her quizzical look, he made a shoving motion. 'No passing buses for me to *fall under.*'

'Oh, that.' The faintest hint of a blush coloured her cheeks, before she straightened her shoulders. 'I seem to remember something about webbed fingers and arsenic, so don't be playing the hard-done-by card with me.' She crossed her arms, drawing his attention to the slimness of her frame as it drew her baggy top taut. 'You started it.'

Scowling at her faulty memory, Owen mirrored her pose. '*You* started it. You called me a colossal arse.'

'That's because you were being a colossal arse. Look, I get that you're some kind of sex god throwing off pheromones left, right and centre, and I'm just the weird-looking local you wouldn't look twice at, but you didn't have to stomp me down quite so harshly just for approaching you.' The colour drained from her face, leaving her skin a waxy shade. Holding her hands out as though to ward him off, she backed up a few steps. 'Oh, God! Get away from me. I can't control my mouth when I'm around you.' She turned on her DM-booted heels and started running.

Well now, that was all very illuminating. It would appear he wasn't the only one feeling a spark of attraction beneath those layers of animosity. And, unlike him, Libby seemed very unhappy about it. A gentleman would turn on his heel and give her time to gather her equilibrium, but as had already been established, Owen was no gentleman. He was a sex god, apparently. Time to throw off a few more pheromones and see what happened next. With a grin he had no doubt most would call smug playing about his lips, he hurried after Libby.

With the difference in their strides, he was only a few paces behind her as Libby rushed through the front door of the chip shop. The clatter of her boots on the tiled floor turned all eyes towards them, including those of the man behind the counter.

41

Mick Stone took one look at Owen and blurted out, 'What the hell are you doing here?'

Thankfully, Libby assumed the question was aimed at her. 'I've come to help you with the late shift, what do you think I'm doing here?' she asked as she edged past the queue to slip around the edge of the counter. 'Give me two seconds to get my coat on.' She placed a quick kiss on her father's cheek and disappeared out the back.

Joining the back of the queue, Owen made a show of studying the large menu on the wall above Mick's head. 'I heard in the pub this is the place for the best fish and chips for miles around and I had to check it out for myself. Anyone have recommendations?' As he'd hoped, the people ahead of him were all happy to offer an opinion and a friendly, if heated, discussion started of the merits of cod over haddock.

Libby returned, still buttoning up a white coat with her wild hair tamed beneath the ugliest hair net he'd ever seen. She took one look at him, bristled, then fixed a brilliant smile on the woman at the front of the line. 'Evening, Rose, what'll it be for you tonight?'

Fascinated, Owen watched as Libby and her dad paid particular attention to each and every customer. Conversations rose and fell like the tide washing on the beach as others waiting joined in with their own observations and chatter. Ten minutes later and he still hadn't made it to the front of the queue, and to his shock it didn't bother Owen one bit.

Had he been in London, he'd have complained long before now, would likely have already walked out in disgust at being kept waiting, but the likelihood of the scene before him unfolding in any of his local takeaways was about on a par with a unicorn charging down Kensington High Street. He'd used the Chinese at the end of his street pretty much every week for the past three years and still didn't have a clue what the couple who ran it were called. Thanks to the ordering app on his phone, he didn't even need to speak to them beyond giving a number and saying thank you when they handed over his usual crispy beef, chicken and pineapple with a side of special fried rice in a white carrier bag. Not that they went out of their way to be chatty, either.

There was definitely a different pace to life down here, and he would have to make some readjustments now he'd be spending more time in the bay. The deal with Sam over his restaurant had come out of nowhere. Owen had been on the hunt for an early morning coffee and come across the plans spread over the kitchen table in the pub.

A day spent poring over the plans for Subterranean had left him genuinely excited by the project. Sam had a fantastic vision, and plenty of top chefs had proven success with regional restaurants. It would be a gamble, but if they could position a couple of features in the right newspapers, the punters would flock to the coast for the chance to say they'd been the first to discover a hot new talent.

As for the chip shop, it occupied an absolute prime piece of real estate right in the centre of the promenade. Like many of the buildings along the seafront, it sprawled over three storeys, with living accommodation occupying the top two floors. He hadn't yet decided whether he'd retain the retail space below, but with a bit of rejigging—and the requisite planning permission— the upper floors could be transformed into a couple of luxury duplexes complete with roof terraces. With some discreet planting, no one would be any the wiser about the terraces and he'd be able to provide a secluded spot for the discerning sunbather without altering the façade of the building.

His eyes strayed to Libby, red-faced from the heat as she lifted a basket of piping-hot chips from the fryer and wondered if he should tell her she'd directly influenced his plans. Her comments about ugly modern apartments changing the appearance of the promenade had stuck with him. It would be important to get the locals on side as any protests from them might put a spanner in

43

the works. Only he couldn't tell her anything about it, thanks to the ludicrous deal he'd struck with Mick about keeping quiet until after Christmas.

The back of his neck itched. When Mick's 'girl' had been some amorphous, unknown individual, Owen hadn't given two hoots about what she did or didn't know about the deal. He'd never referred to her by name during their discussions and it was only during a chat with Sam that morning that Owen had put two and two together. Mick had assured him he was the sole title holder to the property since the passing of his wife, so whatever family drama selling up might cause would be his problem. He'd asked Owen to hold off so he could have one last Christmas with 'his girl', and as the timing had suited him, Owen had no objections.

Now he knew Libby was involved, it didn't sit so well with him, especially when his new business partner was so closely connected to her two friends. It was clear the three women were very close, and if she objected to the sale of her childhood home and place of work, it could make things very awkward for everyone. He'd have to dig a little deeper, try and get to know Libby without giving the game away. Getting a bit closer to her wouldn't be a hardship in the least.

It was finally his turn to be served. With a polite nod to Mick, Owen fixed a big grin on Libby who was doing her best to pretend he wasn't there. 'Evening, Libby.'

The glare she flicked his way all but scorched the skin off his face, but she was saved from responding by Mick. 'You two know each other then?'

Resting one elbow on the counter, Owen turned partly towards him, but made sure to keep Libby in his eyeline. 'Yup. We've met a couple of times in the pub. Just spent the evening together, haven't we?'

Mick's eyebrows climbed high enough to disappear beneath the brim of his white trilby as Libby made a strangled noise in her throat. She coughed, then muttered, 'This is Owen. He's investing in Sam's new restaurant, they were talking about their plans while I was hanging out with Beth and Eliza.'

'The restaurant? I didn't know Sam was looking for a partner.' The concern in Mick's voice was palpable and it suddenly occurred to Owen he might think it would put their own deal in jeopardy.

'He wasn't. I'm staying at the pub while I follow up on *another* investment opportunity and I kind of stumbled across the plans. I've got room in my portfolio for both, and Sam's vision for Subterranean is very exciting.' He made sure to hold Mick's gaze as he emphasised 'another' hoping he would understand he was referring to his purchase of the chip shop. Bloody hell, talking about something whilst not being obvious he was talking about it was too much like hard work. Surely Mick couldn't mean to keep this up until after Christmas?

Mick visibly relaxed, much to Owen's relief. 'He's a grand cook, is Sam. I'm sure he'll make a roaring success of the place.'

'And he was singing your praises, too. Told me you serve the best fish and chips in the county, so I'm sure you'll have something here to satisfy my appetite.' Owen aimed his last remark squarely at Libby and was rewarded with a hot blush, and another of those fantastically filthy glares for his trouble. She had spirit in spades, and he wanted all that fire inside her focused on him. 'What does the lady recommend?'

Narrowing her eyes, Libby reached for a vicious-looking two-pronged fork and used it to spear a battered sausage with enough force to make Owen glad there was a solid counter between them. Oblivious to the tension between them, Mick shook his head. 'We can do a bit better than that. How does a large cod and chips sound, Owen?'

Not wishing to be rude, Owen turned his attention to Mick. 'Sounds great, thanks very much.' He watched as Libby returned the poor abused sausage to the warming container before dishing up a huge portion of chips upon which she laid a long cod fillet

45

wrapped in a pale golden batter. His stomach gave an appreciative rumble as the scent of the hot food hit him.

'Salt and vinegar?'

He waited to reply until she lifted her eyes to meet his. 'Lovely.'
Her lips twitched in spite of herself and Owen wanted to pump
his fist at winning even that tiny reaction from her. 'And I'll take
a Diet Coke as well, please.'

Mick rang up the cost and Owen retrieved his debit card to
pay. 'Well, thank you both for this. I'm sure I'll enjoy every bite.'
With a quick wink at Libby, Owen retreated to the door, clutching
his drink and the large paper parcel. He didn't go far, though. A
lamppost hung above the railing running along the promenade
directly opposite the shop window. Owen perched on the top rail
beneath the bright light, unwrapped his meal and set it on his
lap, and waited.

The chips were hot, crispy on the outside, and fluffy on the
inside. In other words, perfect. Picking his way through the mountain of food, he watched Libby puttering around behind the
counter, serving the next few customers. All smiles, there wasn't
a hint of the animosity she showed him, not even towards a group
of noisy lads who spilled through the door clearly a little worse
for wear. As they staggered out, clutching their food and laughing,
her gaze followed them as they crossed in front of Owen's position. *Any second now...*

Libby froze, jaw gaping and he couldn't resist giving her a
jaunty wave with the chip in his hand. He could almost see steam
pouring from her ears as she very deliberately turned her back.
Satisfied, he turned his attention to the melt-in-the-mouth fish
and didn't look up again until he'd finished every last morsel. It
was enough that she knew he was out there. If he was a betting
man, he would've taken any odds that she wouldn't be able to
resist watching him, and sure enough he caught a flurry of her
white coat turning away the moment he raised his head.

Having crumpled up his empty paper, he drained the last of

his can of drink then hopped down from the railing. A bin sat outside the chip shop, so he crossed the promenade to deposit his rubbish. The shop was empty of customers, and there was no sign of Mick, only Libby making a huge performance of spraying and wiping down the front of the counter. Waiting until she glanced over her shoulder, Owen gave her a little wave then strolled back to retake his position on the top railing. A quick check of his watch told him last orders in the pub had come and gone. He scanned the prom in both directions. Apart from a couple walking their dog, it was pretty much deserted. *Not much longer to wait.*

Resting his elbows on his knees, Owen watched as Libby flipped the closed sign and slid the top bolt home before disappearing out of view. The lights went out, and he waited, eyes straining for any hint of movement inside. After ten fruitless minutes, he slipped down from the railing with a sigh. He'd been so sure she wouldn't be able to resist coming out to speak to him—even if it was only to tell him to sod off. Ah well, Rome wasn't built in a day, and spiky, intriguing little pixies weren't easily tamed which was probably just as well.

Tucking his hands in his pockets, Owen glanced up and down the promenade. Other than security lights mounted high on their walls, the businesses were all dark. He supposed he should return to the pub, but he wasn't the least bit tired. Maybe a walk would help to ease the restlessness inside him. He'd made it maybe half a dozen paces when a soft snick came from behind him. Not wanting her to catch him smiling, he made sure his face was in the shadows before he turned around. 'I thought you were going to leave me out here like a stray cat.'

'It was tempting, but then I was worried you'd start yowling underneath my window or scent marking the steps.' She'd swapped her white coat for a black cardigan hanging loosely off one shoulder to reveal the spaghetti straps of her vest top. Tempted by the soft material, he hitched it up then smoothed his fingers down her arm to tangle with her own. She flinched back. 'Hey, keep your hands to yourself!' She hauled the two sides of her cardigan around her body like a shield. 'Do you think I'm so desperate I'll fall into bed with any man, even one who doesn't fancy me? That you can flash your smile and splash your cash, and the poor little country mouse will swoon at your feet? I might be desperate, but I'm not *that* desperate.'

Owen felt his temper rise in response to her outrageous accusations. 'Christ, you're full of assumptions about me, aren't you? Shame you're wrong on every single one of them.'

'Wrong? Don't make me laugh. What was that all about in the shop earlier, making sure everyone heard that you're investing in two different projects in the bay other than you showing off to all us poor locals? And then spending an hour hanging around outside my door pretending to flirt with me. What are you even doing here? Did you figure out I've got a stupid crush on you and decide to grit your teeth and make the best of it? It's all the same in the dark, I suppose.'

Moving before he knew what he was going to do, he grabbed her around the waist and hauled her against him. 'Can't you just be quiet for one minute?' He mashed his lips down upon hers before she could spew forth any more accusations.

Hands braced upon his chest, she shoved hard against his hold for a couple of seconds before her fingers curled up and over his shoulders to pull him closer. The stubborn moue of her lips softened beneath his to release a little gasp. Shifting his grip from her waist to her hips, her raised her higher up against his body until she hooked her legs around him, the weight of her boots thudding against the back of his thighs. His mouth still locked on hers, he took a couple of staggering steps until he had her pinned against the shadowed wall of a nearby shop.

The scent, feel and taste of her swam through his senses until nothing else existed. When he tested the seam of her lips with his tongue and she yielded for him with a hungry little noise, he feared his knees might give out from the desire spearing through him, and he kissed her like his life depended upon it. Her nails pricked his skin through the cotton of his T-shirt for a long moment before she released her grip to press once more against his chest. This time he let her ease him away.

Gasping for breath, they stared at each other through the gloom. 'But…but you don't like me,' Libby said, her tone full of bewilderment.

'I don't know what gave you that idea, but you're wrong.' He shifted his body where it notched between her thighs to prove just how wrong. 'I like you plenty, Libby Stone.'

Chapter 6

Had it not been for Owen's firm grip upon her waist, Libby might have melted into a puddle of goo right there on the promenade. Perhaps the town council would erect one of those little blue plaques on the wall to record the moment? *It was here in the summer of 2018 that Libby Stone was relieved of her senses by a single kiss.* Confusion wasn't a comfortable state of mind. She liked things straightforward, to know where she stood in life. The sun rose in the east and set in the west, the tides followed the cycles of the moon, a seagull would always try and steal your chips, Owen Coburn was bad news wrapped in a very sexy package. All incontrovertible truths. *Or so she'd thought.* When he was being brash, she could tell herself she'd dodged a bullet, that her bruised feelings would heal soon enough. And then he showed up, flirted with her, *kissed* her until her head swam, even told her that he liked her.

She couldn't think straight, and it wasn't just from his kisses which had been even better than all those fantasies she'd spun about him. Gripped with the sudden panic that perhaps she'd fallen asleep slumped over the counter in the chippy, she unhooked her arms from around his neck and gave herself a pinch. Nope, not asleep.

'What on earth are you doing?' Owen asked.

'Just checking.'

He laughed. The low rich sound vibrated through her threatening to turn her already liquid insides to mush. 'You really aren't like any other woman I've ever met.' She stiffened and would've wriggled free of his hold had his mouth not grazed softly across her own. 'Damn, you're spikier than a hedgehog. That was a compliment, by the way,' he murmured against her lips.

She let herself melt against him once more as he traced his way from her lips to her throat in a series of butterfly soft kisses. 'You really aren't like any other man I've met either,' she confessed.

Owen raised his head and she found herself straining to read his expression in the near dark. 'I'm not what you think I am, Libby. Everything I've got in life has been earned through my own sweat and determination. No one gave me a hand up, along the way. It's taken me eighteen years to get from being a jobbing labourer to having my name above the door of my business.'

Thankful for the shadows, Libby felt her face flush at the hint of accusation in his voice. She'd done to him exactly what she hated people doing to her—judged him by appearance. The designer suits, the confident way he talked about investing in the restaurant like it was no big deal had blinded her. From what he was saying, he'd worked his way up from nothing. She did a quick calculation in her head. 'You must've started straight from school, unless you've got one of those Dorian Grey paintings hiding in the attic.'

'Is that a roundabout way of asking how old I am? I'm 34.'

'Oh.' She'd assumed him to be a bit younger—closer to Sam's age.

'Oh?' His arms slid from beneath her thighs to cup her bottom, the proprietorial hold sending shivers through her. 'Is that going to be a problem for you?'

He was too close, the heat of him too distracting for her poor lust-addled brain, but she couldn't back up when he had her pinned against the wall. 'Why…why would it be a problem for me?' Damn him for putting that breathy note in her voice. She didn't do breathy, she didn't do sweet, melting compliance. And she'd tell him so if he'd just stop touching her like that.

'Because when I get you into bed, I don't want you to suddenly decide the age gap between us is an issue.'

When. Not if. There was not even a hint of doubt in his voice and she liked it far more than she should. 'So arrogant,' she said, scrambling to regain the upper hand.

'Confident.'

'I hate you.' But she was laughing as she said it, and he'd found that sweet spot just beneath her ear with his lips, and suddenly there was no more room for words.

She didn't know how long they stood there in the shadows, the harshness of their breathing and the waves lapping upon the distant shore the only sounds as they kissed and caressed each other. It might have been minutes or a matter of seconds before Owen broke away with a gasp. 'Take me home, Libby.'

Yes. She had her legs unhooked and was sliding back to the floor before reality kicked in. 'Dad's there.'

'Damn.' He smothered his own word with another round of feverish kisses. 'Then come back to the pub with me.'

And do a walk of shame along the promenade in the morning, presuming she could even sneak in and out of there without her friends finding out? 'That's even worse.'

'I *need* you.' Three of the most intoxicating words she'd ever heard spilled from his lips. It was the tone of his voice as much as anything that blew the last of her common sense away. No man had ever spoken of her with such urgency, with such blatant need and just the right edge of demand.

If it hadn't been so long since anyone had touched her like this, if she hadn't been so bloody lonely, she might have pushed him away and run for the safety of her little bedroom above the shop with its walls still the same pale pink of her childhood. But it had. And he was making her body sing with anticipation. For the first time in her life she knew what it was to be the sole focus of a powerful man. 'Come with me.'

Not stopping to think, she dragged Owen down the steps and along the beach to where a row of old beach huts rested against the wall of the promenade. They were a hangover from the Fifties, before the town had grown so popular with tourists. The parish council had refused permission over the years for any more to be built and put a moratorium on who could purchase them. As a result, they'd stayed in the hands of the same families for several generations.

The kids at school whose folks owned them had been some of the most popular thanks to their unfettered access to the perfect hangout spot. Libby had spent many an evening and weekend hanging out in one or other of the gaily painted huts. And if they were lucky… Pausing in front of a bright yellow hut, she stretched on tiptoe and fumbled along the top of the door frame with her fingers. 'Ah hah!'

'Well, aren't you just full of surprises?' Owen said as she unlocked the door and pushed it open. It was pitch black inside, but provided the Tanners hadn't given the place a major overhaul she could still remember the layout.

'Hang on to me.' Extending her hands forward, Libby began to shuffle forward as she pictured the inside of the little cabin the last time she'd seen it. A pair of basket weave chairs on either side, a table in the far left corner piled high with the jigsaw puzzles and old board games, and along the back wall… Her shins brushed against something and she bent at the waist to find the edge of the large cushioned bench. 'There's a seat here.'

Owen gripped her hips. 'I think I like where I am just fine, come here.' Turning her with insistent hands, she expected his kiss to be as intense as the ones they shared on the beach. Instead, it was a long, slow exploration as though now he'd got her somewhere private, all the urgency had left him.

53

She didn't want soft and tender, she wanted fast and furious with no time to think about what she was doing, and who she was doing it with. Frustrated, she pushed at the bottom of his T-shirt only to have him capture her hands and hold them away from their bodies leaving their lips a single point of connection.

'Shh,' he said when she would've protested. 'No rush now, and in spite of what I said there's no need for this to go any further unless you want it to.'

Damn him. She'd wanted him to overwhelm her, to take charge and do with her as he would. That way she could blame him in the morning when the regrets came, and they most surely would. Whatever else Owen might be, he didn't strike her as the kind of man who wanted commitment, and that spelled disaster for Libby. In her heart of hearts, she knew whatever happened between them that night would alter her on some fundamental level. A shiver rippled through her, a portent rather than a thrill. Owen Coburn would not only be her downfall, he wanted her to walk right into his lion's den with her eyes wide open.

Even with all those doubts and fears ricocheting through her brain, there was no hesitation as she freed her hands and hooked them around his neck. 'I want this. I want you. No regrets.'

Had anyone in the history of the world told such a blatant lie to a lover? As they sank down together on the bench, she neither knew nor cared.

'I can't find my T-shirt.'

Raising her head at the sound of Owen's voice was instinctive, and a huge mistake as she bumped it on the edge of the corner table. 'Ouch!' She sat back on her heels and rubbed her forehead. 'I can't find my jeans, or my bra. Whose bloody idea was it to have a tryst in a pitch-black shed?'

'I seem to remember it was yours.' Libby jumped. He sounded much closer to her than he had a second ago. Something warm brushed her shoulder then traced down her arm to place a tangle of material in her hand. 'I found your bra. I was going to keep it as a memento.'

The silly comment helped soothe away the worst of her nerves. 'What were you planning to do with it, nail it over your headboard?'

Owen laughed. 'I thought I'd hang it from the flag pole outside my office, isn't that what victors used to do with trophies captured from their enemies?'

He hadn't moved away so she took a chance and leaned into the muscled heat of his chest. 'We weren't really enemies.'

His arm curled around her back. 'No, not really, although I could've sworn you said you hated me, earlier.'

She'd said an awful lot more than that to him in the past hour. Shocking things; shameless things; things she'd never thought in all of her 26 years, never mind demanded until he'd taken her in his arms. *Don't think about it.* What they'd shared had been too raw, too intense, and if she let herself dwell on it, she'd fall right back under his spell. Thankful for the shield of darkness so he couldn't see the heat burning on her cheeks, she extended her arm to sweep along the floor beside her and touched something soft. 'I think this might be your T-shirt.'

'Thanks.' He didn't seem to be in any hurry to take it from her. Clever, questing fingers slipped under her top to play over the little ridges of her spine. 'Libby…'

Dear God. His ability to put so much temptation in one word should be illegal. 'We should be getting back. If Dad wakes up, he'll wonder where I am.' Mick Stone slept like the dead from the moment his head hit the pillow until his alarm clock went off in the morning, but Owen didn't need to know that. If she let him get her under him again she might still be there when the beach filled up with visitors in a few hours.

His hand stilled on her back for a moment, before he withdrew it. 'Sure. Right, let's try and find your jeans.' Was that a trace of hurt in his voice? It couldn't possibly be. She could count her number of awkward post-coital experiences on one hand which was a damn sight less than him, of that she had no doubt. So, he should be better at this than her. She felt him crawl away, felt the loss of his warmth against her side and was suddenly desperate to scramble after him and tumble them both to the floor.

She didn't though. Instead, she removed her top and began to fumble around with her bra until she had it the right way round to clip it back on. Her top was halfway over her head when Owen gave a little crow of triumph. 'Here they are! Now I just need to work out where the hell you are again.'

Finally dressed, they left the little haven of the beach hut. Libby paused to lock the door and replace the key back in its hiding place before turning to survey the sky. The moon had set, and the first streaks of indigo and pink showed the approaching dawn. She could've sworn they'd only been inside for an hour. 'What time is it?'

Pale luminescence flashed as Owen turned his wrist to study his watch. 'About half three, I think.'

'Bloody hell, come on, I've got to be up in a few hours.' She broke into a jog, keeping the dark outline of the promenade to her left. The lampposts had dimmed to pale orange, another sign of how late—or how early—it was.

When they reached the steps leading up to the prom, Owen grabbed for her hand and tugged her around to face him. Cupping her jaw with his other hand, he feathered a kiss across her lips. 'I'll find us somewhere a bit more comfortable for next time.'

Next time. He said it as naturally as breathing, as though of course they would be seeing each other again. She'd been refusing to think beyond the next few moments, getting dressed, finding their shoes, saying goodbye…only it didn't sound like he had any intention of saying goodbye. The sex had been good. Ha! Who was she trying to kid? The sex had been blow-the-top-of-your-head-off incredible. He'd certainly seemed to enjoy it as much as she had, so maybe he was on the lookout for a repeat performance. Or maybe he was looking for something more.

But what could that be, in truth, because even with him getting involved in Sam's restaurant, didn't he have a whole other life in London? He would be there, and she would be here. They could hook up for the odd weekend, she supposed, until the restaurant was up and running, but then what? It was too much to think about, and she was too tired right then to think about it. Or maybe just a bit scared of how she would feel if that was really all he wanted. She could always ask him and find out. The words stuck in her throat.

'You're very quiet all of a sudden.'

'Am I? Sorry, I'm just a bit tired.' Hating herself for the cop-out, Libby began to make her way up the stairs. 'Well, my bed is calling to me.'

'Hold on, I'll walk you back.' Within two steps he'd caught up with her and taken her hand in his.

They walked in silence to her front door, where she disentangled her fingers ostensibly to fish her key out of her pocket. She had the door open and one foot inside when he stilled her with a single finger beneath her chin. Hopeless to resist, she allowed him to tilt her face up for the briefest kiss. 'Goodnight, Pixie.'

As she crept up the stairs to avoid waking her dad, Libby tried to convince herself it was a good thing that despite his promise of 'next time' he hadn't tried to make arrangements to meet again—and failed miserably.

Chapter 7

Back in London, Owen spent most of the next week glued to his desk as he tried to get on top of everything at work. His weekends were usually spent catching up and reviewing the files and reports on all their projects, so his trip to Lavender Bay had put him behind. It didn't help that his mind strayed to Libby the moment he let his concentration slip. He'd already promised Jack he'd be back for the kid's beach football match, although now he wasn't quite sure why he'd volunteered.

He didn't know the first thing about kids, but there'd been something about the whole mess which had spoken to something deep inside him. Jack's nephew, Noah, had been devastated when one of the other boys told him he couldn't be a part of the fathers and sons football match because he didn't have a dad. What had seemed to be an act of cruelty had turned out to be a misguided attempt by Michael, the other boy, to not be the only child in their class to miss out on the day. Owen knew well enough what it was like to feel excluded from games and class events. None of his foster parents had shown any interest.

Owen had also committed to meeting the bank manager with Sam, so he needed to be sure everything was in hand back here at the office to give him the freedom to not only meet those commitments, but also to spend some quality time with Libby.

By the time Alex came into his office on Friday lunchtime, Owen finally felt like he was getting somewhere. 'Everything all right?' he asked as his second-in-command slumped down in the chair beside his desk.

'Yeah, just about. Bit of an emergency on the Vauxhall site. The foreman's wife went into premature labour, so he had to head to the hospital.'

Owen set down his pen to pay full attention to what his assistant was saying. 'Christ, I hope everything's okay. She's not due for another month, is she?'

'Two weeks. Johnno wanted to work right up to the last minute.' Alex rubbed her eyes, then dropped her head back with a sigh. 'Bob Knox is on that job and he's got more than enough experience to oversee the rest of the day and get the site cleaned up and secured. We already had an agency guy lined up to cover the paternity leave and they've juggled his scheduled to free him up for Monday.'

He might have known she'd have everything in hand. She'd come to him six years ago, frustrated after two years at a larger firm where more than a few old dinosaurs couldn't get their head around the idea of a female quantity surveyor. He'd promised to never ask her to make a cup of tea, and she'd promised he'd never regret hiring her. There'd been other candidates for the job, some with more experience, but his gut had told him Alex would be a good fit. And so it had proven.

From implementing an electronic signing-in system for the sites to help verify submitted timesheets, to championing safety training and even a campaign specifically targeted towards men's health they'd rolled out to all their sites, barely a month had gone by without Alex knocking at Owen's door with a suggestion on how to improve the business. All Owen had to do was keep feeding that hunger in her to progress and both Alex and the company had gone from strength to strength. He'd sent her on every course she'd requested and been paid back many times over with her loyalty and effort.

Three years after she'd started, she'd knocked on his door and confessed to a romance with Nick, a consultant project manager they used to help run some of their bigger projects. Not wanting to lose either of them, he hadn't been a fan of their relationship, but he'd appreciated her honesty and bitten his lip against voicing any protest. Thankfully, his worries had proven unfounded, and he'd even stood up for Nick as his best man at their wedding the previous summer.

'I'll give Johnno a ring later and check in with him. If he wants an extra couple of weeks' leave, I'll cover the cost.'

'Thanks, Boss. I'll give the agency the heads-up that we might want to extend the cover.'

When she continued to sit there but didn't speak Owen swivelled his chair around to face her. 'Something else on your mind?'

Keeping her eyes focused on the ceiling, Alex said, 'You're off down to the coast again this weekend.'

'That's right. I need to finalise the restaurant deal I told you about.' Tilting back his seat, Owen crossed his feet at the ankles. 'Is that a problem?'

Alex shrugged. 'Not for me to say, is it, Boss?'

Owen told her what he thought of that with a sharply raised eyebrow. 'Bollocks. If you've got something on your mind, spit it out.' When he'd first started the company, Owen had been very conscious about watching his language. He wasn't a labourer on site anymore, and he wanted to cultivate a professional environment. He'd stuck to it religiously, until the day he'd come across Alex in the stairwell ranting to herself about an unreliable supplier before she tackled a call with them. He'd given her points for creativity, and they'd agreed to speak frankly to each other behind closed doors.

'Well, it just seems like you're spreading yourself a bit thin. You're in here every morning before me, and when Nick and I drove past last night after we'd been out to the pictures, your office light was still on.' Alex glanced away, then back. 'I don't get the fascination of this Lavender Bay. I had a look online and it looks like any other little coastal town.'

Alex knew a bit about Owen's background, but not all the gory details, and that's how Owen intended it to stay. 'It's personal,' he said, knowing that would be enough to shut her down.

He turned his mind back to the issue at hand. His business was exactly that—both professionally and privately—but that didn't mean he could do what he liked and stuff the consequences. He couldn't be in two places at once, and for all the hours he'd put in that week his thoughts had never been off Lavender Bay for more than a handful of minutes at a time, especially one particular resident. This thing with Libby—not that he was even sure it *was* a thing—was fast becoming an obsession. 'If you think its's becoming a serious issue, I expect you to tell me, okay?'

'Fair enough.' Alex stood. 'You'll be back on Wednesday?'

He nodded. 'That's the plan. Hey, Alex?'

His assistant paused at the door. 'Yes, Boss?'

'How would you feel about a bit more responsibility around here?'

Alex took a step back into the room. 'How much are we talking about?'

'A desk in here, a stake in the company, too, if you want it. We'd have to sit down with the accountant and work it all out so you understand what you'd be agreeing to. There'd be more reward, but potentially more risk to your income so I won't push you into anything. If you'd rather remain a straight employee, we can come up with a package to reflect your extra responsibility.'

The glow of pride on Alex's face lifted something in Owen's heart. She'd proven her loyalty time and again, and it shouldn't have taken a turning point in his own life for Owen to reward her for it. It would also take the weight off his shoulders and give him room to breathe, to devote the time he wanted to on his new venture with Sam. He'd been office bound for too long and getting his hands dirty again felt damn good.

'I don't know what to say.'

'You don't need to say anything yet. Talk it over with Nick this weekend and let me know what you think next week. And if you can talk him into giving up his other clients and coming on board full-time with us, I reckon we can make that work too.' Her excitement dimmed a little, and he thought about what he'd just said, and how it might be misconstrued. 'One isn't dependent upon the other, Alex. You've more than earned a step-up to partner.'

She brightened. 'That's fantastic, really fantastic. Thanks, Boss,' Alex said.

Rising, Owen offered his hand. 'It's Owen from now on.'

Her grin could've lit up half of London. 'Cheers, Owen. You won't regret this, I promise.' They shook hands. 'Right, I'd better go and get on with some work. Don't worry about anything here while you're away, I'll keep on top of everything.'

Owen knew she would, but he didn't want Alex to feel like he was dumping everything in her lap. 'I'll have my phone with me. Don't feel the need to check in, but if anything comes up that you want to bounce off me, just call.'

'I'd better give Nick a ring, too, tell him to put a bottle in the fridge as we'll be celebrating tonight. I might even see if he fancies a weekend away some time before I get too busy.' She beamed at Owen. 'Anywhere you'd recommend, a nice little spot beside the sea somewhere?' Laughing, they shook hands again then Alex left with a decided spring in her step.

Settling back at his desk, Owen picked up his pen and turned his attention back to the project file he was reviewing. As much as he trusted Alex, he wanted everything squared away before his evening train.

'There you are! We were about ready to send a search party out for you. Are you hungry? I've set a plate aside for you because I thought you might be hungry, or maybe you ate on the train? Either way, you sit yourself down, love, and have a drink. I've just rung the bell for last orders, but it's my pub so I can do as I please.' Owen let the flood of words from Annie Barnes wash over him like a soothing balm. It wasn't so much what she said as the way she said it, with real concern as though he was part of the family and not an occasional guest.

The trip down had been a nightmare thanks to a broken air-conditioner in his carriage and a previous service cancellation, so he'd ended up sitting in the corridor for the best part of five hours. He'd stuffed his suit jacket and tie in his bag and rolled up his sleeves, but his cotton shirt still clung to him like a wet rag. He needed a shower and a change of clothes, and possibly a deep tissue massage to get the kinks out of his back, but he needed the foaming pint of lager Annie placed on the bar in front of him more. 'Thanks, Mrs Barnes, you're a lifesaver.' Dropping his bags at his feet, Owen eased his numb arse onto a stool then took a deep draft from his glass.

'Hello, son. We'd about given you up as a lost cause. Here, shall I put those up in your room for you?' Annie's husband, Paul, appeared at his side looking better than the last time Owen had seen him. He'd caught the sun, and the greyish pallor to his skin had given way to a deep summer tan. He didn't know the ins and outs of Paul's health problems, but Sam had mentioned a chronic lung condition had laid his dad low the previous year.

'I can manage them, Mr Barnes. Just let me wash away the dust of the day with this pint and I'll get them out of the way.' Owen nudged his bags closer to the bar with his foot.

'They're fine where they are, love, and so are you,' Annie interjected from the other side of the bar. 'Sit as long as you like. Did you want that plate?'

The heat in the packed pub wasn't any less stifling than the train had been. And it was noisy, to boot. Head throbbing, Owen placed a hand on his belly as it gave an uneasy rumble. The sandwich and crisps he'd grabbed on the way through the station felt like a long time ago, but he was too tired to think about eating just then. If he didn't have anything, though, he'd likely regret it when he woke up starving at 3 a.m. 'Maybe in a few minutes?'

Annie gave him a sympathetic smile. 'Why don't you take that drink up with you and have a shower?'

'Come on, son, I'll give you a hand with these and when you're ready you can join me in the kitchen and we'll see about your supper.' Paul placed a fleeting hand on Owen's shoulder then bent to retrieve the laptop bag and suit carrier from the floor. Too tired to argue, Owen hefted his holdall in one hand, grabbed his pint with the other and followed his host towards the back stairs.

Showered and changed into a pair of baggy cotton shorts and T-shirt, Owen paused at the door to the Barnes family kitchen. 'All right to come in?'

Paul glanced up from where he was bent over by the oven 'Of course it is. I've just turned this up, won't be long now.' He crossed to the fridge and opened it. 'Fancy another beer?'

'Yes, please.' Owen sank down into one of the kitchen chairs and sprawled his legs out in front of him. 'Thanks,' he said, acknowledging the can Paul set down before him. 'You didn't have to go to any trouble.'

'No trouble, son. Sam's next door with Beth, said to let you know he'll be back first thing.' Paul eased himself into the chair opposite and popped the ring on his own can of beer. 'He's talked non-stop about you agreeing to come on board with him about the restaurant. I don't think he can quite believe it.'

Catching the hint of concern, Owen put down his drink and sat forward. 'I'm deadly serious about working with him, Mr Barnes, you don't have to worry I might change my mind or let him down. That's just not who I am. Once I set my mind to something, I see it through.'

'Well, I had to check. Doesn't matter how old they get, I still

64

worry about him and Eliza both. Probably more so now than when they were little. A grazed knee or a slipped bike chain were a lot easier to fix than broken hearts and broken marriages.'

Though he had no experience of it himself, the love Paul held for his children was plain to see. 'Sam and Eliza are lucky to have you and Mrs Barnes in their corner.'

Paul shrugged off the compliment, though there was no hiding the little smile on his lips. 'They're good kids, for all their ups and downs. And what about you, son, who's in your corner?'

'I manage all right for myself.' Owen swigged a mouthful of beer before he said too much.

'That's no good, you've got to have people around who support you. Independence is a fine thing, but not to the point of isolation.'

Owen tried not to let his irritation show. He knew the man meant well, but every word only served to underline what life might have been like had his mother not given him away without a second thought. 'Not everyone gets the choice, though.'

'True enough, son.' Paul pushed to his feet. 'Well, let's see how this dinner is looking.'

A few minutes later, Owen found himself facing a heaped plate of chicken and pasta in a rich, creamy sauce. The fragrant steam rising up wove around his senses and set his stomach rumbling once more. 'This looks great.'

Setting himself down with a small piece of cheese and a couple of water biscuits, Paul smiled. 'Annie thought it would be the easiest thing to warm up for you without sitting too heavy after a long day. How was the journey down?'

Between mouthfuls of the delicious food and another can of beer Owen described his nightmare trip. The conversation segued naturally into talking about the rest of his day and then onto the current projects his company was running. Paul proved an easy sounding board and they were still deep in conversation when Annie wandered in later.

'The bar's sorted. I'll need a hand to put the chairs up tomorrow morning before I do the floors, but everything else is wiped down and the dishwasher's on.' She bustled over to the table, still seemingly full of energy even after a long evening shift. 'Did you enjoy your dinner?' she asked as she removed Owen's empty plate.

'It was perfect, thank you. And thanks again for thinking of me.'

She waved him off. 'It's no bother at all. Right, shall I put the kettle on?'

Paul rose and took the plate from her. 'Give me that. You sit down and I'll make the tea. You should've given me a shout and I'd have helped you downstairs.'

Annie patted his cheek before taking a seat. 'I know you would've, but I was quite happy pottering around on my own. Nice to have a bit of peace and quiet after all that noise. Besides it gave me time to catch up on *The Archers*.'

It was all so bloody normal, and yet as alien to Owen as the perfect sitcom families he'd grown up envying on the television. Feeling like an interloper, he pulled out his phone and tried to focus on an email which had arrived from Alex. Worried that a problem had cropped up already, he was relieved to see it was just an update to say Johnno's wife had had a little girl and both mother and baby were doing fine. He tapped out a quick reply authorising a gift basket and some flowers to be sent, then glanced up to find Annie watching him.

'Good news?'

It was only then Owen realised he was beaming from ear to ear. 'What? Oh, yeah, one of the guys at work has just had a baby. Well, his wife has, I mean. It was a bit of an emergency but sounds like everything's worked out fine.'

'Well, that's a great way to end the day.'

Paul placed a pair of mugs down in front of them, returned a few moments later with his own and resumed his seat. After sharing a quick glace with his wife, he turned to Owen. 'There's something we wanted to talk to you about.'

Owen frowned. What else was there to talk about? 'Look, Mr Barnes, I already told you I'm committed to the restaurant project, there's no need to worry.'

'Yes, I know and I've taken you at your word, son. This kind of follows on from that.'

'What Paul's trying to say is you'll likely be spending a lot more time down here and it's not always easy to make sure there's a room available for you. We're already booked up for the rest of the season and we don't like to turn anyone away.'

Damn. He should've thought of that instead of just assuming he could come and go as he pleased. 'I'm sorry to put you in an awkward position, I'll find myself somewhere else to stay.'

'Oh dear, we're not going about this the right way at all. We don't want you to find somewhere else to stay, we want you to stay with us.'

Thoroughly confused, Owen looked from Annie to Paul. 'I don't understand, you just told me you're fully booked.'

'Well, on the guest room side of things we are, but now that Sam's spending his nights next door with Beth, we thought you might like to use his room when you visit. You can leave some clothing, a wash kit and whatever; that way you can come and go as you need to.'

Taken aback, he took a mouthful of coffee to cover his confusion. They hardly knew him and yet were inviting him to share a part of their home with them. 'Are…are you sure?'

'Of course we are, love. We had a family meeting about it, and everyone thinks it's the most practical solution with you likely to be toing and froing over the next few months.' Annie reached across the table to pat the back of his hand. It was only a fleeting touch, the kind of thing these people shared dozens of times a day and yet it reached deep inside Owen and stirred some unknown longing.

'I…I'm not sure what to say.'

The kind smile on Annie's face slipped. 'Unless, you don't want to?' She exchanged a quick glance with her husband. 'We should have considered you might want to retain your privacy, not be lumped in with the rest of us.' God, she was deflating before him like a tyre leaking air from a slow puncture. 'Well, if you could try and work out your schedule for the next couple of months then we can make sure we have one of the guest rooms available.'

And turn business away, just because he didn't know how to accept an act of kindness. 'No, no, don't do that. Honestly, it'd be fantastic if I could use Sam's room, it'll save me so much hassle not having to lug my kit back and forth all the time. I just wasn't expecting it.'

You'd think he'd given them the Crown jewels the way they were beaming at him. Was this what normal people were like? Doing things for no other reason than to make someone else's life a bit easier? 'I'll pay you board, of course.'

'You most certainly will not! We didn't suggest this so we could make extra money.' Paul looked mutinous.

Owen held his hands up. 'I didn't think that for one moment, but I won't take advantage of your kindness. You must let me contribute something, at least towards meals.'

'Well, I suppose that'd be all right.' Annie sounded slightly miffed about it and Owen knew he'd have his work cut out trying to get her to accept a penny. He'd do it though. He always paid his way.

And, as generous as the Barnes' offer was, it created another problem for him. With enough persuasion, he might have persuaded Libby to sneak up through the guest entrance and into his room, but he couldn't imagine any circumstances where she'd be willing to spend the night with him ensconced in the heart of the family quarters above the pub. He'd have to come up with another solution. It took him the rest of his cup of coffee before the perfect idea struck him. 'As I'm going to be spending more time here, I really need to find a space I can work in. It doesn't have to be big, but I need to be able to secure it.'

Paul frowned. 'I'm not sure what to suggest, we don't really go in for hot desking around here.'

'Hot desking, listen to Alan Sugar over there!' Annie snorted.

Owen grinned. He loved the way they teased each other. There was a familiarity to it which spoke to a lifetime of shared moments and memories. 'I'm not looking to establish an empire, just a quiet space where I can focus on my work.' *And other things.* 'Hmm.' He considered tapping his lip, but decided that would be overkill. 'Do you know anything about those little beach huts along the front?'

Chapter 8

Waking up the previous Sunday morning in a haze of panic and morning-after-the-night-before regrets, Libby had told her dad she had a migraine and spent the day hiding in her room. The first time she'd spotted Owen through a crack in the curtains, she'd ducked away then cursed herself for being a coward. Positioning herself on the window seat so she could see out without being seen, she'd been by turns shocked, excited and finally charmed as he reappeared on the promenade at various times over the day. Torn between wanting to run out and leap into his arms and having to confess to her dad she'd lied to him, Libby had stayed put, consoled with the thought he'd be back the following weekend.

The rest of the week had passed in an agony of indecision and self-recriminations. She had no way of contacting Owen as they hadn't got around to exchanging numbers—whether this had been a deliberate act on his part became yet another question she'd tortured herself with. She could've asked Sam, but how to justify wanting the details for someone she'd professed such a strong dislike for without giving the whole bloody game away? And what was she going to say to him even if she could contact him? One minute she was desperate to lay eyes—and other things—on him, the next she hoped never to see him again. Only that wasn't going to happen, was it, because he was back in the bay again for the weekend.

Nerves turning her stomach to acid, Libby tugged up the hood on an old sleeveless sweatshirt she'd teamed with a pair of frayed denim shorts and hurried along the prom as fast as her flip-flops would let her. Almost tripping over her feet in her desperation to get the hundred yards from the chip shop to the emporium, she cursed the already scorching temperature for making her boots impractical. Approaching the front door of The Siren, Libby paused to scan the busy stretch of pavement before she then scurried past and into the safety of the emporium. The bell door jangled loudly above her head as she leaned back against the door with a sigh of relief at getting past the pub unnoticed. She'd never make a secret agent.

'There you are, we thought you must have forgotten us!' Beth called out brightly from her spot behind the counter. 'Eliza's in the back making a brew.'

Having removed her hood, Libby ruffled a hand through her short hair as she skirted around the counter with a quick smile to the customer Beth was serving. Mrs Bradshaw was the self-appointed chair of the Lavender Bay Improvement Society and made it a point to know everybody's business. There was no way Libby was getting trapped into conversation with her if she could help it. 'I overslept so a cuppa sounds perfect.' She'd have been on time had she not lain awake for hours fretting over what to do about Owen until finally nodding off around 3 a.m., but she kept that juicy titbit to herself.

'Here, take this one and I'll make another.' Eliza thrust a mug into Libby's hands as she entered the back area of the shop which held a tiny kitchenette area and a couple of old armchairs.

Libby sank down into one of the chairs with a huge yawn. 'Thank you,' she managed through watering eyes.

'Late night?' Eliza patted her shoulder sympathetically before perching on the arm of Libby's chair as she waited for the kettle to re-boil.

'Just one of those ones where I couldn't sleep for some reason. Too hot, I suppose.' Though the night temperatures had been oppressive of late, it still felt like a lie.

'You're not kidding. If I didn't have a fan in my room, I don't know what I'd do with myself.' Eliza patted her pocket, pulled out a sugar-pink scrunchie and secured her long curls in a high ponytail. 'That's a bit better.' She brushed a hand over the spiky-ends of Libby's crop. 'When it's hot like this I envy you.'

Horrified at the idea Eliza might be contemplating cutting her beautiful hair, Libby almost spilled hot tea in her lap as she made a grab for her friend's arm. 'Don't even think about it! If it's bothering you, let me put it in a French plait for you, or something.'

'I'm only kidding…well mostly, but I do get a bit bored sometimes of all this hair everywhere.'

By the time Beth joined them, Eliza was settled on the floor cross-legged in front of the armchair and Libby had made good progress with the plait. 'Phew! I didn't think Mrs Bradshaw would ever stop talking.' The three of them shared a knowing grin.

'What was she going on about now?' Eliza said between sips of her tea.

Beth grinned. 'She was telling me about some ruffian with a crew cut and dreadful tattoos she saw coming out the pub this morning, said she was shocked how early some types needed a drink. You should've seen her face when I pointed out it was probably Sam's new business partner and that Owen ran his own development company.'

Eliza laughed, whilst Libby ducked her head, pretending to focus on the plait in her hands as she felt her face flame. If she couldn't hear his name without blushing, she was in big trouble. *Just tell them*. It was on the tip of her tongue to confess all, but when she opened her mouth nothing came out. She knew she was being ridiculous—though they might tease her a bit, there'd be no judgement from either of her friends over her decision to sleep with Owen. Perhaps it would be better to wait and see how things went with him first. If they made a big deal of it and then he made it clear it was a one-off she'd feel even more foolish than she already did. She wasn't lying to them exactly, just withholding information until she had a clearer picture in her own mind of where things stood. *Yeah, yeah, yeah.*

'So why did you want to see us this morning?' Eliza asked, providing a very welcome change in subject as Libby tied off the end of her plait and gave her a pat on the shoulder to let her know it was done. Eliza leaned her head back to blow her a kiss before turning back to Beth. 'Not that I ever mind spending time with you guys, especially as Jack's having a boys' weekend with Noah and his friend Michael.'

Stepping back out into the main shop area, Beth bent to retrieve something from beneath the counter then thrust it at the two of them. 'I got this in the post from one of my suppliers yesterday!'

Libby stared at the thick sales brochure covered in ceramic Santas, packs of greetings cards and novelty bobble hats. 'But… it's only July.'

'I know,' Beth wailed. 'It's hotter than Satan's armpit outside and I'm supposed to somehow get my head around ordering stock for Christmas.'

Reaching forward, Eliza took the brochure and began leafing through it. Libby peered over her shoulder at the pages of cute snow globes, embroidered cushions and baubles. 'There's so much choice,' she said with a shake of her head. 'I had no idea.'

'Neither did I.' Beth slumped into the chair opposite. 'I don't know where to start.'

'These are lovely.' Eliza held up a page of simple wooden table decorations so both of them could see. 'Really simple and elegant. I think they'd fit right in with the kind of stock you've been introducing, Beth.'

A matched pair of figurines caught Libby's eye—a doe leaning down to nuzzle at a fawn curled at her feet. 'Want these!'

'Well, that's your first sale sorted.' Eliza grinned at Beth.

'You're clearly a natural at this,' her friend retorted as the bell above the shop door rang. 'I shall leave you to it.'

Sliding from the chair to join Eliza on the floor, Libby joined her in poring over the brochure. Once they'd had a browse through to get an idea of what was available, they started again from the beginning, turning the corners to mark the pages of items which caught their eyes. 'I love these.' Eliza smoothed her hand over a page of cushions embroidered with slogans of good cheer.

'You could make ones better than that.' Libby had a gorgeous set which Eliza had made to match her favourite bedding as a surprise for her eighteenth birthday. They looked as good today as when she'd first unwrapped them and they never failed to bring a smile to her face whenever she dressed the bed with them. Always an incredibly gifted crafter, Eliza had recently started up her own business making dresses and knick-knacks which Beth was selling through the emporium, as well as homemade soaps and other luxury body products using the lavender Jack produced up at the farm.

Eliza sucked her lower lip between her teeth and began to chew it, her expression thoughtful. 'I hadn't really considered doing seasonal-specific stuff…I suppose I could.'

'Suppose you could, what?' Beth asked as she walked back in so Libby filled her in on her suggestion about the cushions. 'I think that's a great idea. I could sell them for you, or better yet, why don't you take a booth at the Christmas market and sell them yourself?'

Confused, Libby looked between the other two. 'What Christmas market? Nobody tells me anything these days!'

'It's the first I've heard about it as well,' Eliza said.

'The local traders' association sent an email last week suggesting they organise a Christmas market as a way of encouraging visitors to the bay out of season. They want to get enough people to take booths to fill the promenade from one end to the other.' Beth picked up the fallen catalogue and studied one of the pages they'd marked. 'I was talking to Sam about it last night because he's keen to do one for the restaurant, and I suppose that's what made me panic a bit about getting stock organised in time for this place.'

'I'll check with Dad when I get back, see if he's seen it.' Libby let the conversation continue between Beth and Eliza as she thought about the market idea. Her dad could do a fish and chip stall, of course, but perhaps she could take one for herself, do a bit of a test run for the kind of things she wanted to sell as and when she converted the shop to a café. Easy things that people could walk around with like hot sausage rolls and cheese and onion pasties; mince pies and stollen bites for those with a sweeter tooth. 'Maybe I'll take a stall, too.' She outlined her plan. 'If I can show Dad what I want to do is popular, it might go easier on him when it comes to changing directions if he really does decide to retire next year.'

Eliza reached her for hand. 'Have you talked to him about it yet?'

'No.' Libby shook her head, feeling pathetic. 'I know I should, but I can't bear the idea of upsetting him. What if he takes me wanting to change things the wrong way, like I think running the chippy isn't good enough for me?'

'I know how hard it is.' Eliza squeezed her fingers. 'I was terrified of telling Mum and Dad I didn't want to take over the pub from them. It took a bit of getting used to, but they're coming around to the idea.' She gave a wistful sigh. 'They just want me to be happy, and I'm sure it's the same for your dad, too.'

'You're right, I know you're right, I just haven't found the right time to bring it up with him yet. I also don't want him to think I'm looking to push him out of the door, but some nights he looks so flipping tired when we close up that it worries me.'

Eliza tugged her close for a hug. 'It's scary growing up, Libs. I always thought my dad was so big and strong, invincible to everything. When he got sick last year it really brought things home to roost.'

'He's been making good progress, though?'

'Oh, yes, but he'll never be the same. And I look at Mum and she's suddenly got all this grey hair and then I worry about the future. Perhaps I shouldn't be fiddling around with cushions and soaps and should just knuckle down at the pub, so they can have some peace of mind.' She rested her head on Libby's shoulder with a sigh.

Beth hunkered down in front of them. 'What would your mum say if she could hear you, Eliza?' She looked at Libby. 'Or your lovely dad for that matter? If either thought you were giving up on your own dreams in order to please them, they'd be horrified.' A broad smile lifted the frown between her brows. 'Besides, if I can stand up to my mum about keeping this old place rather than selling up and pocketing the cash, then you two have got nothing to worry about!' If you looked up the word mercenary in the dictionary, there'd be a picture of Beth's mum next to it. At least these days her nagging was confined to the odd transatlantic phone call, and then only if it was Beth who bothered to place the call.

'All right, I'll do it!' Libby held up her hands in defeat. 'Now come on, let's get your Christmas stock order sorted out.'

Hunkered down on the floor, the three of them spent the next couple of hours reviewing the catalogue and making a short list of items they thought would work well on the eclectic shelves of the emporium. Beth was up and down like a jack-in-the-box responding to the front door bell of the shop which could only bode well for her business. As they waited for her to return, Libby took the opportunity to stretch out her cramped legs. 'How did the soap-making trial go?' she asked Eliza who'd got up to flick the kettle on again.

A telltale blush heated her cheeks. 'It was very nice, umm, good, it went really well. I was very pleased with the blending.'

Ha! Seeing as how she'd gone up to Jack's farm to use the large workspace in his lavender processing shed, Libby could just imagine how well things had *blended*. It was on the tip of her tongue to say exactly that when Eliza changed the subject. 'So, are you watching the football match tomorrow? I have to work the bar because Mum and Dad already have plans and Beth is hoping it will bring in some extra visitors, so she can't leave the shop. Jack, Sam and Owen could do with a bit of cheerleading.'

The incongruous image of herself dressed in a short dress waving a set of pom-poms as she yelled Owen's name popped into Libby's head. Ducking to hide a blush, she shook her head. 'No, I'm working too. We're hoping for lots of hungry spectators.' Even if the chippy wasn't going to open, wild horses couldn't drag her anywhere near the beach tomorrow. Sleeping with Owen had been a one-off silly mistake. His silence over the past week had been enough to make that clear. She would not be repeating it again.

Chapter 9

'Noah James Gilbert, you stop right there!' Exiting the pub with Sam, Owen found himself freezing on the spot at the shouted command, and he wasn't the only one. Dozens of heads turned to regard the kindly looking woman with short grey hair standing with her fists pressed to her hips in the middle of the prom. Two guilty-faced small boys stood statue still about thirty metres in front of her, heads bowed as though waiting for the sky to fall in on them.

'Someone's in trouble already,' Sam observed with a grin as they watched the woman blow on her nails before buffing them on the front of her pretty peach sleeveless blouse. She turned to say something to Jack who stood beside her laden down with several bags and a large cool box. In moments his expression was as hang-dog as the boys.

By the time they'd made their way to where Jack was waiting for them, his mum had taken both boys in hand and led them onto the beach. Sam clapped Jack on the shoulder. 'Is that your mum? She's terrifying.'

'Here, make yourself useful, will you?' Jack thrust the cool box at Sam, seeming to take no offence. 'And as I recall, your mum can give mine a run for her money.'

Sam laughed as he jogged down the steps beside Jack. Feeling awkward at their easy banter over such an alien topic, Owen gave them a bit of distance. There was no malice in their observations, more a resigned affection. Sam dumped the cool box on the sand then straightened up. 'Don't remind me! We must make sure they never meet, or they'll be plotting world domination within the first half-hour.'

'Too late. Mum's decided to *pop in* to the pub later and see Eliza.' Jack rolled his eyes.

'We're doomed, then, mate.' Sam grinned. 'All mums are the same, right, Owen?'

A tumult of emotions swept through him. Confusion, anger, and more than a touch of shame. 'I wouldn't know.' The all-telling words were out before he could stop them. Not wanting to see surprise—or worse, pity—on their faces, Owen shouldered past the two of them and strode across the beach to where Jack's mum stood with the boys.

Ignoring her curious glance, and conscious of the way he towered over the kids, Owen dropped onto one knee to bring himself to their height and held out his hand. 'Hi, I'm Owen, and you must be Noah.' With the same blue eyes and dark hair there was no mistaking the boy as anything other Jack's nephew.

Taking his hand with a shy smile, Noah shook it then turned to the wary boy beside him. 'This is my friend, Michael.'

Owen studied the boy who was the reason he'd found himself volunteering to help out in the first place. Never a joiner, he'd been unable to ignore the conversation between Jack and Sam a couple of weeks previously in the pub. Owen had felt an immediate pang of sympathy for the kid's plight, though his own many experiences of missing out on stuff had been down to general neglect and disinterest rather than a parent struggling to make ends meet by pulling extra hours driving a taxi as was the case with Michael's dad. Whatever the reason, feeling excluded could seem like the end of the world at his age so Owen had found himself offering to fill the gap. He smiled at Michael but didn't try to force the boy to take his hand. 'Hey, I'm going to be your playing partner for today, if that's okay with you?'

Michael eyed Owen uncertainly, but eventually gave a nod of assent. Relieved to be over the first hurdle, Owen turned his hand to helping set out the blanket, beach towels and other paraphernalia Jack had hauled onto the beach. Sam decided they'd benefit from a couple of sun umbrellas and headed back to the pub with Jack's mum on his arm, promising her an introduction to Beth and a friends and family discount at the emporium.

'I'm going to go and get us signed in.' Jack pointed to where a slightly harassed-looking young woman stood a few feet away, clutching a clipboard. 'See you in a minute.' When Noah slipped his hand in Jack's, obviously intent on going with him, Jack paused to glance at Owen, a question in his eyes.

Owen waved him on. 'Michael and I will be fine, won't we, mate? We can work out our winning tactics.' Patting the edge of the blanket next to him, Owen waited until Michael sat beside him then began to sketch stick figures in the sand as he laid out options of what they could do. He kept it simple, doubting either of them would remember once they got running around but it was an easy ice-breaker and he soon had Michael chattering about the players from his favourite team.

Bastian, Jack's chocolate Labrador, took advantage of their distraction to claim the blanket while no one was paying attention and when Owen glanced over his shoulder, the big dog looked set for the day. He didn't do much more than wag his tail in approval when Sam returned and unfurled the first of two huge umbrellas and bathed their bit of the beach in welcome shade.

As they stood on the sidelines awaiting their turn to play, Owen watched Michael eyeing the other pairs gathered around them. The easy affection connections between father and son were in marked contrast to the slight stiffness between the two of them, and Owen resolved to try harder. He'd volunteered to do this to make sure Michael didn't feel left out, but he was at risk of making him look as out of place as if he'd not been there at all. Squatting down, he placed himself in Michael's eyeline. 'I bet your dad is sorry to be missing out on this today? I'm sure he'd be here if he could, though.'

Michael nodded. 'He works hard to take care of us.' It sounded like words he'd picked up from someone else and had adopted as a mantra to remind himself. 'Jack said if I could score a goal for Daddy, he'd film it on his phone so I could show him later.'

'Then we'll have to make sure you score.' An idea came to him, sure he'd end up looking a bit of a tit, but what would it matter in the big scheme of things. 'Hey, Michael, we should work out a celebration routine for when you do score, just like they do in the Premier League.'

Eyes bright for the first time that morning, Michael grinned. 'Can we?'

'Sure, but let's talk about it over there so no one can overhear and nick our idea.' Owen nodded over to a quieter spot not far from the water and they laid their plans.

By the time their names were called, Michael was raring to go. Delighted at his enthusiasm, Owen took his place beside him in the miniature marked-out pitch. 'Let's smash 'em!' he said, holding up his hand for a high-five.

'No mercy!' Michael smacked his little hand against Owen's as he completed the battle cry they'd come up with, and then the game was on.

It was hot, chaotic and the most fun Owen had had in a long time. At the end of the first five-minute half he was bent over at the waist panting from a combination of exhaustion and too much laughter. Their opponents were pretty hapless, and it was not through want of trying that the score remained goalless. Accepting a bottle of cold water from Sam, Owen chugged half of it down then made sure Michael had a good drink too. Using a towel the other man handed out to him, Owen rubbed the sweat from Michael's face and arms. 'All right, champ?'

'We nearly had them just before the whistle!' Bouncing on his toes, Michael showed no signs of fatigue. 'I'm gonna score for sure next half.' He glanced towards Jack who gave him a thumbs-up, his phone held ready in his other hand.

'I'm ready, buddy, don't worry. Now let's see you score.'

Owen tossed the towel to Sam, the whistle blew, and they were off again. The kid on the opposite team kicked the ball towards his dad, missed his mark and groaned as the ball slid past his dad's foot and over the sideline. Thinking it was a game, Bastian lunged for the football, tugging his lead out of Noah's hand in the process, and scampered off down the beach shoving the ball with his nose. The whistle blew, and Owen joined in the chorus of laughter as a red-faced Jack chased after his dog. That only made things worse, of course, and soon half the spectators were involved trying to rescue the ball from the Lab, who barked excitedly at all his new friends.

'Oh, Mrs Taylor's going to tell him off.' Eyes wide as saucers, Michael had his gaze fixed on the small woman who was marching down the beach towards Jack. From the wagging of her finger, it did look indeed like she was giving him a talking-to.

Owen gave Michael's shoulder a gentle nudge. 'Maybe she'll give him detention.' The boy looked horrified for a moment as though detention was a fate worse than death, before breaking out into giggles that shook his whole body. 'And Bastian, too,' he gasped. 'She'll make him sit in the corner!'

Order finally restored, with Bastian banished back to the blanket and Sam standing guard over him, they recommenced the match. The minutes flew past, and though they pressed forward it seemed they were destined for a goalless draw until Owen dummied a kick to the left, sending his adult opponent in the wrong direction and leaving a free space for Michael to run into. Owen passed him the ball and held his breath as the kid faced off against his classmate who'd dashed back to cover the goal. Michael got his foot perfectly under the ball and sent it flying past the keeper's shoulder and straight into the back of the miniature net.

With a scream of delight, Michael threw out his arms and zoomed around like an aeroplane until he came to a stop facing Owen. They nodded once at each other then exchanged the complicated routine of hand slaps they'd come up with before flapping their arms like a pair of demented chickens as they turned in a circle. Cheers rose from the spectators and uncaring of how ridiculous he might look, Owen turned to them and bowed with a flourish as the whistle blew signalling the end of their match.

'We won, we won!' Michael took a flying leap at Owen who had no choice other than to catch him up in his arms. Flipping the boy around so he could cling to his shoulders, Owen carried him off the field like they'd won the World Cup, not the first-round robin in a kids' friendly.

The rest of the afternoon passed in a whirl of laughter. Owen and Michael made it through to the knock-out stages, but neither were bothered when they lost in their quarter final. The two boys had a whale of a time—when they weren't running around the beach, they were splashing in and out of the shallows with Bastian. The simple joy on their faces hurt and healed Owen's heart in equal measures. Beneath the pang of jealousy that he'd never experienced anything like this as a kid himself was a surprising warmth that he'd played some small part in a special day. Whatever difficulties the boys might have faced, they retained a sense of innocence Owen hoped neither would lose for a long time to come.

When they finally trudged up the beach, clothes stiff with dried salt water, hair full of sand and stinking like only men and boys could do after hours running around in the baking sun, it felt like the five of them were a little band of brothers. It wasn't just the kids; Owen had found himself really enjoying the company of both Sam and Jack. Like light and shade, one full of quick laughter, the other more thoughtful, though no less amusing in his responses, the pair were so easy to talk to that he found himself already looking forward to the many more weekends to come. It'd been a long time since he'd had friends, far too long if he was honest with himself.

The fact Jack had taken on someone else's child—even his brother's kid—filled Owen with admiration. He couldn't imagine being thrust into that situation; he'd never pictured himself having kids and wasn't sure he'd be equal to the task. Mucking around on the beach for a couple of hours was one thing, but the idea of being solely responsible for the health and wellbeing of a child? Owen knew all too well how badly that could turn out and was in no hurry to risk repeating the mistakes of his own past. As fun as the afternoon had been, he wasn't sorry to be handing Michael back to his parents.

Leaving Jack and the boys with a round of high-fives and a big hug from Michael, Owen followed Sam into the pub for a quick pint. He had plans for the evening, but not wanting to risk anyone prying into them, he feigned the need for an early night—even going so far as to persuade Eliza, who was serving behind the bar, to rustle him up a sandwich to take up to his room with a second beer.

A hot shower, a change of clothes and a quick check to make sure the coast was clear, he let himself quietly out the guest entrance down the back stairs and took a circuitous route towards the beach. Stopping the first young lad he spotted, Owen took an envelope out of his pocket and offered it to the boy. 'How would you like to earn yourself five quid?'

Chapter 10

Two days. Owen had been back in Lavender Bay for two whole days and hadn't so much as walked past the front door of the chippy. Libby knew this because she'd spent the same two days with her eyes glued to a certain spot on the promenade railings. It was one thing for Libby to decide it'd been a mistake to sleep with him, it was quite another for him to prove it so blatantly by avoiding her.

The kids' beach football match Owen, Jack and Sam were involved with had finished ages ago. It had been a huge success, or so she'd heard from the scores of families who'd come through the front door for the past couple of hours, tired, happy and starving after hours spent running around in the Sunday afternoon sun. Libby hadn't attended the event herself—though she'd normally have been down there cheering on every team—because the last thing she wanted was for Owen to think she was gawking at him. Bloody man! He had her second-guessing herself all the time and then didn't have the decency to show his face.

Well, at least Sunday was early closing so she only had to hang on for five more minutes and then she could go upstairs and sulk in the bath. She checked the clock: two minutes left, close enough to switch off the fryers. Her hand was inches from the switch when the buzzer beneath the front door mat sounded. With a sigh, and the falsest of smiles, Libby looked up to greet the customer only to find a young boy of about 10 clutching a fiver in one hand and an envelope in the other. 'Can I help you?'

The boy thrust the envelope onto the counter. 'This is for you, and can I have some chips please?'

Libby studied the envelope, but didn't touch it. Her name was scrawled in an unfamiliar bold black script. She didn't need to know the writing to guess who it was from though. 'Where did you get this?'

With a shrug, the boy pointed back over his shoulder. 'Man on the beach gave me a fiver to deliver it to you.' His face clouded. 'Did I do something wrong?'

Shaking her head, Libby scooped a large portion of chips into the centre of the pile of paper in front of her. 'Well, your mum probably wouldn't like you accepting money off a stranger, even for something as simple as delivering an envelope, would she?'

His face fell even further. 'No.'

Poor kid, it wasn't his fault a certain someone had taken advantage of him. 'Hey, don't worry. It's just a friend of mine messing about, but I think you should be more careful in the future, and you should tell your mum about what you did. Now, do you want salt and vinegar on these?'

'Yes, please.' Clutching his chips and the change from his precious five-pound note the boy slouched from the shop.

The second he'd cleared the steps, Libby swung the closed sign and bolted the door. For the next half an hour, she ignored the envelope and stuck diligently to her clean-up routine. If Owen thought he could ignore her and then she'd come running, he was in for a disappointment. She had a hot bath and an e-book she'd pre-ordered ages ago waiting for her, and that was the only thing she planned on reading. With a huff, she swept the envelope into the just-emptied bin, turned off the lights and brushed past the beaded curtain hanging between the shop and the back area.

She made it halfway upstairs before coming to an abrupt halt. Wasn't she just as guilty of ignoring Owen? Worse, really, because at least he was making an effort to communicate. Two steps back down and she froze again. Why send a letter rather than come in person? Perhaps he wanted to let her down gently and thought it would be easier in writing. The idea he might not want to see her again tied her stomach in knots and she started back up the stairs, not ready to face that possibility.

Her foot hovered above the final tread. But what if he did want to see her, but was worried she would *reject* him? 'This is ridiculous!' Stomping almost hard enough to put her foot through one of the treads, Libby marched back down and into the shop to snatch the envelope out of the bin.

'Everything all right, lovey?'

At her dad's voice, Libby stuffed the envelope in the front pocket of her trousers then turned around. 'What? Oh, everything's fine thanks.' When he stared at the waste bin still clutched in her free hand, she plastered on a smile. 'I thought I'd lost one of my rings so was just checking the bin.' The clean, empty bin. God, she was a terrible liar.

Either her dad hadn't noticed or was too nice to say anything about her odd behaviour. 'That's a shame, lovey. I'm sure it'll turn up once you stop looking for it.' It had been his solution for finding lost things for as long as she could remember, and the familiarity of it was enough to brighten her mood.

Hooking her arm through his, she rested her head against his shoulder. 'Wise words, Dad.'

'What're your plans for this fine evening?' he asked as they made their way upstairs to their family home. 'There's one of those crime series you love starting tonight, if you fancy it?'

Conscious of the envelope burning a hole in her pocket, Libby demurred. 'I'm not sure, Dad. I've been stuck in all day, so I might pop out for a bit of fresh air.'

'Whatever you like, lovey. Shall I DVR it and we can watch it later?'

'Sounds like a plan. I'm going to get changed, I'll see you in a bit.' With a quick peck on his cheek, she hurried up to her private haven on the second floor.

Most of their accommodation sprawled over the first floor, but Libby had chosen one of the attic rooms as a child. Then, as now, she'd loved the view it afforded out across the sea. Her dad had extended the windowsill to create a bench seat which her mum had covered in gaily coloured cushions. It was her spot. For thinking, dreaming, or spying on gorgeous, frustrating men. Whatever her mood was, curling up on her little bench always made her feel better.

Sinking down on one of the tattered cushions, Libby drew out the crumpled envelope and stared at it. Five minutes—and a failure to develop any kind of X-ray vision—later, she gave into temptation and ripped it open. Her eyes scanned the brief note, little bubbles of excitement fizzing inside her.

Mr Owen Coburn cordially invites Ms Elizabeth Marie Stone to join him for supper this evening at 8 p.m.

Location: Third hut from the left, The Beach, Lavender Bay.

Dress code: clothing optional

Clothing optional? He should be so bloody lucky. With a skip in her step, Libby headed to the little en-suite bathroom her dad had installed when she'd turned 12. If Owen wanted to see her naked again he was going to have to work for it, but best to be prepared…just in case.

With a quick rub of her palms against the front of her best jeans, Libby glanced over her shoulder, then tapped on the door of the beach hut. The beach around her was mostly empty. Those who'd finished their holidays would be well on their way home by now, and the locals would be going through their regular Sunday evening routines. The door swung back and her breath caught at the sight of Owen clad in an olive green short-sleeved shirt which turned his tanned skin to a delicious shade of caramel. He'd teamed it with a pair of cream chinos and his feet were bare. It really was criminal for a man to be so good-looking. 'Hi.' It was about all she could manage.

'Hi.' He scrubbed at the back of his neck with one hand. 'I wasn't sure you were going to show.'

That admission of uncertainty did more to disarm her than anything else. 'After such a charming invitation, how could I resist?' She gave him a quick once-over. 'I see you didn't follow the suggested dress code either.'

He laughed. 'Can't blame a man for trying.' Stepping back, he swept his arm wide. 'Come on in.'

Scanning the room, two thoughts crossed her mind in quick succession: one, he really was trying, and two, she was in deep trouble. A bed with an old-fashioned brass frame dominated one half of the small space, its mattress draped in a mish-mash of patchwork quilts, blankets and cushions.

Not wanting to think too hard about how comfortable it looked, her eyes skipped over to a battered wooden desk with an old captain's chair in front of it and a mismatched cabinet beside it. The top of the desk held several platters of cold meat, cheese, olives and a crispy-topped cob loaf. Beside a couple of china plates draped with cotton napkins sat an ice bucket with what looked like a bottle of champagne nestled inside it and a pair of mismatched glasses. A bowl of strawberries and a pot of clotted cream adorned the cabinet. 'What's all this?'

Slipping past her, Owen lifted the champagne from the ice and began to twist off the wire cage covering the cork. 'I did promise you supper.'

'Yes, but how did you manage'— arms outstretched, she turned in a half-circle —'all this?'

With one of the napkins wrapped about the cork, Owen eased it from the bottle's neck with the softest pop, rather than the brash, showy bang she might have expected from him. Another point in his favour—they were beginning to rack up. 'The furniture I picked up after touring around the local antique shops yesterday afternoon.'

'Antique shops?' Had he been shopping at the emporium? That would be bound to raise questions with Beth.

'*Not* the one you're thinking of, don't panic.' Owen handed her a glass full of sparkling golden liquid. 'The food, I sourced from the local supermarket through one of those click-and-collect orders.'

He was still missing the point. 'But how did you get access to this hut?'

'Oh, that?' He gave her a disarming smile. 'I asked the Barneses about how I might go about renting one.'

'You did *what*?' Humiliation burned across her cheeks. What on earth had he told them, that he wanted a…a love shack?

'If I'm going to be spending more time down here, I need an office I can work from in peace. I can rig up the laptop to my phone for internet access, and I quite fancied something with a sea view.' He reached for her free hand. 'Annie and Paul are letting me stay in Sam's old room which is incredibly generous of them, but completely ruinous to my plans for you.' He pressed a kiss to her palm.

Relief flooded through her, leaving her giddy before she'd taken so much as a sip of her champagne. 'What kind of plans would those be?'

Sliding his arm around her waist, her pulled her close. 'Lots of nefarious plans which require adherence to the dress code.'

'You're very sure of yourself, aren't you?' Her words might have held more impact if she hadn't cuddled closer to his chest.

'When it comes to you, Libby, I'm not sure of anything other than I can't get you out of my head.'

Oh, Lord. He knew all the right things to say. A pang of worry marred her excitement at the effort he'd gone to. Perhaps he knew

90

what to say because he'd had a lot of practice. She wasn't exactly an expert when it came to relationships. What if this was all just a bit of flash to make sure she fell into his arms? What if he had a girlfriend back in London and she was just a convenient amusement for when he was staying in the bay? He leaned down for a kiss, but she stopped him with a hand to his chest. 'Don't hurt me, okay?'

'Hurt you?' His arm fell away. 'What kind of a man do you think I am, Libby?'

'That's the point, Owen. I have no idea. I don't really know anything about you.'

A deep groove etched between his brows. 'I'm not one for all that soul-baring, "tell me all about your feelings and I'll tell you all about mine" crap. Can't we just be two people having a good time together?'

There was a tension to his words, and she wondered exactly what it was he was trying to hide from her. She tried again. 'I'm not expecting you to bare your soul to me. I just meant that I don't know anything about your life in London, or what your interest is in Lavender Bay.'

Owen sank down on the edge of the bed, eyes fixed on the glass he held between his fingers. 'I have my own company which I built from scratch after starting out as a builder's mate. I own a one-bedroom flat in an anonymous high-end development in Canary Wharf, which I share with a half-dead spider plant, and by own, I mean I have a mortgage large enough to give myself nightmares. Half the other apartments are empty because they've been bought as investment opportunities or tax write-offs so I have no neighbours that I've ever met. I eat out most nights because the meals for one section in the supermarket is the most depressing place on the planet. I date the right sort of women and take them to the right sort of places and I'm bored shitless by the whole bloody lot of it.'

Wow. She wasn't sure what she'd been expecting, but this

wasn't it. At least she had her dad and her friends, a community she fit into and was an integral part of. People who would always be happy to hear her voice if she called them. She couldn't imagine anything worse than the empty, lonely life he'd just described to her. A couple of steps brought her close enough to stand between his legs. 'I'm definitely the wrong sort of woman then because as much as I love the effort you went to this evening, I'd have been just as happy with a bag of salt and vinegar crisps and a glass of house white in the pub. I don't do materialism.'

Leaning back on one elbow so he could look up into her eyes, Owen waved the glass in his free hand towards the discreet logo sewn onto the front of his shirt. 'That's a shame, because I'm a study in materialism.'

'Bollocks.' Libby nudged his knee with hers. 'You're the most real person I've ever met.' There was a vitality to him, a strength of will that made him stand out in the crowd. She'd called it confidence, arrogance even, but that wasn't it at all. He was a man who knew himself for what he was and wore it well. If she wasn't careful, she'd get caught up by his sheer force of personality and be swept away. 'Being around you scares me a little bit,' she admitted.

He sat up so quickly champagne spilled over the back of his hand. Eyes wide with horror, he stared at her. 'I scare you? Christ, Libby, that's the last thing I want to do.'

'Not like that!' Cupping his cheek, she smiled down at him. 'You have a lot of presence, and sometimes that's a bit overwhelming. I feel like it'd be easy to lose all sense of myself when I'm with you.'

Owen's hand found her hip. 'Now it's my turn to call bollocks. You've got personality in spades. You're not like any other woman I've ever met.'

'So you keep telling me, and that worries me, too. I don't want to be some novelty or amusement.'

His fingers slid down to squeeze her bottom. 'Because there's nothing novel or amusing about mermaid hair.' There was such a sweet smile on his lips, it was impossible to be offended.

His hold on her firmed, urging her down until she straddled his lap. 'That's better. I couldn't do this with you all the way up there.' Leaning forward he brushed her lips with his, a sweet glide of temptation that brought every inch of her to life with the spark of delicious memories. 'There's no nefarious plan here, I promise. I fancy the pants off you, and I think that's mutual. Let's just have some fun and see where things go, okay?'

'I'm overthinking all this, aren't I?'

Owen took her glass then placed it together with his own on a little bedside table. 'On the grounds that there's no way for me to answer that without getting myself in trouble, I'm going to distract you instead.'

'I like the sound of that.' Libby let herself sink deeper against him as she wound her arms about his neck. A loud buzzing came from the desk behind them, and she turned to glare at Owen's mobile. 'I *don't* like the sound of that.' As though on command, the phone fell silent and she turned back to him with a grin. 'Now, where were we?'

To her disappointment, Owen's attention was fixed behind her, a frown etched its way between his brows. 'I should probably just check that.'

Ugh. She hadn't counted on him being a workaholic, but then again she knew that running your own business didn't always mean keeping to regular office hours. With a sigh, she started to rise from his lap. 'If you need to work, I can leave you to it.'

'What? No, don't go!' His hands tightened on her hips, holding her in place. 'That was just an email alert, I can check it later. My office will call if it's something really urgent.'

'Great, so if it starts ringing, what will you do, put me on hold? Way to make a girl feel special.' Libby pulled herself away from his hands and stepped away. She'd dated a man before who'd been more interested in his phone than in her, and sworn she'd never do it again.

'Hold on a sec.' Owen stood, crossed to the desk and picked up his phone.

And that was her cue to leave. 'I'll see you around.'

Arms locked around her waist. 'Where are you going?'

Turning in his arms, she eyed him warily. 'What about your phone?'

'It's off.' Keeping her held against him he walked backwards until the bed hit the back of his knees then fell back onto it, taking her down with him. 'You've got my complete and undivided attention.'

Warmth curled inside her. 'Is that so?'

Still a bit breathless from being on the receiving end of Owen's complete attention, Libby rested comfortably in the crook of his arm eating occasional strawberries from the bowl he'd propped on his chest and listening to the gulls' cry as they dipped and soared over the evening tide. The tiny hut was like a space out of time, the real world only a step and yet miles away. Lilac, orange and red painted the patch of sky visible through the small square window above the bed. 'I could stay here forever,' she said with a contented sigh, before biting her lip. She needed to play things a bit cooler, not come over quite so eager. Sure, he'd gone to a lot of trouble tonight, but she couldn't afford to read too much into it. Trying to keep her body relaxed against his, she hoped he'd take it as a throwaway comment.

Tilting the bowl on his chest towards him, Owen peered at the last couple of strawberries. 'You've already eaten most of the food so that might be a bit of problem.'

Relief flooded through her, and she told herself to stop second-guessing everything and just enjoy the moment. Stealing one of the strawberries, she popped it into her mouth. 'Not for me. I'll laze around here, and you can channel your inner hunter-gatherer and go out on foraging trips.'

With a chuckle, Owen dropped a kiss on the top of her head. 'I'm not sure Lidl existed in prehistoric times. Besides, I thought it was the woman's job to tend and care for her man?'

Sitting up, Libby grabbed a pillow and bopped him on the head. 'Let this be the first of many disappointments for you, because I can barely look after myself.'

She'd expected another laugh from him, but the look on his face as he shoved the bowl of strawberries to one side and tucked the pillow behind him to sit more upright was anything other than amused. 'Don't do that.'

'Do what?'

'Make yourself the butt of the joke. You work so bloody hard. Don't think I haven't noticed all those hours you spend on your feet. And I bet you take care of your dad too, on top of everything else.'

Taken aback at the vehemence behind his words, Libby reached for her glass of champagne and gulped the last mouthful. 'I didn't think I was doing that. I thought we were just messing around. Dad and I take care of each other, like we've always done. We've always split everything down the middle at work and at home. Though just lately he's been trying to do more than his fair share.' With a sigh, she scrubbed a hand through her hair. 'He gets on these periodic guilt trips, like he thinks he robbed me of my youth or some such nonsense. It's been much worse since Beth and Eliza came home.'

'How so?'

'He's always on at me to go out and spend time with them, like we're still teenagers. I'm not a kid anymore. This is my job, my life and I'm happy with the responsibility of it. I can't get him to see that, though. Working in the chippy was good enough for him, and his parents before that, so why shouldn't it be enough for me?'

'Is it enough for you?' When she frowned, he held up a hand. 'That's not a criticism, I'm just asking if it's really what you want and that you're not just saying it because you think it's what's expected of you.'

She knew what he was trying to say, but it was hard to stop her next words from sounding defensive. 'I've got plenty of plans for the future, but they all revolve around staying here in the bay.'

'And have you told him that? He's probably just trying to make sure you enjoy a better life than he had. That's what all parents want for their children—or so I've heard.'

That wasn't the first time he'd made a reference like that, and she wondered anew what else lurked behind the confident face he turned towards the world. Whatever his personal issues might be, he was right about one thing: she hadn't told her dad about her plans for the future. And it was something she'd have to address with him sooner rather than later. Stretching over, she snagged the champagne bottle from the bucket they'd placed on the floor, and said as much. 'You're right, I need to talk to him.'

Owen tucked a hand behind his head, drawing the muscles in that side of his body tight. With a lazy smile that did all sorts of ridiculous things to her insides, he gave her a nudge with his foot. 'Of course I'm right. I always am. Now pour me some more of that champagne.'

'Ugh, you're *so* bossy.' She needed to stop making it sound like a compliment. Her feminist credentials would be withdrawn if she kept melting every time he issued a command.

She shared the remaining champagne between their glasses—making sure she added just a bit more to her own glass—then settled next to him against the pile of pillows. It was time to take control of the situation, make it clear she was putting no expectations upon him, that she wouldn't be running straight to Eliza and Beth to tell them about her new boyfriend. 'Would you be offended if I asked if we could keep this just between us?'

'A clandestine and sordid affair?' Humour sparkled in his eyes, and she saw no sign of offence, thank goodness. She wasn't ashamed of being with him, but she didn't want their friends getting the wrong idea and reading more into it than there was. *And not just them, either.*

'Not sordid, just private.'

Owen slung an arm around her shoulders and pulled her close to whisper in her ear. 'Just a little bit sordid?' He caught her lobe with the edge of his teeth making her shiver in delight.

'I might be persuaded.' She wriggled away from his lips before she did something unforgivable like spill her champagne, or let slip the turmoil he stirred up inside her. 'Cheers.' She tilted her glass and he clinked them together.

'Cheers. Here's to us.'

'To us,' she echoed. *For as long as that might be.*

Chapter 11

Every free moment he had over the next few weekends was spent with Libby. When he couldn't be with her, he found himself daydreaming about her. When his phone buzzed during the long, lonely evenings in his flat, he resented the fact she wasn't there to tell him to switch the damn thing off. Even his enthusiasm for the restaurant project was starting to wane. He couldn't let Sam down, though, so he'd forced himself to spend the whole day in the sweaty heat of the old skittle alley helping him rip out the old fixtures and fittings.

'That's the last of it,' Sam said with a groan as he knuckled his back. 'I reckon we've earned a beer.'

Owen checked his watch. Libby was covering the early shift in the chip shop and would be finished in a few minutes. 'I might take a pass on that, mate, if you don't mind. I've got a few things to catch up on, so I'll head down to the hut once I've had a shower.' It didn't feel right lying to him, but he'd promised Libby they could keep things on the down-low.

Sam shook his head. 'Don't you ever stop?' There was no censure in it.

'Joys of being the boss, as you'll find out for yourself soon enough.' Owen tied the top of the last rubble sack and stacked it in the corner with the other rubbish. They'd booked a Wait and Load skip for Monday so there wasn't much more to be done until then.

'Don't remind me.' Sam clapped him on the shoulder. 'Thanks again for pitching in like this, I didn't expect you to get your hands dirty.'

Tugging off his work gloves, Owen tucked them into the back pocket of his filthy jeans. 'A bit of hard work never killed anyone, and I don't believe in paying someone to do something I can do just as well myself. This project will start eating up our money soon enough.'

'That's very true, but I'm glad you're here all the same. Well, if you're sure about that beer, I'm going to grab a shower and go and see my gorgeous girlfriend.'

Me too. 'I'll catch you later.'

A shower and a quick change and ten minutes later Owen perched on the railings a few feet along from the chip shop. Libby let herself out the front door with a wave over her shoulder then started along the prom, hands tucked into the pockets of a pair of black-and-white tartan trousers she'd teamed with a black vest top. He felt a smile stretching his mouth at the shock of scarlet hair feathering around her face. She'd been at the bloody hair dye again. Thinking back to his early days on the building sites, he stuck two fingers in his mouth and whistled his appreciation. 'All right, love, fancy a drink?' He'd tried hard over the years to smooth the rougher edges of his accent, but he exaggerated them for her now.

Jerking to a halt, Libby stared at him in surprise before glancing around. A few early evening strollers were watching them, but no one he recognised. Striding over to him, she folded her arms across her chest. 'I thought we were meeting in the hut?'

He slid down from the railing to curl an arm around her waist and tug her close. 'What if I said I couldn't wait a moment longer to see you?'

Eyes bright, she shook her head. 'I'd say you were full of it, or after something.'

Grinning, he hooked his fingers through the belt loops of her jeans and spread his legs so he could settle her between them. 'I'm always after something, but I thought we could take a stroll along the beach first.'

'That sounds nice.'

Keeping one arm around her waist, Owen steered them along the prom towards the step that led to the beach. His nose started itching, probably from all the dust and dirt in the skittle alley and he drew a white handkerchief from his pocket. Releasing his hold on her, he turned away to blow his nose.

When he turned back she was giving him a funny half-smile. 'How is it that you're the only man I know other than my dad who still uses a hanky?'

Shrugging, he folded the cotton into a square and tucked it away once more. 'One of the few helpful lessons I learned from Mrs Travers was to always keep a clean handkerchief in my pocket.'

'Mrs Travers? Who was she, one of your teachers?'

His harsh bark of laughter seemed to echo off the quiet buildings behind them. 'You could say that, I suppose. Mrs Travers was my foster mum for about six months until the social worker found out she was a proponent of cold baths and starvation techniques as part of our training regimen.' *Okay...*soul-baring hadn't been on his agenda, but it was out there now, and he was so tired of pretending he had everything together. For reasons he couldn't fathom, he wanted Libby to know him—the real him.

'Foster mum? What happened to your parents?' The gentle concern in her voice felt like a stroke over his skin.

Not sure how much he wanted to say, he kept it to the barest of facts. 'I was given up at birth; got bounced around the system until I was old enough to get myself out.'

'I...I can't imagine.' Her voice took on a harder, almost angry tone. 'How old were you when you were with this Mrs Travers?'

'I went to live with her a couple of weeks after my ninth birthday. Hers was the seventh foster home I'd been in by then.' At her gasp, Owen shrugged. 'It wasn't the worst place I lived, and when it all got too much, I had Mr Buttons to cry to.' When she blinked up at him, he realised what he'd let slip. Embarrassed, he kicked a small pile of sand by his foot. 'He's just some silly teddy bear. I don't know where he came from, only that I've always seemed to have him. He's got this row of buttons on his chest, so I called him Mr Buttons.' And that was all he was going to say about that. She didn't need to know that the tattered old bear still sat on the chest of drawers beside his bed. 'Come on, let's walk.'

Having made their way down to the beach, they removed their shoes. Dangling his trainers from the fingers of one hand, he took Libby's free hand with the other. They strolled in silence for a few minutes before Libby halted at the edge of where the sea lapped against the sand. The fading sun glinted off the vibrant colour of her hair as she stared down at neat toenails painted the same vivid red. 'I don't know what to say to you,' she admitted on a sigh. 'I mean, I never know what to say to you, but now it's even worse.'

Dropping his shoes onto the sand, Owen bent to pick up a pebble and send it skipping out across the waves. Beneath the glorious splendour of a sky streaked in glorious shades of pink, purple and orange, the terrified little boy who'd been shunted from pillar to post seemed almost like a stranger. 'There's no need to pity me, Libby, it was a long time ago and I'm still the same colossal arse slash sex god you know and love.'

She laughed. 'You're so bloody arrogant.' On her lips, it didn't sound like an insult.

'Confident.' He countered, wondering if this was going to become one of those inside jokes other couples shared.

She nudged a gentle elbow into his ribs. 'Irritating.'

Owen snagged her elbow then swung her around until they

were barely inches apart, the palm of his other hand splayed across her lower back in case she had any idea of escape. 'You can be, but I'm willing to overlook it.' Ducking his head, he pecked a kiss on the tip of her nose, then another on her cheek, her temple, the delicate skin of her ear.

A shiver rippled through her, but she didn't pull away from him. 'Wh…what are you doing?'

Turning the kiss on her lobe into a little nibble, he murmured, 'I would've thought that would be obvious, Miss Stone. I'm seducing you.'

There was that little shiver again, and he chased it down the side of her neck with his lips. Her skin was so soft, and he knew he'd found his latest obsession. He began to skim his way back up to her ear, keeping the pressure a gentle question rather than a demand. 'God, I love you like this,' he murmured into the curve of her shoulder. 'All sweet and soft and pliant.'

She quivered like a rabbit spotting a predator, torn between freezing and flight. 'No one's ever called me sweet before.'

Owen pulled back to meet her shy gaze through the floppy fringe she wore like a shield. 'Maybe I'm the first one to see past the camouflage.' Blowing softly, he stirred the colourful strands to reveal her periwinkle eyes.

Her shoulders were up in an instant. 'It's not camouflage, this is who I am.'

Capturing a scarlet-streaked lock, he smoothed it behind her ear. 'It's *part* of who you are, but it's not all you are. And you can't deny you use your appearance to manipulate people's first impression of you.' When she opened her lips to protest, he pressed a finger against them. 'That's not a criticism, Pixie, I do the exact same thing with my designer suits.'

The tension melted from her frame as she gave him a little nod. 'Mum used to do my hair every morning. Even when she got really sick, she still insisted. I used to sit on the side of her bed while she brushed it out then plaited it into all these intricate

designs. The other girls at school were always jealous of it. After…'
She glanced away, swallowed, then met his eyes once more. 'After
she died, my dad tried his best, but he was all fingers and thumbs.'

She didn't need to elaborate. He could already picture her with
wonky pigtails trying to put a brave face on what must have been
a devastating loss. Christ, he had a hole in his heart where his
mum should be, and he'd never even met the woman. How much
worse to have known such love and to have it wrenched away?
'They teased you.'

Libby nodded. 'A couple of them cornered me after school. I
ran all the way home in tears, but when I got there I couldn't
bring myself to tell Dad why I was so upset. I didn't want to hurt
his feelings, so I went to the chemist that weekend and bought
a load of cheap dye. My hair was almost down to my waist at
the time, and I hacked it off with the big scissors Dad uses to
trim the fish fillets.' She laughed, a wet painful sound that struck
Owen like a blow to his solar plexus. 'God only knows what he
must've thought when he saw me, but all he said was "You look
nice, lovey" and asked me what I wanted for my tea.'

He knew how cruel kids could be to anyone who looked a bit
different. When he started secondary school, the money his social
worker had slipped him to spend on his uniform had been confis-
cated by his adoptive parents and spent in the local corner shop
on vodka and cigarettes. He'd ended up in what the school secre-
tary had been able to put together from the lost property box.
Too-short trousers and a jumper three sizes too big had set him
up as a prime target for the bullies. By the end of the first day,
the trousers had a hole in the knee, and Owen had spent his first
of many afternoons in detention for fighting. When he'd got
home, there'd been no warm welcome waiting for him, though.

Using the edge of his finger, Owen caught a tear before it could
spill off the edge of her inky-black lashes. 'Sam told a story the
other week about your dad storming up to the school when they
threatened to send you home because of your hair.'

She leaned back to study him. 'You were talking about me?'

'I might have made an enquiry or two when I first came back.' And found out much more than he'd bargained for in the process. He should ease off before they took a step they might not be able to come back from. Talking about stuff like this was almost unbearably intimate, far more so than the sex they'd been enjoying together. Things would be a whole lot simpler if he made a joke and coaxed her back to the hut for another night of passion. It was the percentage decision, and would make things a lot easier when it came to dealing with his purchase of the chip shop in a few months' time.

He hadn't made it this far in life playing the percentages, though. Owen relied on his gut—the way he had when he'd walked away from the deal with Alvin Taylor. And his gut was telling him there was something special about this funny, feisty woman. He'd just have to feel his way carefully and try not to show her too many of the vulnerabilities he masked from the world too quickly. Not an easy prospect. Her gentle response to the little bits he'd told her about his upbringing so far made him want to spill the whole ugly truth out at her feet. He took her hand before he did just that. 'Come on, lets walk some more.'

'I love the feel of sand between my toes.' She wiggled them with a happy sigh. 'Especially after a long day.'

Owen splashed his feet in the light, foamy waves coming in on the evening tide. 'Idyllic', that was the word people used for places like this. Under the breathtaking palette of the sky, it was easy to believe it. But he knew from bitter experience not to be deceived by appearances. When he'd first looked up his birth records and begun dreaming of escaping from London to find his roots, this was exactly the kind of scene he'd painted in his head. It couldn't really be this perfect though, life never was. 'Don't you ever get bored living in the same place all your life?'

A scoff told him what she thought of that. 'Spoken like a true city boy.' She gestured towards the water. 'How could I ever be bored with this? The sea has a million different moods, so every day is different. You should see it in the middle of a storm. I come down here and the full force of nature is on display; it's breathtaking, like I'm standing on the very edge of the world.'

He could picture her, wild hair blowing, laughing as the rain lashed her cheeks pink and the wind threatened to lift her off her feet, and swore to himself he'd be standing there beside her the next time. 'It was a stupid question. I've moved around so much it's hard to understand what it must be like to belong somewhere, I guess.' *Until now.*

Chapter 12

As they strolled along in the deepening twilight, Libby tried to put herself in Owen's shoes, and found it next to impossible. Though the loss of her mum had devastated her, she'd still had all those precious years with her first. Not once had either her mum or dad left her feeling anything other than adored and cherished. It sounded like Owen had never had that from anyone. Conscious he didn't show many people this marshmallow belly of vulnerability, she tried to feel her way carefully around the subject. 'I can't imagine what it must've been like being shunted from place to place. Were any of them okay?'

Owen shrugged. 'A few of them weren't too bad, but none ever felt like home either.' Tucking his hands in his pockets, he scuffed his toes through the sand. 'And I did my damnedest to make sure they didn't feel like home, too. Acted out, skived off school, got in a bit of bother with the police. It was all going to fall apart sooner or later, so in a twisted way it was my way of controlling how and when it happened.'

The sheer rawness of his voice hurt to hear, and Libby took a few paces away to give him time to gather himself. She wasn't sure she wanted to hear quite so much truth. Would he expect her to do the same, to dig up all the ugly little skeletons in her own closet? Not that she had anything on the scale of what Owen had been through, but there were still those little parts of herself she didn't share with anyone—not even Beth or Eliza. Whether it was the shadows cast by the moon over the sand, or the man behind her, she was in danger of cracking open those hidden parts and putting everything out on display. If she didn't like those nasty little bits, how could she expect him to?

'Well, that is not how I saw this evening going.' With a mocking little laugh, Owen grabbed her hand and tugged her into his side. 'You're a dangerous woman, Libby Stone, or maybe the moon's casting some kind of spell on me to reveal all my dark and dirty secrets.'

It was so close to her own thoughts, Libby found herself laughing. 'If you don't show me yours, I won't show you mine, deal?'

'Deal.'

Owen slung his arm around her, tucking her tight against his body and she leaned into him for just a moment before pulling away to grab his hand and tug him towards the surf glowing white on the dark, grey sand. 'Come on!' Even with the current hot spell, the water was still chilly enough to illicit a little shriek as she splashed into the shallows. 'Bloody hell, that's cold!'

Retreating a few paces, Libby kept just her toes close enough for the waves to touch though Owen stayed ankle deep, seemingly uncaring of the water soaking the bottom edge of his jeans. 'If I lived here, I'd do this every night. It's like we own the whole beach,' he said, glancing back at her over his shoulder.

'If you plan on doing this in December, you're on your own. There's this massive charity swim for the local hospital on Boxing Day so you could always join those lunatics.' What was she saying? Just a couple of hours ago she hadn't even wanted him to stick around for the rest of the weekend never mind thinking about longer-term plans.

'I'm always up for a challenge. I take it you've never participated?'

She shook her head. 'No chance. Dad does it every year, and it takes the rest of the day to thaw him out afterwards. They raise money for the local hospice, which is a cause close to our hearts, so I work the crowds who come down to watch the swimmers— shake a collection bucket, that kind of thing. Did I mention it was fancy dress?'

Owen laughed. 'Really? I bet it's a fantastic spectacle.'

Libby grinned, the memory of fifty plus ballerinas in all shapes, sizes and ages charging into the freezing sea loomed large. 'They have a theme for the costumes, too. They started off all dressed as Santa and it kind of morphed from there. If I remember rightly, it's fairies this year.'

'Fairies? Christ! You wouldn't catch me dead in a set of wings and a tutu.' Reaching back, Owen tangled their fingers together. 'You said fundraising for the hospice is close to your heart. Is that because of your mum?'

Libby nodded. He'd likely not notice the slight movement in the dark, but it was all she could manage thanks to the lump which seemed to form in her throat any time she thought about those terrible few weeks at Mulberry House. Oh, the nurses and other volunteers had been amazing, and they'd done their very best to make sure her mum's last days had been as comfortable as possible, but she still took a diversion to avoid walking past the place.

Warm arms enfolded her in a hug. Resting her cheek against Owen's chest, Libby closed her eyes and let the spicy scent of his aftershave and the steady beat of his heart beneath her ear soothe her. He brushed a kiss to the top of her head. 'Sorry, I didn't mean to stir any bad memories.'

'It's okay. When it comes to birthdays, anniversaries and stuff I can prepare myself for it. It's the random conversations which catch me off guard. Besides, I'm the one who mentioned the charity swim which started all this, so it's hardly your fault.'

'I still don't like to see you upset.' Owen chafed his hands up and down her back a few times then stepped back. 'Let's talk about something more pleasant. Where do you see yourself in five years' time?'

The abrupt topic switch caught her off guard for a second, but she decided to roll with it. 'Here, of course. If things go to plan, Dad will retire next year so the shop will be mine.'

'So you don't want anything to change? No far-flung shores you're desperate to explore?'

Her back was up in an instant at the implied criticism she read in his words. 'Is there anything wrong with that?'

Owen held up his hands. 'No, no, not at all. Hey, don't get the hump with me, not when we were getting on so well. I'm genuinely interested.'

He sounded sincere enough, but Libby was tired of justifying her choices. What was the big deal about moving somewhere else? Beth, Eliza and Sam had all tried it and wound up back in the bay, none the happier for their experiences. 'It's not like I've never set foot over the county border. My aunt lives out in Spain and we've holidayed there every year since I was little. Her husband is a local, so we had the proper immersive experience not just sunburn and sangria. I love my cousins, but I don't want to live their lives any more than they're desperate to up sticks and move to the bay.' She sighed. 'Sorry, was I yelling by the end of that?'

Owen stuck a finger in his ear and wiggled it around. 'I'm sure the ringing will stop in a minute.'

'I'm sorry, it just feels like no one seems to understand that not leaving the bay doesn't mean I don't have dreams of my own.'

Gathering her hand in his, Owen knelt then pulled her down to sit beside him. 'Tell me.'

Hesitantly at first, and then with more confidence as her sheer excitement took over, Libby outlined her plans to turn the fish and chip shop into a café. 'I think there's a lot of scope to branch out—picnic baskets for those who want to stay on the beach rather than eat inside, special afternoon teas for things like Mother's Day. I'd offer Simnel cakes and hot cross buns at Easter, and mince pies and Christmas cakes in the winter. Birthday cakes to order, there's no limit other than the number of hours in the day.'

Owen was quiet for long enough to set the nerves fluttering in Libby's belly. When he finally spoke, it was to voice one of her biggest worries. 'Won't people miss the chippy? I'm not trying to rain on your parade, but with something so popular, there's bound to be a few grumbles.'

'I've already thought of that. There's another takeaway on the High Street which does a mix of pizza and kebabs. We've always been careful not to impinge on their menu, and they've done the same for us. I've had a quiet word with Davey and they'd be more than happy to expand and provide fish and chips as well, as long as I give them Mum's secret batter recipe. I won't be depriving people of what they want, I'm giving them another choice.'

She glanced sideways, wishing she had more than the pale moonlight to rely on so she could get some idea of what he was thinking. 'It's not just some random whim. I've been saving for years, so I'll have enough to pay for the decoration and refit—well, if I do most of the work myself that is.'

Bracing his hands behind him, Owen stared out across the waves. 'I can tell it's not a whim; it's clear you've done a lot of work on this.' He was silent again for some time, and when he spoke again there was an odd note in his voice. 'You said once before that you had plans to talk over with your dad and now I get what you meant. Have you told him yet?'

Libby deflated like a soufflé taken too soon from the oven. Burying her face in her bent knees, she muttered, 'Not yet.'

'Oh.'

'Yeah, oh.' Sighing, Libby grabbed a handful of sand then let it trickle slowly through her fingers. 'I know I need to get on with it, but I can't bear to hurt his feelings. I don't suppose selling fish

110

and chips is many people's idea of a stellar career, but all those portions of cod and battered sausages kept me fed, clothed and a safe loving roof over my head. I don't want him to feel like his life's work isn't good enough for me.'

'I'm sure he wouldn't think that.' Taking her hand, Owen brushed the remaining sand from her palm then raised it to his mouth to press a soft kiss in the centre.

Heat radiated from that single spot to spread through her. Drawing her hand free, she closed her fingers as though she could capture the tenderness in that touch and keep it safe forever. She could wish for an ounce of his confidence, too. How did he manage it, after everything she suspected he'd been through from the few brief hints he'd shared of his past? 'What about you, Owen, what about your dreams?'

With a laugh he pushed to his feet. 'I'm not one for dreams.'

God, it was enough to break her heart, though he wouldn't thank her for the pity. Accepting the hand he held out, she let him help her to her feet while she tried to compose herself. Once she was sure she could keep her voice light, Libby hooked her arm through his and began to stroll along the beach. 'If you weren't following a dream, then what brought you here to Lavender Bay?'

He was silent for a long moment. 'I came to find my mum.'

Stunned, Libby pulled up short. 'She's from around here?'

With a tug of her hand, Owen kept walking up the beach towards the row of huts. 'According to my birth certificate, but I've not found any trace of her.' His hollow laugh held far too much pain. 'Not that I've tried too hard to find her. There's only so much rejection a man can take in his life.'

She felt the cut of those bitter words like a whip against her skin, and her next question was tentative. 'What about your dad?'

Owen gave a quick shake of his head. 'He wasn't named on the birth certificate so unless I can find my mum, I don't suppose I'll ever know.'

Libby fell silent, trying to get her head around the idea of not knowing something so fundamental as who your parents were. It was alien to the point of near-impossibility. Clearly, Owen was hurting a great deal about it so she would need to tread carefully and curb her own curiosity.

They reached the hut and Owen unlocked it and ushered her in. 'Hold on.' Using the light from his phone screen, he found his way across to the bed to switch on the fairy lights Libby had bought one day on a whim to wind through the bars of the old iron bedstead.

Pushing the door closed, she leaned back against it. 'If you don't want to talk about your mum, you don't have to.' He didn't respond beyond a quick nod.

Having tossed his trainers in the corner, Owen hitched himself up onto the bed and patted the space beside him. 'Come here, I need to hold you.'

Libby dropped her boots by the door and scrambled up to curl into his side. 'I missed you this week.' It was still an effort to admit those kinds of things to him, but it felt like they'd taken a step forward in their relationship over the past hour. Her suggestion to keep things between just the two of them had seemed like such a good idea at the time, but each weekend that past made her regret it more. Not telling Beth and Eliza had begun to weigh on her, too—an omission was still a lie at the end of the day.

At first, she hadn't expected it to last beyond a handful of encounters so keeping it quiet had been an act of self-preservation. Only Owen had kept texting to check on her schedule, and sending details of his, and one weekend had rolled into the next. When they couldn't avoid spending time with the others without rousing suspicion, Libby felt so awkward she could hardly bring herself to meet his eyes, never mind speak to him. She kept waiting for him to say something about it, but he never did and now it felt like she was trapped in some Groundhog Day loop. She loved the precious hours they spent together like this, but she wanted more. *Just tell him you're ready to go public.*

As she opened her mouth, Owen shifted to cover her body with his. 'I missed you, too. Now come here.' His lips found hers and their bodies moved together in a pattern that had become as natural to her as breathing. Tomorrow, she'd tell him tomorrow...

Chapter 13

The summer flew past. With Alex finding her feet back in London, Owen split his weeks between there and the bay. His days were spent working on the restaurant, and his nights waiting for Libby to finish work and join him in the hut. In the few hours in between the two, he'd continued to try and find any trace of his family. The town librarian had been helpful in pointing out a few books which dealt with local history, but she'd only been in town for about ten years and didn't recognise the name Blackmore. It had been the same at the local paper—a search through their database hadn't yielded any results, but they didn't go back more than twenty years. He wasn't quite desperate enough to spend hours trawling through their older records which had been transferred to microfiche, but not yet digitised. The war memorial told a terrible story of whole generations of sons wiped out—but again, no Blackmores. Thoroughly depressed, he was running out of ideas and the sweet oblivion he found in Libby's arms was all that kept his spirits up.

They took it in turn bringing supper for each other. His particular favourite had been the previous weekend when they'd sat side by side in the doorway of the hut eating chips and sharing a can of cream soda. Afterwards they'd lain on the bed fully clothed and kissed and cuddled like a couple of teenagers as they talked nonsense about their day. They'd dozed off at some point, waking in the early hours to sneak back into their respective beds.

At first, her request for secrecy hadn't bothered him as he didn't want the others interfering in their business any more than she did. As the weeks passed though, and she insisted on maintaining an icy façade whenever they were together in company, it began to grate on his nerves. He liked Libby. Liked her more than anyone he'd known in a very long time and he wanted to move their relationship onto a firmer footing than a few stolen hours here and there. But how to do that without spooking her or indeed her father was a puzzle he hadn't quite found a solution for.

Gentle questioning had revealed she still hadn't spoken to Mick about her plans to take over the chip shop and convert it, and it was obvious her dad was equally reticent about discussing his future retirement plans. Having already signed a contract and made a down payment to Mick, Owen felt torn between the competing needs of the two of them—and his own deep-seated need to buy and hold a piece of the bay for himself.

Several opportunities had come and gone where he could've quizzed Paul Barnes to see if he had any recollection of a Deborah Mary Blackmore, but when it had come down to it, Owen had chickened out. Asking around in the community was his final avenue of exploration, and who would know better than the landlord whose family had run the pub for generations? By not asking, Owen didn't have to admit he'd come to a dead end in his search.

Besides, the status quo was fine just as it was, or so he kept telling himself. He'd made some good friends, was starting to find his feet within the community, and for the first time in a long time he was happy. There was no need to rock the boat, to dig around the past and risk stirring up the unpleasant truth his instincts told him lay at the heart of the mystery surrounding his birth mother. Better not to know than taint his growing appreciation for the bay, and its residents.

It was also easier to pretend there was a tragic tale to be revealed than the possibility he'd find a woman with a happy family who'd been content to forget the mistakes of the past. It nagged at him, though. In the quiet hours when he didn't have Libby's sweet warmth curled into him providing a distraction, the gaps in his past gnawed away at the edges of his new-found contentment.

How could he make a future for himself when he didn't know who the hell he really was? He felt like a chameleon, changing his outer self to blend in depending on his environment. Or an actor playing different roles. During the week, he was the hard-nosed businessman ready to strike a deal for the right money. Over the long weekends in the bay, he was the carefree entrepreneur willing to throw himself into helping a friend realise his dream. And during those long sultry nights, he was Libby's secret lover. He was all those things, and none of them. He was a bloody mess.

'Earth to Owen, come in Owen.' Sam's jokey comment stirred him back to the present and he glanced over his shoulder with a frown.

'What's up?'

With a shake of his head, Sam pointed to the wall behind Owen. 'I should be asking you that seeing as how you've been painting the same spot for the past five minutes. Is everything all right?'

Bending to dip his brush, Owen turned his attention back to the wall. 'Yeah, fine mate. Just got a lot on my mind.'

'Fair enough.' He thought Sam was willing to leave it at that, and they worked in silence for a few minutes until Sam coughed. 'Look, I won't pry, but if there's anything you want to talk about, you know I'm here for you, right? I know this started out as a business venture, but it doesn't feel like that anymore. Well, not to me, at least.'

'Me neither.' God, how had he ended up in this situation? All those years of self-reliance had been terrible preparation when it came to having real friends for the first time in his life. He'd had business acquaintances, employees such as Alex who he got on well with, and willing women to warm his bed a plenty. What he'd no experience of was being around people who didn't want or need anything from him other than the apparent pleasure they found in his company. Not sure what else to say, Owen carried on painting until he reached the corner—and the end of the paint tin.

As he sealed the empty can and carried it carefully to the area they'd set up for waste storage, he thought about the two men who'd recently become an integral part of his life in the bay. Sam was an open book, as friendly and eager as Jack's lunatic chocolate Labrador who'd taken a shine to Owen for no reason he could fathom out. He was no more an animal person than he was a people person, but that didn't deter Bastian from making a beeline for him whenever he was in the vicinity. Jack was quieter, with a more reserved character, but Owen had no doubts about the sincerity of his intentions. And as for his little lad…Noah fairly ripped his heart out every time he gifted Owen with one of his sweet little smiles. There was so much trust in the boy, so much generosity in his heart even after what must have been the devastating loss of his father earlier in the year. Owen found himself torn between wanting to shield the boy and a desperate need to warn him that life would cut him down if he didn't toughen up.

He was just returning with a fresh can when a commotion from the pub above them had he and Sam exchanging a worried look before they both made a run for the stairs. 'What is it, what's wrong?' Sam pushed his way through the group of customers milling around a red-faced man.

'Trouble on the beach, some kid stuck out on the rocks. Your Eliza's out there with him.'

Without waiting to hear more, Sam was out the door and sprinting down the promenade, Owen hard on his heels. A jostling crowd blocked their path, mobile phones all pointed at the drama unfolding on the beach below. After a few moments trying to weave their way through, they abandoned any attempt at politeness and began shouldering through the crowd.

'Oi, watch it!' A disgruntled man made a grab for Sam, his face red with anger.

Owen stopped him with a hard hand on his shoulder. 'Back off, mate, that's his sister down there.'

Holding up his hands, the man backed off and those around them must have heard Owen's comment as they melted away giving them a chance to slip through to a clear spot at the edge of the railings. 'Jesus Christ.' There were three figures out towards the end of the rocks. Eliza was easily identifiable from her sandy curls streaming in the breeze. She had a small, dark-haired boy held in her lap and a man with matching brown hair crouched beside them. 'What the hell are Jack and Noah doing here?' Owen didn't know the ins and outs of the situation, but things between Jack and Eliza had recently hit a rough patch and he'd heard Eliza crying herself to sleep on more than one occasion.

Sam was already lowering himself over the edge of the prom and down onto the rocks and Owen followed him down. 'Steady.' Sam grabbed his arm as the sole of his boot skidded on a smooth bit of stone.

'Thanks.' Checking his balance, Owen tried to rein in the adrenaline pumping through his system and plot a sensible route over the rocks. 'Look.' He pointed. 'If we work our way over to the left, there's that flatter section which looks a bit easier.' He hoped it sounded more confident than he felt because all he could see were jagged edges and small gaps just waiting to twist an ankle, or worse.

'All right.' Sam cupped his hands around his mouth. 'Hang on, we're coming,' he called out.

They'd barely made it five metres when Jack started shouting to them. 'It's bloody treacherous down here. Stay where you are!'

Owen stopped short and made a grab for Sam who seemed intent on carrying on. 'Wait up, mate, you heard what Jack said.'

'We can't just leave them out there!' Sam made to shrug him off, but Owen held firm.

The wail of sirens sounded in the distance. 'Listen. The emergency services are on their way. If we go tearing out there, we risk being two more people they have to rescue.'

'I can't just do nothing.' Sam continued to protest as Owen steered him back the way they'd come.

'Why don't you go up and meet the ambulance, and I'll see if I can clear some of this lot out the way, then?'

With the assistance of a couple of men in the crowd, they hauled themselves back up onto the promenade and Sam loped off towards the main road. Owen turned to one of the guys who'd helped him up. 'Give us a hand with this lot, will you?'

Together they began pushing the gathered people back. A few grumbled, but a couple of others joined in and with outstretched arms they managed to make enough room for the vehicles to approach. A police car arrived first. A male and female officer emerged, tugged on matching fluorescent vests and took over the crowd control. Sam jogged up, a pair of paramedics on his heels.

To his relief, the trio on the rocks were slowly making their way back to the promenade so Owen concentrated on keeping the section of the crowd nearest to him out of the way as the paramedics set up and Sam gave them Eliza and Jack's details.

The next few minutes were a mad flurry of activity as first Jack and Noah were helped up and into an ambulance, and then Eliza. Beth, Libby and Mrs Barnes arrived, only adding to the noise and chaos as they fussed over Eliza. Their arrival brought renewed interest from the crowd who started pushing and shoving to get a better view of what was going on. Owen caught an elbow to the face as some idiot reached past him with a selfie-stick trying to film the action. Furious, Owen gave him a shove. 'Piss off! What's the matter with you?'

He'd had enough. And he wasn't the only one as a white-faced Libby rounded on the crowd. 'It's not a bloody soap opera, those are my friends, my family…'

The words choked off on a sob, and everything fell away in Owen's visceral need to get to her. Shoving through, he caught her in his arms. 'I've got you.' She struggled against him for a few seconds before clinging to him like a barnacle. Every sob wrenched her body against his, cutting him to the quick. At a loss for what else to do, Owen buried his lips into her hair. 'They're all right, everyone's all right,' he said over and over, praying it was true. Eliza seemed fine apart from a nasty cut on her leg, and from the bit he'd glimpsed of Jack and Noah they'd both been lucid, though the little boy's face had been pinched with pain when Jack carried him past.

Something cold nudged his hand, and he glanced down to find a mournful-looking Bastian sitting at his feet, his lead dragging on the floor. Keeping one arm around Libby, he bent to gather the lead. Calmer now, Libby wriggled out from under his arm and moved away as Beth and Sam approached.

He tried to catch her eye, but she resolutely turned away. Jesus, were they still going to maintain this ridiculous façade? They were both free agents, so why was she so desperate to pretend there was nothing between them? He'd had just about enough and was ready to tell her so, when a modicum of common sense stopped him. Now was not the time or the place, but once he got her alone there'd be a reckoning. Taking a deep breath, he turned to Sam. 'Everyone okay?'

Sam shrugged. 'Eliza's going to need a couple of stiches and they think Noah's broken his arm.'

'What the hell were they all doing out there? I thought Jack was up to his eyes in the harvest.' No one had any answers.

Eliza limped over. 'Can you drive me to the hospital?' she asked her brother.

He nodded. 'Of course.'

Owen watched as the paramedics closed the door on the ambulance and prepared to leave. As they were closing, he caught a glimpse of his friend's bleak expression. 'Jesus Christ, did you see the terror on Jack's face? That's one of the many reasons I'm never having kids.' Silently cursing himself for that slip of the tongue, Owen clamped his mouth shut. His own bitter experience had been enough to put him off having a family for life, but he didn't need to be blabbing about that just then. He couldn't imagine being in Jack's shoes, suddenly thrust into a position of sole responsibility for a child because fate had dealt yet another cruel hand.

A shudder ran through him about how much worse it could've been, and he turned back to Eliza before his thoughts could take a morbid turn. Noah would be fine and there were more practical considerations to be tackled. 'What can I do? If you're going to be stuck up at the hospital, do you want me to help out behind the bar? I've never pulled a pint, but I can tidy up, keep the fridges stocked or whatever.' He tried once more to catch Libby's eye, but she seemed fascinated with the multi-coloured laces in her boots. *Bloody stubborn woman.*

Eliza gifted him with a sweet smile before wincing once more over the pain in her leg. 'No, it's fine. Josh is working tonight so him and Mum can handle everything. Someone needs to retrieve Jack's Land Rover from the car park and take it back to the farm, though. It's their biggest harvest day so his mum is probably swamped.'

Grateful for something to do that would not only help out, but also put a bit of space between himself and Libby before he did something stupid like grab her in front of everyone, Owen held out his hand. 'Consider it done. I'll stay up there as long as she needs me.' He tugged Bastian's lead which was still wrapped around his wrist. 'Let's get you home, eh, mate?'

Eliza handed him the keys. 'Thank you. Sam and I should be

able to swing by and collect you on the way home from the hospital.'

He shrugged. 'Don't sweat it, I'll doss on the sofa if needed. Do you know Jack's reg number?'

She shook her head. 'It's black, though, and probably covered in mud.'

'Like every other bloody Land Rover. I'll just point and press until one of them unlocks.' Sam and Beth gave him a quick smile, but Libby still refused to look at him. Inwardly seething, he strode off.

He was maybe twenty feet away when Libby shouted after him. 'Hold up, I'll come with you.'

Still annoyed with her for snubbing him in front of the others, Owen kept on cutting his way through the busy promenade towards the car park, so it was a red-faced and slightly out of breath Libby who caught up with him as he paused to peruse the jumble of cars. 'Didn't you hear me? I said I'd come with you.'

Gripping the keys hard enough to hurt his fingers, Owen scowled. 'I didn't want to risk us being seen together in public. What would your friends think?'

It was Libby's turn to frown. 'They're your friends too, and I'm not sure what you're making a big fuss about.'

His eyes alighted on a Land Rover more abandoned than parked on a patch of rough grass at the back of the car park. 'Don't play me for a fool, Libby. The moment Sam and Beth appeared you backed away like a scalded cat. How do you think it makes me feel when my girlfriend won't allow me to comfort her in public?'

She froze in the action of dragging a hand through her hair, wild strands of pink and yellow spilling every which way. 'Girlfriend?' She sounded stunned, as though he'd said something outrageous.

'Well, what the hell else is this?' He gestured wildly between them. 'Come on, we've been spending every free moment with each other for weeks now.' Frustrated at her seeming shock, Owen marched towards the black four-by-four, activated the central locking and yanked open the driver's door.

She mirrored his action on the passenger side, their eyes meeting over the central console. 'You…you never said anything.' The confusion in her tone matched the furrow on her brow.

'I didn't think I needed to, I thought it was obvious.' Owen hesitated. What if he'd read it all wrong and Libby really didn't want anything more serious than a fling? 'But maybe we're not on the same page at all.'

'I'm not sure we're even reading the same book.' Releasing the door, she wrapped her arms around her waist. 'I don't know what you want.' Her voice had dropped to barely a whisper.

With a sigh, Owen slid into his seat then reached out a hand to help Libby do the same. 'I want to be with you, and not just when we can sneak away and be alone. I don't want to hide how I feel about you from the others.'

She stared at his outstretched hand for a moment before taking it. 'I don't want to hide it either, not really, but it's easier for you.'

Starting the car, he braced a hand behind her seat as he half-turned and began to reverse the car out of its awkward position. It was only once he'd manoeuvred them out of the car park that he picked up the conversation. 'How do you mean, it's easier for me?'

He caught her shrug out of the corner of his eye as he looked for a space to join the flow of traffic on the main road. 'Libby?' Facing towards her side window she muttered something into the hand supporting her head.

'What was that?'

With a huff, she turned to face him. 'I said that you won't be the one picking up the pieces.'

Thoroughly confused, he steered the car to the kerb and stopped. 'What on earth are you talking about?'

She threw her hands up. 'Oh, come on, Owen. Once you've finished whatever it is you're doing down here in the bay, you'll be back off to London and I'll be the one left behind having to face everyone.'

Realisation dawned. 'You think I'm just going to up and leave you once I've concluded my business here?'

'What else am I supposed to think? You turn up out of nowhere and barge your way into my life being all sexy and annoying and completely impossible. I still don't know anything about you other than your name and a few snippets of tragic backstory, yet I'm supposed to somehow interpret that as you being willing to make a romantic commitment to me?'

Women and their desperate need to uncover every little secret! 'You're being ridiculous. I've told you more about myself than I have anyone else. What burning questions do you still have?'

'Where the hell do I start? You've not said one word about trying to find your mum since you first mentioned her, not even a name. I know I said you didn't have to talk about it, but I hoped you'd trust me enough to let me support you. Are you even still looking for her?' Libby drew in a ragged breath. 'And what happens after the restaurant refurbishment is finished and you've got no excuse to keep coming down here every weekend? You can't tell me you'll be schlepping up and down on the train every week just to see me. I like you Owen, I really like you and I'm terrified you're going to break my heart.'

Something inside him broke, words spilling out without thought to their consequences. 'Her name's Deborah Mary Blackmore and I haven't looked for her because I'm fucking terrified about it. What if she doesn't want me, Libby? What the hell do I do then? I've been convincing myself that owning a property here is enough for now, that it's still making a connection to my roots.'

Chest heaving, he grabbed the steering wheel as he battled to get himself back under control. When he could speak without

124

shouting, he started again. 'When Beth wouldn't sell me the emporium I left in the spring thinking to put this place behind me, and for a few weeks everything was fine. Then out of the blue I got a call from someone offering me a second chance to invest so I came back and then everything started to snowball. The restaurant, getting to know the others, connecting with you. Before I knew where I was, I felt like I had everything I'd been looking for. If I find Deborah and she doesn't want me, I don't see how on earth I can stay here. And then what will I do about you? Your life is here, your future is here, how could I ask you to leave all that behind for a man that no one else in the world has ever wanted?'

'Oh, *Owen*.' He heard the snick of her belt unfastening and then she was tugging his hand free from the wheel, so she could clamber across his lap to face him. Gripping his cheeks with her palms, she forced him to meet the shocking azure of her gaze. 'You have to stop trying to deal with all this on your own. If you find Deborah and she doesn't want you in her life, she's a damn fool.' She shook him gently. 'You're a good man, Owen. Maybe no one else has bothered to tell you that before, but it's true and I'm here to remind you any time you need it. As for the rest, we can work it out as long as we have each other. Tell me I have you.'

Owen had no clue what he'd ever done to deserve this gift of a woman. Maybe she was the universe's way of trying to balance things out. 'You do, I swear it, Libby. For as long as you want me, I'm yours.'

Her mouth found his, her hands hooked around his neck pulling him closer until the auto-lock mechanism on his belt stopped him. One hand fumbling to undo it, he buried the other one in her hair, tilting her head to find the perfect angle as he took control of their kiss.

A loud *beep* shocked them both, and they broke apart. 'What the hell?'

Looking sheepish, Libby shifted in his lap. 'I accidentally leaned back against the horn.' She started to giggle, her body shaking against his causing all sorts of pleasant sensations to ripple through him.

'Come here.' He reached for her, intent on picking up where they'd left off, when someone knocked on the window next to his head.

'Bloody hell!' Libby shrieked, and the car horn blared once more, none of which impressed the police officer staring at the two of them. He pointed at the panel on the door and Owen pressed the button to open the window.

'Hello, Officer.'

'Good afternoon, sir. Are you aware you're parked in a drop-off zone?'

Oh, shit. Owen mustered up his best smile and tried to pretend there wasn't a woman straddling his lap. 'Sorry about that, we were having an argument and I didn't want to drive while distracted.'

Stoney-faced, the police officer looked from him to Libby and back again. 'Well, it seems you've patched things up, so might I suggest you continue the rest of your…discussion elsewhere?'

'Yes. Of course. Again, I'm very sorry.' Owen tried to edge a giggling Libby off his lap, wincing as her foot caught a particularly delicate part of his anatomy. 'Oof. Right, we'll be on our way.'

'Very good, sir.' Christ, did they teach all cops to have a face liked a smacked arse? The officer continued to stare at him, and Owen wondered what else he wanted.

'We'll be off then,' he said again, reaching for the ignition.

The officer cleared his throat loudly. 'Forgetting something, sir?' He nodded downwards. 'It's been an offence to drive without wearing a seat belt since 1983. Let's not add that to a public display of lewd behaviour.'

'No, no of course not. Thank you.' With a quick action, he fastened his belt then started the engine. The road was thankfully clear enabling him to pull away from the kerb before the cop found something else to accuse him of. 'Jesus, that might have been the most humiliating experience of my life.'

A choked sound came from beside him and he risked a quick glance over. Tears were streaming down Libby's face as she clutched her sides. 'Lewd behaviour?' She giggle-snorted.

He felt a laugh bubbling in his chest. 'Look, I know I wanted us to go public, but there has to be a better way to do it than getting ourselves arrested.'

Chapter 14

Within half an hour of arriving at the farm, Owen had Jack's mum, Sally, eating out of the palm of his hand. Clearly worried about her grandson, the arrival of some practical as well as moral support had her smiling and laughing as Owen lavished her with effortless charm and good humour. After a quick briefing on the most immediate tasks, Owen had disappeared off to the processing shed to supervise and assist with the unloading of the lavender harvested by the team of local volunteers from surrounding farms. Libby found herself in a beautiful farmhouse kitchen helping Sally pull together an evening meal for the workers. Any worry that she might be intruding had been dispelled within the first few minutes of them arriving with the Land Rover. For all she must be desperately worried about her grandson, Jack's mum had such a warm way about her that Libby soon felt like she'd known her forever.

To combat the heat from the Aga, they'd opened the back door and the windows above the double sink unit. Pretty lace curtains fluttered in the breeze, giving the impression of cooler air coming in at least. Positioned before a wide wooden chopping block, Libby surveyed four still-warm crusty loaves. 'Do you want me to slice all this bread, Mrs Gilbert?'

Sally looked over from the other side of the sinks where she was preparing a large green salad. 'Save one for now, my dear, and we'll see how we get on. There's a basket in the cupboard underneath that you can use. Just pop a tea towel over it.'

They pottered around for the next half an hour, laying the table, checking there were plenty of cold drinks stacked in the fridge to soothe parched and dusty throats. Libby did her best to keep up a stream of easy chatter, asking questions about the farm and complimenting the kitchen. The latter wasn't difficult as she was half in love with the spacious room with its sturdy pine furniture and terracotta tiled floor. There was a warm, homely feel to it—exactly the kind of look she wanted to recreate when it came to her plans for the teashop. How nice for people to feel like they were wandering into a friend's kitchen rather than a shop. 'Do you think I could take a few photos of your kitchen, Mrs G?'

Sally glanced over her shoulder from her position before the Aga. 'Whatever for?'

'I don't know if Jack told you, but my dad and I run the chip shop on the prom?' When Sally nodded, she continued. 'I've set my heart on turning it into teashop one day and I'd like to capture something of the fantastic, homely feel of your kitchen in the design.'

'Well, that's a lovely thing to say, you snap away, dear.'

Libby had just put her phone away when deep voices and laughter came from the rear yard and Owen appeared at the head of the workers from the shed. Sally shooed them straight back into the yard, clothes brush in hand, and made them brush the worst of the dust and lavender heads from their clothing before they were allowed into the kitchen. A neat row of boots soon lined the little utility room between the back door and the kitchen, and hands and faces were rinsed in the large sink out there. 'Are you going to inspect our nails, Sal?' one of the men said with a grin as he held out his hands to show her.

'Sit yourself down and behave before I decide not to feed you!' With a flap of the tea towel she'd had draped over one shoulder, Sally herded the workers towards the long kitchen table.

Slipping into the chair beside Owen when he patted the seat, Libby reached out to wipe a streak of dust he'd missed from his cheek. 'How did you get on?'

He captured her hand and pressed a quick kiss to the palm. 'Great. These guys knew what they were doing and were very tolerant as I bumbled around trying not to get in the way.' His self-deprecating comment hit the perfect tone with the others.

'For a city boy, he did all right. Not afraid to get his hands dirty,' the man opposite said as he offered the salad bowl across the table to them.

Owen grinned. 'I'm not that long off the building site myself. I know all about getting dirty for a living.'

'Mind your backs.' Sally placed a huge ceramic dish filled with bubbling lasagne in the centre of the table to a chorus of cheers and compliments.

The aroma of melted cheese and rich tomato sauce filled the air, setting Libby's stomach rumbling. 'This looks fantastic, thank you, Mrs G.'

'Dig in.' Sally was halfway into her seat at the end of the table when her phone rang. 'Excuse me for a moment.'

With one ear to the conversation around the table, Libby kept an eye on the back door through which Sally had disappeared to take her call. When she didn't return after a few minutes, Libby nudged Owen and indicated she was going to check on her. He nodded, then redoubled his efforts to engage everyone at the table in the conversation to keep them distracted.

Libby was a couple of steps from the back yard when the sound of soft sobs reached her. Hurrying out, she placed a gentle hand on Sally's arm. 'Mrs G?'

Turning, Sally smiled at her through her tears. 'Oh, don't mind me, dear, I'm just being silly. Jack said Noah's going to be okay, but he's staying in overnight. I know Jack can handle everything, but I hate that I'm not there for them.'

Taking her hands, Libby gave them a comforting squeeze. 'You being here holding the fort will be a huge weight off Jack's mind. Owen's going to stay with you, so you won't be on your own.'

'He's a good boy.' Sally cupped her cheek. 'And you're a good girl. Jack's lucky to have such lovely friends to rally around.'

'I'd stay too, but I need to get back to give Dad a hand in the shop tonight. I'll be back first thing, though, to lend a hand wherever I can.' If Jack and Noah were staying overnight, they'd need some stuff. 'Come back and eat, and then maybe you could put a few things in a bag for Jack and Noah? Owen's going to drop me back off in town, so we could swing past the hospital first.'

'Yes, you're right, I should've thought of that. I don't know what's the matter with me.'

Libby hooked her arm around Sally's shoulder. 'You've had a horrible shock, so it's not surprising if you're not thinking quite straight. Come on, let's go and grab some of that gorgeous lasagne before that pack of beasts in there scoff it all.'

Though she wouldn't have wished the circumstances which brought it about, Libby enjoyed the next couple of days helping out at the lavender farm. Noah's accident had really spooked Jack, and Eliza was determined to show him that he didn't have to manage everything alone. Libby had been happy to be roped in along with the rest of the gang. Spending time with her friends was never a hardship and she found the process of extracting the essential oil from the delicate purple flowers fascinating. Sally was patient and knowledgeable, and once her grandson was back home proudly displaying the cast on his arm to lots of attention, she visibly relaxed. Even Libby's dad got in on the action— pitching up with fish and chips for everyone and staying to lend a hand. Glancing across, she couldn't help but smile at the look of intense concentration on his face as he made sure the labels he was sticking to the bottles of oil were positioned exactly right.

Turning her attention back to her own task—she and Beth were helping Sally to decant the oil into the bottles—Libby lost herself in the rhythm of the mini production line they'd set up. So absorbed was she in measuring out the exact amount, she missed Owen's approach in among the general cacophony of chatter and music from a radio blasting out by the door. The sudden press of his arm around her waist made her jump, and a little shriek escaped her. 'You scared the life out of me!' she exclaimed, trying to wriggle away as he aimed a kiss to her lips. When he didn't release her, she leaned closer and whispered, 'Not here.'

It wasn't that she wanted to hide things between them anymore, but she'd never been one for big public displays of affection, and the pointed looks and grins both Beth and Eliza aimed at her any time Owen came anywhere near her set her face burning with embarrassment. Some of the light fell from Owen's eyes, and she reached up to pluck a stray sprig of lavender from the shoulder of his T-shirt and turned it into a soothing caress of apology. It wasn't his fault she'd made such a big deal about hating him to her friends. The humble pie was hers to eat, not his. Popping up on tiptoe, she pressed her lips to his ear. 'You, me and a bottle of wine at the hut tonight.'

Mischief and delight glowed in his smile, sending her heart fluttering. 'You've got yourself a date, Miss Stone.'

'Oi, stop your slacking and get back to work!' Sam's laughing yell drew all eyes to them and Libby made a concerted effort not to duck her head when Owen brushed a kiss over her lips.

'Just taking a little refreshment break, keep your hair on.' There was a distinct strut to his step as Owen headed back to where he, Sam and Jack had been taking it in turns to fork the huge pile of lavender into the processing vat.

'We need to talk,' Beth said, nudging Libby in the ribs.

'Oh, yes we certainly do,' Eliza added from the opposite side of the table where she was stacking the completed bottles into boxes ready for transportation to the wholesaler.

They both looked as delighted for her as Libby felt, so although there would be some merciless teasing, she could tell they were on her side. Warmth suffused her. There'd never been a time when the three of them had all been content in their relationships; how nice it would be to gossip together without one of them—and it had usually been her—feeling left out. It felt like a real turning point, a maturing for all of them. Beth and Eliza were taking charge of their lives and building their own businesses, and she'd be able to join them in that too one of these days.

On that thought, her gaze strayed automatically back to her dad. His expression of concentration had been replaced with a worried frown, which he was directing straight at her. Libby twitched her lips into a smile, expecting to see his face brighten the way it always did when their eyes met, but to her disappointment, her dad jerked his eyes down to the bottles in front of him. Telling herself she was reading too much into it, she waited for him to look back up.

And waited.

Minutes passed, but Mick kept his attention firmly locked on the work before him. Every time Libby glanced across, his head was down. The ball of hurt in her middle expanded. Her dad was never one for sulks and silences, never really one for bad moods in general. Added to that, she couldn't think of anything she'd done that would've upset him—unless he was unhappy about her and Owen, but that didn't make any sense. He'd never been bothered about her dating before, and she might still live at home, but she was a grown woman in every sense. Taking a deep breath, she forced herself to shrug it off. She was probably making a fuss over nothing. It was still punishingly hot; maybe he just wasn't feeling too good.

Worried now for his health, Libby made her way around the table to his side. 'Everything all right, Dad? Can I get you a cold drink?'

With only the barest glance towards her, Mick shook his head. 'I'm fine, lovey, but I think I need to be getting back. Lots of prep to do before the evening shift.' Straightening up, he wiped his hands on a cloth he'd picked up from the bench. 'Say goodbye to Sally and the others for me. I'll see you later.'

She stared after his departing back, stunned. Not in all her years had her dad ever said hello or goodbye to her without giving her a kiss. Heart in her mouth, Libby chased after him, catching him next to their little white van. 'Dad, what's the matter? What have I done?'

Looking uncomfortable, Mick fiddled with his keys. 'It's not you, lovey.'

'Then what is it? You've got me really worried here.'

He folded his arms. 'How long have you and Owen been *involved* with each other.'

The inflection in his tone was sharp enough to make her flinch. 'A few weeks, just since he's been back in the bay.'

It was his turn to look shocked. 'So he's the one you've been sneaking out to see.'

Sneaking out? Upset and confused by his overreaction, it was Libby's turn to snap. 'Come off it, Dad. If I was 16 rather than 26 then you might have some room for concern. Just because I don't choose to flaunt my love life in front of you—because I was under the apparently mistaken impression we respect each other—it doesn't mean I'm doing anything to feel ashamed of. We're both free agents.'

Taking her arm, Mick walked them further away from the open door of the shed. 'You don't know anything about the man. You don't even know what he's doing here in the first place.'

This conversation was taking a very strange turn. 'What's the matter with you? You're talking about him like he's a Russian spy or something. For your information, I know exactly why he's here.'

The blood drained from his face. 'You can't *possibly* know.'

What on earth was he talking about? As far as she knew, her dad and Owen had exchanged barely half a dozen words. And even if he somehow knew about Owen being given up as a baby by some mystery woman from the bay, why would he care? The most dreadful thought popped up in her head, and it was so horrifying Libby thought for a moment that she might throw up. Father unknown might be exactly the kind of thing a woman would write on a birth certificate if she'd been having an affair with a married man… 'Oh my God! You're not…' She shook her head. 'No, you can't be.'

Mick reached for her. 'Come on now, lovey, I can explain.'

Oh, no, no, no, no, no! Her mum and dad had been proper childhood sweethearts with eyes for no one else since they'd first held hands in the playground. How many times had he told her that story? How many times had she comforted herself with the fact that for all her mum had died so young, they'd at least shared a magical true love almost their entire lives. But what if that wasn't true?

Holding up her hands, Libby backed away. 'You told me you'd only ever been with mum.' It had come up during an excruciating conversation when Mick had sat her down at 15 and attempted to give her 'the talk'. They'd both been dying of embarrassment by the end of it, but it had been just one of the many times her dad had negotiated the minefield of raising a daughter on his own, and she loved him for it.

Mick frowned. 'What's that got to do with the price of fish?'

She was nearly crying now—life couldn't be this cruel, it couldn't be! 'Owen wants to settle in the bay because he's looking for his birth parents. His mum gave him up when he was a baby and all he knows about her is a name and that she came from around here. The only reason you could possibly know about

135

that is if…' She choked on a sob. '…Is if you're *his* dad, too.'

'What? Oh, no, lovey. No! Come here now.' Mick gathered her shaking frame into his big bear hug. 'Shh, it's nothing like that. Nothing at all. Goodness, talk about getting the wrong end of the stick. What a bloody muddle we're all in.'

The stream of reassurances eventually got through to her, and Libby raised her tearful gaze to meet his. 'You're not his dad?'

Mick gave a half-laugh. 'Absolutely not. I wasn't lying to you about me and your mum, so you can put that nonsense right out of your head. I just don't want you falling for the first bloke who comes along and catches your eye. There's a big wide world out there, lovey, and I want you to take the time to explore it before you think about settling down.'

Giddy with relief, Libby clutched onto her dad as her knees wobbled. 'Oh, God!' She started to giggle a little raggedly as she tried to swallow back her tears. 'I thought I was going to be sick! You seemed so dead set against me and him being together that I assumed it must be because of something awful. I know there's a big world out there, Dad, but I'm very happy with my little corner of it. Owen hasn't made any promises to me, but I have a really good feeling about us. He's a great guy, once you get to know him.'

Mick gave her a little shake. 'You're only saying that because you've never been given the chance to get out there and see for yourself. I know I held you back, I still feel terrible about you having to stay here while your friends went off to university and beyond. But that's going to change, and very soon.'

Not this old chestnut. He had such a selective memory sometimes. Libby might have been devastated when Eliza and Beth went off to university, but only because she'd hated being separated from them. She'd never had any academic ambition, and exams had been an absolute horror show. She'd be up all hours revising, and then the moment she'd sat in her seat the answers had slid from her brain leaving her shaking and sweating. Putting herself through any more of that had been her idea of a night-mare.

Mick knew all that. He'd been the one to mop her tears when she'd been so sure she'd failed every one of her GCSEs, and the one who'd bought a bottle of champagne to celebrate what would've been a very mediocre set of passes as far as most other parents had been concerned. How many times did she have to go through this with him? 'Dad, please. I love my life here in the bay. I know my place, and once you're ready to retire then I'll be more than happy to take over from you.' She took a deep breath. Now seemed like as good a time as any to talk about it. 'I've got a few ideas, actually, for things I'd like to do with the shop in the future. That's if you wouldn't mind...'

'No! You've got to stop this, because it's not going to happen.'

Shocked to the core, Libby stepped back. She'd known the idea she wanted to change the chip shop might be a bit of a hard sell at first, but she'd never expected he'd refuse out of hand to even listen to her. 'Dad, please. Let's go home and I can show you what I've got in mind.'

'That's enough, Elizabeth. I know you think you've got it all worked out and you're convinced you are content here, but that's only because you don't know any better. Once the shop is sold, you'll have enough money to do whatever you want! You can go to Europe, go to the States, even. The world will be your oyster.'

Sold? He couldn't possibly mean it. The world gave an alarming lurch and Libby had to brace her hand on their little white van to stop herself keeling over. 'Tell me you're joking.'

Mick shook his head. 'It's no joke. I've already found a buyer and it's all signed and sealed. On the stroke of midnight on New Year's Eve, the shop will have a new owner.'

She couldn't believe her ears. How could he possibly have done all this behind her back? She thought back to those shifty meetings he'd gone off to, the ones she'd stupidly believed were him going off to meet a lady-friend and been excited for him. Instead, he'd committed the ultimate betrayal and sold not just their business, but their home out from under her. 'But where will we live?'

Mick's face flushed a dull red. 'I'm going to stay with Val and Eduardo in October to do a bit of apartment hunting.'

'In *Spain*? You don't even plan on retiring here in the bay? Bloody hell, Dad, who even are you? I can't believe you kept all this from me. I thought we told each other everything.' She was crying hard now. Beyond the shock of it all was a deep hurt that he'd not confided in her about any of these plans, when they'd always told each other everything.

'You didn't tell me anything about your new boyfriend, so I'm not the only one who's been keeping secrets.' His harsh tone softened. 'I'm so sorry, lovey. Please, let's not fight. I didn't think you'd take on so.' He patted her shoulder, his face a picture of abject misery.

'Then why didn't you talk to me about it first?' Libby dug around in her pockets and eventually unearthed a clean—if crumpled—tissue. Blotting at her face, she gasped in a couple of breaths as she tried to swallow down more tears.

Mick wrung his hands. 'Since the day your mum passed, being here in the bay has been an agony for me. I kept waiting and waiting for it to get better, for my heart to get used to her not being around, and it never has. If it hadn't been for needing to keep you close to your friends, I'd have packed us both up and moved somewhere else straight away. By the time it felt like you might be okay to manage on your own, it was too close to retirement for me to bother. So I held on, even though every corner I turn is a constant reminder of your mum. Even now there are some nights I sleep in the chair in my room because the thought of lying in the bed we shared is too much for me.'

Libby couldn't imagine it. One of the things she loved so much about Lavender Bay was that all her memories of her mum were here. There were some days when she found it hard to recall every detail of her mum's face, but that didn't matter so much when a stroll along the prom brought back learning to ride a bike, or the weekend they'd built the world's biggest sandcastle—or so it had seemed to her, Eliza, Sam and Beth. That was one of her most favourite memories, the four of them brown as berries from hours in the sun as their parents took it in turns to supervise. They'd had a huge picnic lunch on the Sunday afternoon. That weekend had been full of smiles and laughter, when they'd believed themselves invincible and their innocence had still been untouched by the harsh realities of life.

Any time she was sad or lonely she wrapped herself up in the blanket of those memories, of the garden-fresh scent of the Timotei shampoo her mum always used, the decadent crack of a spoon through the crunchy top layer of a Wall's Viennetta ice-cream dessert—the height of luxury and sophistication to Libby's childish palate.

She'd always assumed her dad sought similar comfort in his own memories—but evidently not. 'Ah, Daddy, why didn't you ever tell me how hard it was for you here?'

Mick held out his arms. 'And why would I do that, my angel girl? You needed to be here, and that was all that ever really mattered to me.'

Libby snivelled into his shirt, absorbing the heat and scent and love of the one man who'd been her rock through everything. That once dark hair might be peppered with silver, his solid frame a little looser in places than it had been, but he was still a solid wall of reassurance. 'So, you really want to go away?' she asked when her tears had abated once more.

'I don't know, lovey, but I have to try something. It's not like you need me anymore.'

'Don't ever say that. Don't ever even think it, because I'm always going to need you.' She straightened up. 'If you need to get away, I understand, but can't we find a way for you to do it without selling up?'

Mick gave a sad shake of his head. 'My pension's enough for me to live on, but I need some of the money from selling the shop to buy a place for myself, and I want you to have the other half to treat yourself. You've worked hard since the day you left school, and it isn't right. I know it's my fault you've been deprived of so many chances, and this is my way of putting that right.'

She started to protest once more, but he held his hand up. 'I won't be moved on this, Libby, so don't even try. You've trusted me this far to know what's best for you; trust me just once more.' He touched a broad, calloused finger to her cheek. 'You've got a few months to get used to the idea. Let's not waste them by arguing when you could be spending the time planning the trip of a lifetime. No more tears now, promise me?'

With a nod and a watery smile, she let him go and when he glanced across just before driving away, she made sure to give him a wave to show him she was all right. It was a lie. She'd never been so far from all right in her life. All her plans and dreams lay scattered at her feet among the discarded stalks of lavender littering the yard. He didn't understand, and she didn't have the words right then to make him see. But he was right about one thing: she had a few months and she would spend them doing her damnedest to find a way out of this mess. If her dad wanted to sell the shop, then fine. He could sell it to her.

Needing a few moments to calm down, Libby took herself off to the farmhouse to use the bathroom and wash her hands and face. A quick check in the mirror showed only a bit of redness around her nose, something she could blame on a sneezing fit caused by the dust or the overwhelming scent of lavender in the processing shed. With a pinch on the arm for courage, she jogged back to join the others. No need to tell anyone about what her dad was planning, not until she'd figured things out for herself. They all had enough on their plates and if she was going to do this, it would be under her own steam. To prove to not only her dad, but herself that she could.

Chapter 15

'This better be bloody worth it,' Owen grunted to Sam as the two of them wrestled with opposite corners of an enormous rectangular fish tank.

'It will, trust me. A couple of inches your way and it'll be just right.' Sam huffed his fringe from his eyes, seemingly unconcerned about the death stare Owen was levelling at him.

'That's what you said twenty bloody minutes ago. Whose idea was it to stick a bloody fish tank in the middle of a restaurant, anyway?' Owen braced a shoulder against the tank as he shuffled backwards.

'It's an aquarium, not a fish tank—at least that's what we've put on the website. And we wouldn't be having to move it if some smart-arse hadn't decided to change the specs for the seating.'

Owen couldn't decide if it was the utter calmness of Sam's tone or the fact he was absolutely right that made him want to punch his business partner on the nose. The fact that Owen was the smart-arse in question didn't help matters either. 'Those booths I found are going to look fantastic,' he grumbled.

A supplier he'd worked with for years had got wind of their plans to create a high-spec restaurant in the unlikely venue of an old skittle alley beneath Sam's parents' pub in the tiny seaside town of Lavender Bay and made contact. His firm had recently designed some composite low-backed booths which could be customised in a variety of materials and colours. The deal he'd offered in return for cross-promotional images and a booking on opening night for him and his wife had been too good to refuse.

Unfortunately, the change meant some rejigging of the already agreed layout of the restaurant and the resultant shifting of the fish tank. And an increase in the budget, though Owen had decided to swallow that himself. 'I should have checked everything on the CAD before I suggested the change.' The specialist software allowed Owen and his design team to reproduce the layout for all their projects on the computer, so they could plan interiors to pinpoint accuracy.

Sam shrugged one shoulder, dismissing the issue. 'I'm not the one complaining, mate. I love the samples for the booths, and this is exactly why I needed someone with your experience on board. If you started messing around with the menus, that might be a different story.'

As if he would. The restaurant had been Sam's dream for a long time and he'd been well on the way to achieving it on his own terms before Owen had volunteered himself as a partner in the project. 'I'll leave the food and drink to you Mr Cordon Bleu.'

Sam grinned. 'I never get tired of hearing that.'

Once upon a time, when he'd been young and stupid it was the kind of thing Owen might have taken the mick about. These days, he was a big believer in aiming high and shouting about every damn achievement along the way. 'I don't blame you, if it was me I'd have it tattooed on my arm.'

Sam laughed, then straightened up with a groan. 'I reckon the tank will be fine here, and if it's not I don't care anymore.'

'Aquarium, not tank, remember?' Owen couldn't resist the little dig. 'Right, what do we have to do with the damn thing now?'

'Nothing, thank God. Mr Gould from the pet shop is a

serious…' Sam waved his hand in the air like he was searching for the correct term. '…Fishologist.'

'*Fishologist?*'

'Aquarianist, maybe? I dunno. Whatever. He's mad about fish and when I told him about this I thought he'd faint with the excitement. I gave him the dimensions for the ta—*aquarium* and a budget and he's doing the rest. He'll be in tomorrow to check it over and get it up and running and he's even volunteered to teach me how to take care of the fish once they're installed.'

Owen couldn't help but shake his head. It was exactly what he should've expected. In London, it seemed like most people wouldn't give you the time of day unless there was a profit in it for them. Not that he'd ever gone out of his way himself. He liked Alex and her husband well enough, would happily go for a beer with any of his site crews to celebrate the successful end of a project, but he'd never been a great one for hanging out for the sake of it. Forging friendships had never seemed that important, and he'd never thought his life lacking until he'd seen the other side of the coin.

In the bay you couldn't move two feet without someone popping up and offering their help—whether you wanted it or not. Barely a day had gone past without some friend or neighbour sticking their head around the bottom of the stairs to check on their progress, and half the time they ended up with a paint brush or a hammer in hand.

The new seating would be installed in the next couple of days and then they'd be onto the final dressing of the place which Owen was taking the lead on so Sam could turn all of his focus to their opening night which was now less than a fortnight away. For the first time since he'd founded his own company, Owen had taken a leave of absence. Alex was proving more than capable of overseeing everything, and the two of them still kept in touch with regular meetings over Skype, but the day-to-day running was out of Owen's hands.

From now until opening, Subterranean would be his primary focus. Well, apart from Libby, of course. She'd been a bit subdued for a couple of weeks, but whenever he asked what was wrong all he got was a bright smile and the same 'I'm just a bit tired' excuse. He'd wondered if her dad had said anything about selling up but was at a loss as to how broach it without admitting his involvement. He'd promised Mick he'd keep his mouth shut until after Christmas, and he was stuck with it.

He still wasn't sure how he was going to explain away his involvement with the deal when she did eventually find out. Keeping quiet felt like a betrayal, but at the end of the day nothing would change for Libby—she could do what she wanted to the shop and would still have a roof over her head. His appetite for converting the chip shop had waned now he'd fully come to understand how much it meant to her. Turning her out just wasn't on the cards. He might not be turning the quick profit that a conversion and sale would bring him, but the money he would save by not converting the place could be ploughed into another project instead. A lower, but longer-term return from the rental income would still fit into his overall investment portfolio—he'd just have to find a way to convince her to accept him as her landlord. *No problem. No problem at all.* Owen scrubbed a hand over his short hair. Unless he could find a way to really sell the idea to her, she was going to bloody kill him.

Straightening up, Sam rubbed the base of his spine. 'Isn't it a bit too convenient that today's the day when Jack had urgent business at the farm?' With the harvest well and truly over, Jack had been repaying their assistance by lending a hand with getting the restaurant ready for opening day. Both Sam and Owen had told him repeatedly it wasn't necessary, but Jack had enough pride for the three of them combined and wouldn't hear of it.

The Barnes' weekly planning meetings had expanded further still to include Jack and Sally and now rotated between the pub and the farm as Annie Barnes and Sally took it in turns to host a Sunday afternoon buffet. Owen's participation had been expected from the start, and more often than not Libby tagged along so she could keep up to date with what everyone was doing.

Foundations were being laid for an extension to the processing shed which would house a new workshop for Eliza, who currently had stuff split between her room in the pub and a spare room in the Gilberts' farmhouse. They were forever fielding calls for things she'd left at one place or the other and needed 'right now!'

A local firm of builders were ripping out the inside of the old farm cottage ready for Sally to take up residence in her self-titled 'granny annexe'. At hers and Jack's request, Owen had helped with the redesign and sat in on the interviews to find the right building firm, but other than that he was leaving the oversight in Jack's very capable hands. His offer to source materials at cost through his business had taken some persuasion to accept, but it felt like the least he could do. Their wholesale acceptance of Owen was still something of a shock. Somehow, he'd ended up a part of a huge sprawling family group and he still couldn't quite believe his luck.

Things with Libby were good—more than good, in fact—even if she had been a bit distant of late. It wasn't surprising, really, given how much time he was spending on the restaurant, but she'd assured him she was happy to see him even if all they did was tumble onto the bed in the beach hut and sleep more often than not. They were trying to make the most of it whilst they could. September was moving into October and the heat of the summer had faded with the last of the tourists. Even with the extra quilts and blankets they'd added to the bed, it would soon be too cold to spend their nights in there. They had a little portable heater but leaving that on overnight was too big a risk.

He'd been making enquiries about a few of the holiday rental apartments to see if anyone would be willing to lease him one on a longer-term basis, but he hadn't had much luck. Most of the owners used the low season to carry out maintenance and repairs, or already had plans for friends and family to visit. He didn't want to keep switching around from place to place, so he would just have to keep trying. He'd grown used to falling asleep with Libby in his arms, and he wasn't willing to give that up without a fight.

They were expecting one last bump in visitors for the half-term holidays, and they'd timed the opening of the restaurant for the first weekend to maximise footfall. Invitations had been sent out to a handful of local dignitaries, critics from national and local press and friends and colleagues of Sam's from the restaurant world. Rather than a grand opening night, they'd opted to offer a selection of dates over their first week which was being branded as a showcase. Neither of them was expecting to make a lot of money over the winter months, but it would be a great way for Sam to trial dishes and for them to iron out the kinks which came with starting any new business.

Sam's phone began to ring. 'I wonder what Eliza's forgotten this time,' he said with a groan as he retrieved it from his back pocket. He cast a quick glance at the screen then swiped it. 'Sam Barnes.'

Not Eliza then. As Sam continued his side of the conversation, Owen started to move away to afford him a bit of privacy but was waved to a standstill. 'No, that sounds great, Moira. Yes, I'm sure we'll have time if they're all willing to put a couple of evenings in next week. Everything will be in place by then, so they'll be able to familiarise themselves with the layout.'

When deciding on staff for the restaurant, they'd both agreed to utilise local talent as much as possible. Sam had approached several colleges in the area running catering and service industry courses with a view to offering part-time employment for their students. Moira, a tutor at the college in the next town over, had several students who lived in the bay, making it an ideal option for all concerned.

'All sorted?' Owen asked as Sam ended the call.

'Yes, mate. They're coming in Wednesday and Thursday next week, and Moira's offered to come with them to act as a bit of an intermediary until everyone's settled in.'

'That's a good idea.' Owen didn't have much of a clue about wrangling teenagers, and he doubted Sam did either. He'd made equality and harassment training compulsory for everyone he employed—including himself. The building industry had a terrible reputation for sexist behaviour and attitudes, though plenty of companies like his were doing their best to turn that around. He didn't have much experience in the catering world, but he wanted everyone who worked for him to enjoy it. Sam struck him as a pretty laid-back guy, but he'd never seen him in action in the kitchen when the pressure was on. 'Hey, Sam? You don't morph into Gordon Ramsey when you're cooking, do you?'

Shaking his head, Sam laughed. 'Not my style. I worked for a chef like that once in my very early days and it was the worst experience of my life. Don't get me wrong, I'm no pushover, but screaming at people just isn't me.'

'Thank God. Look, we can't do much more here until the furniture arrives so I'm going down to the hut for a few hours to work up some draft contracts. I'll run them past my legal team and send them to the college for comment as well. We've done some trainee placements on our sites, so I've got a lot of the standard terms and conditions on file already.'

'That might be the sexiest thing anyone's ever said to me.' Sam paused. 'Oh sorry, I drifted off at the mention of the word contracts and was thinking about Beth.'

'Nice. And I think that's my cue to go. I've got the phone if you need me.'

'No worries. I'm going to lock up here and go and make a mess in Beth's kitchen for a few hours. Fancy coming round for a drink later?'

Owen shrugged. 'Let me find out what Libby's up to first, and I'll let you know, okay?'

'Sure, sure, I know what that means. You two will end up in the love shack, and that's the last we'll hear of you.'

Raising an eyebrow, Owen fixed Sam with an unrepentant stare. 'Not everyone has a nice, cosy bed in a nice, private flat to share with their girlfriend, so don't give me a hard time, okay?'

'I hear you.' Sam held up his hands in truce. 'But it would be nice to get the gang together without one or other of us being in crisis mode. I'm going to give Eliza a ring and see if she and Jack are free. Make it to the flat by eight and I'll even feed you.'

'Now if you'd just said that in the first place…' Owen grabbed his phone, wallet and keys from a nearby table and headed for the door. Pausing at the bottom of the steps, he glanced over his shoulder at Sam. 'I'll pick up some wine on the way. White or red?'

'Yes.'

With a laugh and a wave, Owen jogged up the stairs.

A fierce wind tore along the promenade, sending odd bits of rubbish swirling and making Owen glad for the thick fleece sweatshirt he'd donned that morning. Stretching out one foot, he stamped on a sheet of newspaper as it went dancing past on the wind. Two more sheets barrelled past him, so having pocketed the first sheet he went chasing after them. As he continued to make his way along the prom, he came across several more sheets which he stopped to gather. He hated seeing rubbish anywhere, but particularly somewhere as beautiful as the bay. There were plenty of bins posted along the prom, painted in the same glossy black as the railings to help them blend in. Stopping at the nearest one, he stuffed the newspaper down inside to prevent it from being carried off again.

'Oh, I'm so sorry, is that my paper?' Owen glanced up to see a flustered older lady approaching him. She clutched a messy bundle of screwed-up papers and supplements still in their plastic wrap against her chest with one hand, the other full of shopping bags. 'The wind caught me by surprise as I came out of the newsagent's and I ended up dropping it. Before I knew it, bits were flying everywhere.' Red-faced with distress, she tried to gesture with her hands, almost losing grip of one of the magazines.

'Here, let me help you.' Taking the stack, he knelt to sort and straighten the pile into something more manageable, talking to her as he worked. 'I'm sorry, I've thrown half of your copy of *The Times* in the bin. I didn't realise.'

'Oh, not to worry. I saved the puzzle section, so that's the main thing.' With a bit of effort, Owen wrestled the remaining stack into a shopping bag she held open, then brushed off his knees. 'You're very kind,' the woman said, her eyes almost disappearing in a crinkly smile.

'It's nothing, really. Now, are you sure you can manage all this, or can I give you a hand?' It hadn't escaped his notice how white her fingers were from the weight of her shopping straining them.

'I haven't far to go, just up to Baycrest. It was too nice a day to stay cooped up, although I wasn't expecting it to be quite so windy.' She adjusted the brightly coloured scarf covering her white curls then tilted her head to one side. 'Do I know you?'

'My name's Owen Coburn. You might have seen me around the place, I'm working with Sam Barnes from The Siren. We're opening a restaurant together, you might have heard about that?'

'I've heard all about it from Joe—that's Sam's grandfather. He's got a flat at Baycrest just a few doors down from mine. I must say it sounds very exciting, if a bit fancy for the likes of me, but that's not it.' To Owen's surprise, she gripped his chin between two fingers and turned his first one way then the other. 'No, there's something about you, young man, I just can't put my finger on it.'

Excitement churned in his gut. Could this be the breakthrough he'd been looking for? Telling himself to not get ahead of himself, he tried to keep his first question casual.

'Have you lived in Lavender Bay for a long time, Mrs…?'

'Collymore,' she supplied. 'But you can call me Doris, dear. If you count seventy-eight years as a long time, dear, then I'd say so. Born and raised here.' She pointed vaguely in the direction of the shops. 'Lived next door to the Methodist chapel until the day I was married, then moved into one of the old fishing cottages where I remained until the day my Ned passed. I couldn't stand to be there on my own, and there are plenty of young families in need of good homes, so I packed myself off up to Baycrest. Best thing I ever did. I miss my Ned something awful, but it's lovely to be surrounded by friends. I have all the company I want, and when I'd rather be on my own I can just shut my front door.' She gave a little laugh. 'Listen to me giving you my life story! Why did you want to know how long I've lived here?'

This was it. He'd told himself it didn't matter, that he didn't need to go rummaging around in the past anymore, but the way his heart was pounding right then told him that was a load of rubbish. He wanted to know. He *needed* to know. 'I heard I might have some distant relatives around these parts, but I don't know anything about them.'

'Oh, how interesting. What did you say your surname was again, Coburn?' Her eyes crinkled at the edges, then she shook her head. 'Can't say that's a name I can place, dear, sorry.'

'The family I'm looking for is the Blackmores.'

Her head jerked up, and a tingle shot down Owen's spine. 'Doris?' he prompted when she didn't say anything.

'Sorry, dear, I was wool-gathering. Happens to us all at this age. Let me ask around and I'll get back to you if I hear of anything.'

Disappointment crashed over him like a tidal wave, threatening to suck him under. He should've known better than to get his hopes up. 'No, that's fine. I think I might have the name wrong. I'll double-check my facts first.'

She patted his arm once more. 'There's no harm in my asking, there's not many families around these parts that one or other

150

of us doesn't know. Don't fret, dear.' That was easy for her to say. Owen gave himself a mental kick in the arse. There was no point in being mad at Doris; none of this was her fault.

They reached the bottom of the entrance leading to Baycrest. 'Stairs or ramp?' he asked.

'Ramp, I think. Walking in all that wind has worn me out, but I can manage fine from here.' She unhooked their arms and held out her hands for her bags.

'If you're sure?'

'Absolutely. You've been more than enough help, dear. Come down here now, let me give you a kiss. I can see Lillian twitching at her net curtains so let's give her something to look at.'

He couldn't help but laugh, she was a real sweetheart. Bending his head, he let her peck his cheek. 'It was lovely to meet you, Doris.'

'You too, Owen, dear. Come for tea next week, that'll really set the tongues wagging! Let's say next Wednesday at four o'clock. I'm in flat three on the ground floor. There's a buzzer at the main entrance.'

'I might just do that. Take care now.' He waited at the bottom of the path until he was sure Doris was managing on her own, then headed back the way he'd come. A dark cloud blotted out the weak warmth of the sun, turning his mood as grey as the weather once more.

Chapter 16

Denial wasn't just a river in Egypt, it had become the default state of mind in the Stone household. Both Libby and her dad had done a fine job of ignoring the looming sale of the chip shop, choosing to go about their daily business as though their entire world wasn't going to change in just a few more weeks. The only thing she was doing differently was not hiding her relationship with Owen. Although he hadn't said as much, she could tell her dad still had reservations by the way there was always a short pause before he responded when she told him she was off to meet Owen.

There was no ignoring things when her dad had taken his suitcase down from the loft that morning, however. Still bound and determined to look for a new home in Spain, he would be heading off in a couple of days to stay with his sister and her husband to begin the hunt. With the house to herself, she could invite Owen to stay with her, but that would mean explaining her dad's plans.

Libby sighed as she tugged her jumper down over her knees and blew on the ends of her fingers. The little heater wasn't doing much to warm up the hut, but she needed space to finalise her business plan for the café. Though Owen had given her a key, this was the first time she'd ventured to the hut without having any arrangement to meet him. She just needed to get out of the house for a bit and find a space to think.

She had a meeting with a mortgage broker next week and was trying to be confident about her chances of success. With her dad planning to give her half the proceeds of the sale, her intention was to apply for a mortgage worth about seventy per cent of her best guess of the market value for the property. It was a bit of a shot in the dark, given how tight-lipped Mick was being over the deal he'd struck, but she hoped it would give her enough money to compensate him and have a little bit left over to invest in her plans. Trying to ignore the little voice in her head telling her she was wasting her time, she turned her attention back to the spreadsheet she was working on.

Lost in a sea of numbers, the sharp snick of the door latch opening took her by surprise. Hand over her racing heart, she swivelled in the captain's chair to face the door as a rosy-cheeked Owen let himself in. He stopped dead. 'Oh, I didn't know you'd be here.'

Feeling like an intruder, she unhooked her legs from inside her baggy jumper and leaped up. 'Sorry, I thought you were going to be busy at Subterranean all day.'

After shutting the door against the brutal wind outside, Owen sank onto the edge of the bed. 'No need to be sorry, we've done as much as we can do until the seating arrives, so I thought I'd get some paperwork sorted.' He glanced at the laptop behind her. 'Looks like I'm not the only one.'

Needing to hide the blush creeping up her cheeks, Libby tucked her nose into the loose neck of her jumper as she sank down in the old captain's chair beside the desk. 'Just fiddling around with a few ideas, nothing important.' She felt stupid for not just telling him the truth, but she was still worried he'd pull some white knight act and offer to do something ridiculous like buy the shop.

Her tummy did a funny twist. Perhaps he'd just shrug, tell her it was time to move on, maybe even use it as a way to persuade her to follow him to London. If he was even still thinking of them in that kind of way. She just didn't know.

Their heartfelt declarations to each other after Noah's accident on the beach hadn't moved things forward in the way she'd hoped, and she wondered if Owen was experiencing the same doubts now plaguing her. They'd fallen into this semi-casual routine, snatching a few hours here and there together, and he'd still given her no firm indication of his mid- to long-term plans.

Once the last of the fit-out works were completed and the restaurant was up and running, there would be no need for him to spend so much time in the bay. He still had his business in London to run, and though she'd been sincere in her declaration they'd work things out, in the cold light of day she just couldn't see *how*. His life was there, hers was here.

Perhaps it was time to stop pretending and accept the fact theirs was a romance with a limited shelf life. A delicious, decadent treat to be savoured and enjoyed, something they could both look back on with fondness. She swallowed a sigh. That might be possible for him, but not for her now she'd gone and fallen head over heels in love with him.

'A penny for them.'

Blinking, she realised she'd just been sitting there staring at him like a gormless twit. 'Sorry, I was miles away.'

'Not anywhere nice from the look on your face.' He moved from the bed to squat beside her, his broad palm engulfing one of her knees. 'What's the matter, Libs? You look as rubbish as I feel.'

Uncurling herself from the chair, she slipped down into his lap, curling her arms around his neck. 'Nothing, really. I've just got a few things I need to sort through.' Tilting her head back, she petted his cheek, noted the grim tightness around his eyes and mouth. 'Never mind me, are you okay?'

His brows drew closer together. 'I don't like it when you put me off like that.' She opened her mouth to respond, but he pressed his thumb down to stop her. 'Don't mind me, I'm in a shitty mood and looking for a fight where there's not one to be had. I thought I might have a lead on my mother, but it didn't pan out.'

'Oh, Owen, I'm so sorry. Do you want to talk about it?'

He shook his head. 'Nothing to talk about, really, just me jumping the gun. I thought it didn't matter, that I'd put the idea of looking for her behind me. It shouldn't matter this much. I *hate* that it matters this much.'

The raw pain in his voice cut her like a knife. Reaching to cup his face, she tried to stroke some of the tension from his jawline with her thumbs. 'Tell me what I can do to help.'

'Distract me.' His lips closed over hers to give her one of those slow, teasing kisses which sent her pulse fluttering and all thoughts flying from her head other than the beating need to be with him, under him, around him. She knew they should stop, that they were both using sex as an avoidance technique, but she just wanted to escape for a little while.

Owen eased back, heat and laughter sparkling in his eyes. 'If this was a romance movie, I'd perform some feat of acrobatics and be able to stand up with you in my arms and carry you over to the bed.'

Giggling, she pressed their foreheads together. 'It's all about equality these days, so maybe I'll throw you over my shoulder and carry you instead.'

His lips found her ear, sending delicious shivers through her which had nothing to do with the chilled air in the hut. 'Or we could stay right here.'

'Mmm, that sounds like a much better idea.'

With lots of pauses for kisses and caresses which warmed her blood and sent her senses spiralling, they managed to divest each other of their jeans and underwear. Owen's hands snaked beneath her jumper to cup her breasts. 'I love how you fit me,' he murmured against her throat. 'Like your body was moulded exactly for my hands.'

155

Sighing into his touch, Libby let her head fall back as she let Owen chase all her worries away in a rush of heat and tenderness. Whatever might be wrong in her life, being here with him like this *worked*. There was no effort to it, no hesitation anymore after so many moments spent together learning the patterns and rhythms of each other's bodies.

A partnership, he'd said, and in her head she added another word—lovers. She'd shared a bed with men before, but Owen was her first lover. The first to put her pleasure before his own, as she did for him, together building something beautiful, and breathtaking, and right.

Head on his shoulder, hips still locked around his, Libby tried to catch her breath. Owen's hand played over the outside of her thigh raising a trail of goose bumps in his wake. A tiny aftershock rippled through her, everything still sensitised until even the light dance of his fingers felt like too much. Another shiver, a third, and she lifted her head as it slowly dawned on her that it was now the cold sinking into her bones rather than anything else causing them. Reality hit in a wave of discomfort, from the ache of her knees pressed into the wooden floor beneath them to another blast of wind sneaking through a gap in the boards of the wall behind her. She shifted, causing Owen to stir and they staggered up to crawl under the mountain of quilts on the bed.

'I'll be glad when we don't have to do this anymore,' she said as she snuggled into his side.

Propping himself on one elbow, Owen raised a quizzical brow. 'That's not exactly a vote of confidence.'

With a laugh, she reached out to cup his cheek. 'Don't worry, it wasn't a critique on your performance, just the location. Dad's going away for a few weeks to see my aunt and uncle, so I'll have the place to myself.'

Owen's eyes lit up. 'Are you trying to seduce me with promises of all this *and* central heating?'

'Is it working?'

His hand slid down her back to cup her bottom. 'Oh, yes.'

Little bubbles of excitement filled her. It wasn't just the thought of getting to spend a whole night with him, it was all the other stuff that usually went with a relationship. They'd be able to curl up on the sofa and watch rubbish on the television or sit at the kitchen table and share a bite of supper as they talked about their days. 'I could cook you a proper meal, no more picnics and takeaways.'

Settling onto his back, Owen tucked her in closer to his side. 'Or, I can cook for you. As long as you like either spaghetti Bolognaise, chicken curry or bacon sandwiches because that's the extent of my kitchen repertoire.'

'Tell me again why you're getting involved in the restaurant business?' She was teasing, and he picked up the lightness in her question from the grin on her face.

'I'm in it for the money and the girls.' Turning his head, he claimed a kiss. 'Sam's invited us round to the flat for dinner tonight, if you fancy it? He was going to give Eliza a call, see if her and Jack are free.'

The six of them together sounded good. More than good, it sounded like they were a real couple. It was the kind of thing she, Beth and Eliza had dreamed of when they were young, before life had taken two of them away. They were back together, finally fulfilling those girlish plans. 'It sounds great. I'll have a word with dad, but I'm sure he can spare me.' Things were winding down in the shop. Now the tourists had gone home they were back to relying on the locals for trade, so it didn't take two of them to manage an evening shift. He'd be more than happy to give her a night off before he left her to handle everything on her own. Probably be glad to escape the horrible tension that had built between them.

If she could get some joy from the broker, maybe she should seize the initiative and make a start on the conversion works whilst her dad was away. They often closed for a few weeks before Christmas to deep clean the shop and carry out all the maintenance jobs they'd put off during their busy time. If she could show her dad something tangible, surely he'd see how serious she was about making a go of it. Until the moment he handed over the keys, there was still a chance to change his mind. She had to hold on to that belief.

'Come in, come in, it's so good to see you.' Beth met them at the back door of the emporium, engulfing Libby in a huge hug.

Laughing, Libby squeezed her back. 'You saw me yesterday, silly.' Releasing Beth, she edged to one side to give Owen room to bend down and peck a kiss to Beth's cheek.

'I brought wine, as instructed.' He held up the bottles held in each hand.

'See, I knew there was a reason I liked you,' Beth teased. She stretched her left hand out to take one of the bottles and that was when Libby saw it.

'Oh. My. God. What is that on your finger?'

The glittering band was almost eclipsed by the sparkle in Beth's eyes. 'It's just a ring.'

'Just a ring?' Their eyes met and suddenly they were clutching each other and shrieking at the tops of their voices. Tears stung the back of Libby's eyes as she grabbed Beth's hand for a better look. 'It's beautiful, and perfect for you.' Instead of a central gemstone, a delicate pearl nestled in a filigree flower studded with diamonds. Unique and stylish, it was exactly the thing her friend would've chosen for herself. 'The boy done good. I suppose you'll have to keep him now.'

Blinking tears off her lashes, Beth giggled. 'I suppose I will. Come on up, Sam's banished me from the kitchen, so I was starting to get lonely.'

They were just stepping over the threshold when the back gate swung open to admit Eliza and Jack. In a matter of moments, they were screaming and crying again as Beth flashed her ring at Eliza.

'I think they might be like this for a while,' Libby heard Owen say to Jack. 'Maybe we should leave them to it.'

'Good idea.' The two men edged their way around their group hug and wandered upstairs to the flat Beth and Sam now shared.

'Right, now they've gone you must tell us everything,' Eliza said as she made enough room in their huddle to lift Beth's hand to study the ring. 'Oh, gosh, it's perfect.'

Libby nodded. 'I said exactly the same thing. I assumed you must have had something to do with your brother's sudden outbreak of good taste, and was going to yell at you later for not letting me in on the secret.'

With a laugh, Eliza shook her head. 'Nothing to do with me. Somehow my lug head brother managed to get this right all on his own.' She gave Beth's hand a little shake. 'Come on, spill the beans.'

Beth blushed. 'He asked me this morning. Well, asked might be stretching the truth. He'd put the ring box on the bathroom sink before we went to bed last night. Normally he's up and about first thing so he can get out for a run, but this morning he was just lounging around in bed. I couldn't work out what was going on until I walked into the bathroom and saw the box. My hands were shaking so badly, I nearly dropped the ring down the plug-hole!'

'Well, he would've been able to impress you with his plumbing skills—that is how he won your heart,' Libby said with a grin. Not long after Beth had inherited the emporium and the flat above it, she'd had a near disaster with the kitchen sink and Sam had happened to turn up just in time to save the day.

'He certainly has his uses.' The expression on Beth's face was so saucy, Libby couldn't help but burst out laughing.

Eliza pulled a face. 'Oh, yuk! That's my brother, remember?

159

Come on, let's get out of this wind and get some wine open so I can wash that image out of my head.'

They found the three men gathered on the landing outside the kitchen door, clinking bottles of beer together. 'If you'd given me a proper hint, I'd have brought some champagne,' Owen was saying. 'And you were so casual about the dinner invitation, we nearly didn't bother.'

Sam took a quick mouthful of his beer, his eyes fixed on Beth. 'My fiancée made me promise not to breathe a word about it.'

Damn, if Libby was ever on the receiving end of a look like the one he was giving Beth, she'd likely melt into a puddle of goo. She glanced at Beth, who was looking ready to swoon, or grab Sam by the hand and drag him off to the bedroom. Raising her hand, Libby waved it between the two of them. 'That's enough of that, thank you very much. I'm only here because I was promised food.'

Sam raised his beer to his brow in a little salute. 'Yes, ma'am. Owen, do you want to open one of those bottles and pour a drink for our ladies?' *Our ladies.* A throwaway comment, but it gave Libby a funny little feeling in her stomach. She caught Owen's gaze, and oh, boy, goo didn't even begin to describe it. There was a seriousness to his expression, a promise in his eyes that sent a shiver down her spine. Blushing, she broke the eye contact before she did something stupid like ask him when it might be their turn. It was too much, and way too soon for her to even be thinking like that.

Libby allowed the others to usher her into the living room, grateful to escape. She soon found herself perched on the arm of the sofa, as Beth and Eliza chattered a mile a minute about possible dates for the wedding. When Owen approached with a glass of wine for her, she took it with a brief smile and hoped he wouldn't notice she'd deliberately placed herself in a position where he couldn't sit beside her. He trailed his fingers down her arm in a soft caress before circling back around the room to lean against the wall where Jack had positioned himself.

The empty armchair seemed to mock her. Positioned at a right-angle to the opposite end of the two-seater sofa, there was no practical reason for her not to be sitting in it. Whenever they had a girls' night, though the order they sat in might change, the three of them always sprawled across that corner of the room. Telling herself she just wanted to keep close to Beth, Libby draped a casual arm around her friend's shoulders and leaned down to break into the wedding conversation. 'I'm not being a bridesmaid unless my dress has at least four layers of ruffles.'

'And puff sleeves!' Eliza chimed in. Within moments they were shrieking with laughter over an internet search Beth had typed into her phone.

'Ooh, tartan!' Beth said, before heaving a mock-sad sigh. 'If only one or other of us had any kind of Scottish roots.'

'It doesn't look like that's stopped any of this lot. I like the idea, I could dye my hair to match.' Eliza choked on a mouthful of wine she'd been taking in an unfortunate bit of timing as Libby spoke. Jack was beside her in an instant, only allowing her to wave him off after he'd rubbed a soothing hand up and down Eliza's back.

A waft of delicious spices preceded Sam's entrance into the room bearing a platter covered in hors d'oeuvres. Bending at the waist, he placed them down on the coffee table beside a stack of small side plates already neatly covered in cocktail napkins.

Libby crowded forward along with everyone else, her eyes dancing with delight over the selection of delicately furled smoked salmon bites, butter-soft pastry parcels and cocktail sticks skewering olives, feta cheese and prosciutto. It was hard to know where to start. As she leant forward to snag a plate from the stack the room started to swim before her eyes. Sparkling lights danced across her vision, and she had a vague impression of Owen shouting her name as the Wurlitzer in her head stopped spinning and everything went black.

161

Chapter 17

Bright. That was the first message her brain sent her even before she'd opened her eyes. Blinding light stabbed at her irises, and she clamped her lids down with a wince. Why was someone shining a torch at her?

'Libs?' Beth's voice came from somewhere to her right, and she rolled her head towards the sound, regretting it instantly as the queasy feeling in her stomach kicked into overdrive.

'Feel sick,' she managed to get out before a strong arm was hooked behind her and she emptied the meagre contents of her stomach into a cardboard tray shoved in front of her in the nick of time. Shuddering against the bitter taste in her mouth, Libby risked a glance through her tangled fringe to see her worst fear realised as her eyes met Owen's worried gaze. Great, just great; such a glamorous look puking your guts up in front of your incredibly sexy boyfriend. A hot flush rippled through her and she swallowed hard against another bout of nausea. 'Sorry about that.'

'Nothing to be sorry about.' He eased her back against a pile of hard square pillows before putting the tray somewhere out of her line of sight. 'How are you feeling?'

'Like I got hit by a truck which then reversed over me for good measure.' She accepted a glass of water with a straw from him and sipped a little, grateful to wash the bile away. 'My hand hurts,' She flexed it against a tight pull across her skin, only then registering there was a drip taped to it, a clear tube snaking from it towards a stand beside the bed. 'I'm in hospital?'

'You keeled over at Beth's.' Owen's fingers fluttered over her hair, barely touching as he smoothed back her lank fringe. 'Gave yourself a right whack on the coffee table as you went down.' Libby raised her hand towards her forehead only for him to capture it and ease it back onto the crisp white sheets. 'Don't touch, you've had a couple of stitches.'

'What happened?' She glanced from Owen to Beth. 'The last thing I remember is Sam coming in with those lovely looking hors d'oe—oh, Beth! I've ruined your party.' Mortification flooded her veins. She'd never fainted in her life before, and what a bloody time to pick for her first swan dive.

'Shh, don't be silly. No one cares about that, we just want to make sure you're all right. I'll let the nurse know that you're awake.' Rising from her seat, Beth disappeared behind the blue and white flowered curtain.

As though she'd broken some kind of spell, Libby became aware of the noises coming from the other side of the little blue cocoon. Muffled voices in hushed conversations, the squeak of someone's shoes on the hard-tiled floor and from somewhere to her left the regular hush-hush of some kind of breathing apparatus.

'Do you want another drink?' Owen offered the water to her again, but she shook her head. Her stomach still didn't feel too clever and the last thing she wanted was to be sick in front of him again.

'I must look a fright.'

Bending to kiss the top of her head, Owen smiled. 'You look great. The perfect shade of ghostly white if you were in the mood to revisit your teenage Goth roots.'

163

That earned him a laugh which quickly changed into a groan as her head began to throb again. She raised her hand in an automatic reflex only to have him stop her once more before she could touch her tender scalp.

When he laid her hand back down, he kept it trapped beneath his own, his thumb stroking back and forth across her knuckles. 'You scared the shit out of me, Libs.' The huskiness in his voice called her attention from their joined hands up to his face. Thick lines of worry marred his normally smooth forehead, and for the first time she noticed the streak of blood down the front of his pale-blue shirt.

'Oh no, I made a mess of your shirt.'

He glanced down as though unaware of the stain, then back up to her. 'You bled like a stuck pig. Thankfully the paramedic said that was quite usual for scalp wounds. They were brilliant actually—the same crew who sorted out Noah when he hurt himself that time on the rocks.'

'They'll have to start offering us a friends and family discount at this rate.' It was a weak attempt at a joke, but she couldn't bear the worry etched into his face. 'I'm okay, Owen, really.'

'Thank you, Doctor Stone, but I think I'll wait for a proper medical opinion, if you don't mind. You were pretty out of it in the ambulance. Do you remember any of that?'

Libby almost shook her head before stopping herself in the nick of time. 'No. Like I said, I remember Sam coming in the room and then nothing until I woke up just now.'

The curtain rings jangled on the rail as the material was swept open and a smiling nurse in a burgundy and white uniform approached, Beth close on her heels. 'Ah, you're back with us then? Let's take a look at you.'

She bustled around, checking Libby's drip and the monitoring screens behind her and then finally Libby herself. 'Your friend said you vomited?'

'Yes. When I first woke up.'

'Hmm. Well the doctor will be along in a few minutes, but you might have a concussion from the bump you took to your head. Are you still feeling sick?'

Libby nodded, then winced. 'I really need to stop moving my head.' Sucking in a deep breath to settle her stomach, she met the nurse's kind gaze. 'A bit queasy, but not like I need to be sick, if that makes sense?'

The nurse smiled. 'I know what you mean. Have you managed a little drink?' Libby pursed her lips at the thought. 'I can get you a few ice chips, if you'd rather? That'll keep your mouth fresh without having to swallow anything if you don't feel like it.'

'That would be lovely, thank you.'

'All right, Ms Stone, I'll be right back with those and the doctor. You just relax, and we'll get you sorted out in no time.'

Chapter 18

The fact Libby seemed lucid enough did little to comfort Owen. He didn't think he'd ever get over the horror of watching her drop from the arm of the sofa and knowing he was too far away to break her fall. The bloody corner of the table had done that. A shudder ran through him as he recalled the terrible sound of her head striking wood. When he'd crouched beside her, she'd been so still and so pale, her pallor a terrible contrast to the bright red of the blood seeping from the cut above her hairline. *Where the hell was the bloody doctor?*

He needed some answers. Normal, healthy people didn't just faint like that. Hadn't Libby said she'd never done it before? God, what if she was really ill? Her dad was supposed to be going away in a couple of days and it would be up to Owen to take care of her. He'd never had to be responsible for the wellbeing of another person. Well, not anyone he truly cared about the way he did about Libby. Panic gripped him unlike anything he'd ever experienced. *Where was the damn doctor?*

Thankfully the curtain swished again before he could work himself into a proper frenzy, and a small woman with deep brown skin and inky-black hair pulled up onto her head in a severe bun appeared alongside the nurse from earlier. She gave a brief nod

166

to both Owen and Beth before turning her focus on Libby. 'Good Evening, Ms Stone, I'm Dr Banerjee. It's good to see you're awake. Perhaps if your friends could excuse us, we can have a chat about what happened to you this evening?'

The nurse lifted one edge of the curtain back. 'I can show you where you can wait, if you like? There's a drinks machine in there. Can't recommend the tea, but the coffee's not too bad.'

A part of him wanted to protest, to insist he should stay and find out what the doctor had to say. But the rational bit of his brain which was still functioning reminded him he didn't have the right. Giving Libby's hand one final squeeze, he met her eyes and hoped the smile on his lips was somewhat reassuring. 'I'll be outside, if you need anything.'

Wide-eyed, she nibbled at her bottom lip but didn't do anything other than nod at him. She looked so pale and small against the white sheets, he wanted to crawl in beside her, hug her close, and promise her everything would be all right. But the nurse had an eyebrow raised at him and Beth had already slid past her to the other side of the curtain. 'Thanks,' he said to the nurse as she lowered the curtain behind them and held out a hand to indicate the way to the family room.

'I'll let you know when you can see her again. Try not to worry.' With a kindly smile the nurse was gone, her Croc-style rubber clogs squeaking on the tiled floor.

The door swung closed behind her with a *whump*, leaving him and Beth in a small, stale-aired room with nothing more than a couple of sad spider plants and a scattering of dog-eared magazines for company. 'Do you want a drink?' Beth crossed the room towards the vending machines in the corner.

'Not really.' Sinking down on an institutional-looking blue couch, Owen grabbed the nearest magazine and began to flick through it. The pages of soap gossip, recipes and tell-all life stories blurred before his eyes. What if it was something really serious? Why else would the doctor have asked them to leave?

He didn't realise he'd voiced his fears aloud until the cushion next to him sank down and Beth put a gentle hand on his shoulder. 'I'm sure it's just a procedural thing. We're not relatives and even if we were, they have to be so careful about stuff like patient confidentiality.'

Owen nodded. He was being a sap. He should be the one comforting Beth, not the other way around. As much as he cared for Libby, he didn't get a monopoly on worry. The girls had all been friends since they were little kids. 'Sorry, I lost my mind for a minute or two then. I just…' He squared his shoulders against another shudder. 'She just looked such an awful colour when she went down.'

'I'm sure she'll be okay.' It sounded too close to a prayer for his liking.

Beth pulled her phone out of her bag and stared at it. They'd both switched them off when entering the ward as per the signs posted everywhere. 'I should call the others, but I don't know what to tell them.'

'You could let them know she's awake and talking. Maybe don't mention the being sick part until we know a bit more?'

She seemed to brighten a bit at his suggestion. 'Yes, that's a good idea.' Rising, she wandered over to where a small window looked out upon the corridor and began speaking into her phone. Settling back into the lumpy couch, Owen closed his eyes and let the soothing soft tone of her voice wash over him.

'Mr Coburn?' Sitting bolt upright at the sound of his name, Owen found the nurse watching him from the doorway. 'Ms Stone is asking to speak to you.' She cast an apologetic glance at Beth who'd taken a couple of steps towards her. 'Just Mr Coburn for the time being.'

Swallowing around a sudden lump in his throat, Owen exchanged a bewildered look with Beth as the nurse ushered him back towards the ward. The curtains were still drawn around

Libby's bed space and he wasn't sure what to make of that when most of the others on the ward were open with patients reading or staring at tablets. A deep sense of foreboding gripped him, but he shoved his way through the curtains before he had a chance to get himself spooked again.

They'd propped Libby up with a couple of extra pillows, and he was relieved to see there was a little more colour in her cheeks. The flush deepened as she watched him approach to perch on the side of her bed. 'How're you doing?' He took her hand, raising it to his lips to blow warm air over the frigid tips of her fingers. 'You're cold, do you need an extra blanket?'

She clenched her hand around his for a moment before easing it free and letting it fall back at her side. 'No, I'm fine.' Her voice sound weak, and there was something about her expression he couldn't quite get a handle on. 'The doctor said I can go home in the morning, provided I have a decent night.'

Relief flooded through him. 'Nothing serious, then?'

Her lips quirked in a funny half-smile. 'I wouldn't say that, exactly.' She glanced away. 'I'm sorry, Owen.'

He tilted his head trying to catch her gaze, but she seemed fascinated by the patterned curtain to the left of the cubicle. 'I told you before, it's not a problem. I'm a big boy, I can handle a bit of vomit.' He'd expected her to laugh, or at least manage a grin, but instead her eyes shuttered closed. She looked so closed off, as remote to him as if she were on the other side of the world not mere inches away. 'Libs, what is it, sweetheart?'

Her throat worked up and down. 'I want you to know, I don't expect anything from you. It's an accident, just one of those stupid things, but I know how you feel about this, so I won't expect you to be involved.'

He had absolutely no idea what she was talking about and told her so. 'I feel like I'm in a play without a script.'

Opening her eyes, she rolled her head to face him and the

169

look of abject sorrow in her eyes struck him like a blow. 'I'm pregnant.'

Oh. Shit. 'But how?' He couldn't stop the ridiculous question, nor the one that followed hard on its heels. 'Is it mine?'

Flinching like he'd slapped her, Libby narrowed her eyes at him. 'The usual way.' She turned her head away. 'Like I said, I'm sorry.' She pulled her hand away and a voice in his head screamed at him to grab it, some sixth sense screaming to him that if he didn't hold on to her, she'd slip away from him forever. He didn't move quickly enough, and she curled her hand behind her head making it impossible for him to take it again.

'It's not like you did it on your own.' Ignoring the chant of *baby, baby, you're going to have a baby* currently on a loop in his head, he took another breath and waited until he could speak calmly before asking. 'What do you want to do about it?'

'Growing up, I always hated being an only child. Mum and Dad were older when they had me, and she told me a bit about the terrible time she'd had conceiving, and how they'd always viewed me as their miracle baby.'

Christ. What must it be like to have been wanted that much that someone viewed you as a miracle, rather than a curse? Owen would never know. His birth parents had never wanted him, and as for the pair who'd finally adopted him and given him a name, well, there were worse things than death, as the old saying went.

With a sigh, Libby continued. 'I didn't want to be the miracle, I wanted to be a normal kid with brothers and sisters and since then, I've always dreamed of a brood of my own.'

Here he was trying to get his head around the prospect of one baby and she'd gone and said the word brood. That didn't imply a couple, or even three. It sounded like the makings of a five-a-side bloody football team. The back of his shirt dampened with sweat at the prospect. How was he supposed to deal with that? The only lessons life had taught him about raising kids would land most people in jail. An afternoon running around kicking a ball about was one thing, but actually being responsible for the health and wellbeing of a child? There was no chance. 'I can't do it.'

Her soft gasp of pain almost ripped him in two, but when she spoke, her words were calm. 'I don't expect you to.'

Gut punch. Never mind the doubts he had about his ability to be a half-decent father, Libby had already judged and found him wanting. He sucked in a couple of shaky breaths fearing he might be the one to vomit this time. She had no faith in him, no expectation he'd step up and do the right thing. He was flawed, and she knew it.

'I'm tired now, I'd like to get some rest.'

'Can I get you anything before I go?'

'I'm in a hospital surrounded by doctors and nurses.' *And, I don't need you.* She hadn't said as much, didn't need to.

Embarrassment burned in his gut, and he rose stiffly. 'Do you want me to come and collect you tomorrow?' He didn't even have a bloody car, but surely someone would lend him one for an hour or two.

She shook her head. 'Dad's coming to fetch me, I've already spoken to him.' She hesitated, then licked her lips. 'He doesn't know about the baby, and I want to keep it that way for now.'

Owen frowned. 'You can't mean to let him go away on holiday and not tell him?'

Her eyes narrowed. 'That's between me and him. I won't be the cause for making him stay somewhere he doesn't want to be.' She glanced away. 'Not again.' The last two words were said more to herself than him, but they revealed a shocking truth. She knew about Mick's plans to sell up, and she hadn't confided in him about it.

In his gut he knew he was being a hypocrite, but he'd sworn to Mick he'd keep his secret. He could think of no good reason for Libby not to tell him about it the moment she knew, but plenty of bad ones. Like she didn't trust him, or didn't think he was an important enough person in her life to be worthy of her confidence. Not sure he could take another blow and remain standing, Owen backed up. 'I'll call you tomorrow. Sleep well.'

'Can you ask Beth to come and see me?' A wash of bitter jealousy swept through him. He bet Beth knew about the sale of the shop, and bloody Eliza too. Thick as thieves the lot of them, and now no doubt they'd be the ones she turned to about the baby.

Owen clenched a fist. If Libby thought she could dismiss him from her life like some casual summer romance which had run its course, she was in for a bloody rude awakening. He'd never given up on something just because it was difficult, and he wasn't about to start now when the stakes were higher than ever. Not trusting himself to speak, he simply nodded, then ducked beyond the curtain.

172

Chapter 19

'Are you sure you'll be all right, lovey? I don't like the thought of going away when you're feeling poorly.' Mick hovered beside her bed wringing his hands, his face the very picture of abject misery.

Libby nodded, and told him for the tenth time in the past five minutes that she'd be fine. 'I just had a funny turn. The doctors think my blood sugar went a bit haywire from not eating much yesterday and then I must've leaned forward too quickly. Apart from a bit of a headache, I'm right as rain.' It wasn't exactly a lie. The doctors had checked her over and pronounced her fit and well. She tried to keep her eyes from straying towards her bag where she'd tucked the copy of that morning's scan carefully between the sheaves of information the nurse had thrust at her— everything from recommended diet sheets to detailed guides on how her baby would be developing over the next few weeks. *Her baby*. A tiny flutter of excitement stirred in her belly.

Mick's big hand patted her shoulder. 'It'd be no trouble to postpone my trip.'

'Dad…'

'All right, all right, I know I'm fussing, but I'm still allowed to do that, aren't I?'

Trying to fight back a sudden rush of tears, Libby blinked hard and smiled up at him through her lashes. 'Of course you are, I'll never get too big where I won't need my dad to take care of me. And you can still do that, you'll only ever be a plane ride away.'

A delighted smile split his broad features. 'I'll make you a brew and then leave you in peace.' Her phone pinged. 'I expect that'll be someone else wanting to make a fuss of you.' He backed away to the door and then paused. 'I won't mind if you have Owen to stay whilst I'm away. In fact, I'd probably feel better knowing he's around to keep an eye on you.'

Salt water stung the back of her eyes again. She'd not seen hide nor hair of Owen since he'd walked out of her hospital room. She hadn't expected him to be thrilled about the baby, but his utter rejection of getting involved had broken something inside of her. Rationally, she could understand how his past would affect his thinking when it came to a family, but the cold blankness on his face was a look she'd never forget. *Or forgive.* 'We're... umm, we're taking a bit of break.'

Mick's face fell. 'Not because of what I said before, I hope? Because believe me, he was a bloody marvel last night. He was the one who sent Jack and Eliza along here in case I needed to close up and come and see you.'

A bloody marvel right up until the moment she'd really needed him. 'No, Dad. Nothing to do with that. We just rushed into things a bit so I'm taking a step back. We're still good friends.' The lie tasted bitter on her tongue. 'Beth and Eliza are popping in to see me in a bit.'

That bit of news brightened him up, at least. 'Well, they know the way up by now. I'll fetch you that tea.'

Libby let her head fall back on the pillow, her gaze tracing over the familiar cracks in the ceiling plaster. She shifted one hand towards her stomach before letting it drop back on the bed. There was a tiny little human growing inside her right that minute.

The logistics of it were blowing her mind. She swallowed hard. They were also making her a little bit squeamish.

She heard the creak of footsteps on the stairs outside and was just pushing herself back into a sitting position when Eliza appeared around her half-open door, a couple of mugs in hand. 'Hello, you.'

Libby smiled. 'Hello, you.'

Eliza placed the mugs on the bedside table then folded her legs beneath her at the other end of the bed. 'Well, aren't you full of surprises?'

'Apparently so.' A loose thread on the blanket caught Libby's eye and she began to fiddle with it, running it through her fingers over and over again. 'Did you see Owen this morning?'

A frown marred Eliza's creamy forehead. 'You haven't spoken to him?'

Unable to speak, Libby shook her head.

'Then you won't know he's had to go back to London on urgent business.'

'Oh, I see.' She hated herself for being right about him. There'd been a tiny kernel of hope left that after a night to get over the shock, he might step up to the plate, but apparently he'd made a run for it.

She sighed. None of this was his fault. He hadn't asked for this and she wouldn't tie him down with her decision to keep the baby. It hadn't even occurred to her for one moment that she wouldn't go through with the pregnancy. She'd meant what she'd said to him about wanting a brood, and whilst these weren't circumstances she'd have chosen to begin her family, she would treat the baby as the gift it was.

'I'm not sure you do see,' Eliza said carefully. 'He was pretty devastated when he came home from the hospital last night and wouldn't speak to any of us, just went straight to his room. He got a phone call from work during breakfast this morning, and he was absolutely torn up about it. He wasn't going to go until I promised him I'd be here to keep an eye on you.' Leaning forward, Eliza gathered her mug into her cupped hands and blew across the surface. 'And what's this about not wanting to tell your dad? What's going on in your head, Libs? I can't work you out at all.'

'Dad needs a break. I'm not a little girl anymore, I can deal with my own problems.' God, it was all such a bloody mess. Clutching at her hair, she gave it a tug as though the little bite of pain would somehow bring some sense to her riotous thoughts. 'I'm glad Owen's gone. It's best all round if we end it now.'

'But why, for heaven's sake?' Eliza looked genuinely bewildered.

'Because he doesn't want to have children. He said as much that day on the beach when Noah had his awful accident and Jack was beside himself with guilt and worry. And he told me straight out last night that he couldn't do it.' Leaning forward, she placed a hand on Eliza's leg. 'We both know what it's like for a child having to cope with a parent who resents them.' They fell silent as they contemplated the terrible time Beth had had growing up with a mother who'd gone out of her way to make Beth feel like a constant inconvenience.

Eliza sighed. 'Maybe he didn't really mean it. We all say things off the cuff when a situation is theoretical. It was bound to be a shock, just give him a bit of time to get his head around it.'

She didn't understand, because she didn't know the whole picture, but it wasn't Libby's place to share Owen's secrets. He'd told her about his own difficult childhood in confidence. 'I don't think it's going to make any difference.'

'You can't know that! Just give him a chance, Libs.'

Libby tugged a handful of hair in frustration. She could pretend to only have the baby's best interests at heart, but this was about self-preservation as much as anything. 'And what if I do that and he ends up resenting me and the baby for trapping him here? What if he decides to try, even though I know he doesn't want to, and then he leaves me in a few years' time because he hates me and the life I've forced him into?'

'Stop that! You're not forcing him to do anything. If he comes back and says he wants to be with you *and* the baby, then why not give yourself a chance at happiness?'

She knew Eliza meant well, but it was easy for her now she and Jack were all loved up and about to move in together. 'Not everyone gets a happy ending, it's not that simple.' She glanced up through her fringe. 'I love him, Eliza. More than I knew it was possible to love another human being. If I don't let him go now, I'm afraid it might break me into more pieces than I'll ever be able to put back together again. I can't take that risk. Not for me, and not for this baby.' She clasped a protective hand around her still flat stomach. It still didn't seem real, that there was the potential for a whole living breathing person floating around in there somewhere.

'Oh, Libby.' In an instant, Eliza had her arms wrapped around her, rocking her as she cried. 'This is exactly why Jack tried to break things off with me after Noah's accident. We can't withdraw from life in the hope it stops us from getting hurt. And imagine what you might be giving up. A whole lifetime of happiness with a man you love, and if my eyes are any judge, a man who absolutely adores you too.'

'You don't understand.' Libby hiccupped through her tears. 'It doesn't matter how much you love someone, or how hard you try, there's no guarantees in life. Look what happened to Mum and Dad, and now he wants to leave me, too…' She clamped a hand over her mouth and bent double as though she could hold in all the pain threatening to spill out of her.

'What? Oh my God, Libby, what are you saying? I thought your dad was going on holiday?' Eliza gripped Libby's face between her palms and lifted it. Using her thumbs, she wiped the tears from Libby's cheeks. 'Shh. Come on now, calm down a minute and tell me what's going on.'

Libby took a couple of snivelling breaths, coughed and tried to speak more slowly. 'He…he's g…g…going to look for somewhere to live. He w…wants to leave the bay.'

Eliza's hands fell away, her sage-green eyes wide with shock. 'You're not serious?'

Grabbing a handful of tissues from the box beside her bed, Libby wiped her face and blew her nose, nodding all the time at Eliza. 'He told me he can't bear to be here without Mum. That it's been a nightmare all these years since we lost her, and he only stayed so I could be here with you and Beth.'

Tears welled in Eliza's eyes. 'He really said that to you? I can't believe it. Oh, how awful for him, and for you, too. Oh, Libs, what will you do?'

Libby shook her head. 'I don't know. He's already found someone to buy this place. Keeps going on about how he's denied me a life of my own all these years and that we'll split the money so I can go travelling, or some other such rubbish he's convinced himself I need to do.'

'But what about your plans for the teashop?' Eliza grabbed her arm. 'And how long have you known about all this?'

Feeling a bit sheepish, Libby looked away. 'A few weeks now.'

'A few weeks! Why the bloody hell didn't you tell us?' Eliza gave her arm a little shake. 'Libby Stone, I'm completely bloody furious with you! We're supposed to be your friends and you've kept all this from us.'

'Kept all what from us?' Beth said as she entered the room. 'What's going on, Eliza? I could hear you shouting from halfway down the stairs.'

Red-faced, Eliza sat back on her haunches. 'I'm sorry, I didn't mean to raise my voice.' She turned her attention back to Libby who was about ready to melt into a puddle and slide off the side of the bed if it meant she could avoid the hurt and accusation in her best friend's tone. 'I can't believe you kept this to yourself.'

Beth sank down on the other side of the bed. 'Kept what? She only found out about the baby last night, Eliza. Give her a chance to catch her breath.'

'I'm not talking about the baby. I'm talking about Mick planning to sell up and retire to Spain. Madam here's known about it for weeks and didn't think to share the news.'

'*What?*'

Libby held her hands up in surrender. 'Don't you start as well, B, I really don't think I can stand it if you're both mad at me on top of everything else. I didn't keep it a secret to hurt either of you, I just wanted some time to try and sort things out for myself. You're both really busy trying to get your businesses established, and then there's the restaurant and Jack's farm, and all...' She trailed off, her once robust reasons sounding ridiculous now she voiced them aloud.

'Oh, Libs.' Beth took her hand. 'You silly thing. We're never so busy that we don't have time to help you. Look at all you've done for the two of us over the past few months.'

She shrugged. 'Yeah, but that was different.' It sounded weak to her own ears, but it *had* been different. Libby had been so excited to have them both home, she would've done anything to help them get re-established. 'Besides, I wanted to prove to myself that I could work it out on my own.'

Eliza and Beth exchanged a look of exasperation. 'If this was one or other of us saying that to you, there'd be hell to pay.' Eliza softened her tone. 'We don't want to take over, nor to make you think we don't trust you to cope with this, we just want to give you the same support you've always given us.'

'Well, now I feel bloody awful,' Libby grumbled, making the other two laugh.

'Good!'

'So you bloody should!'

It was Libby's turn to laugh. 'Oh, girls, what the hell am I going to do?' With a wail, she collapsed into their arms for a huge hug.

'It's a big gamble,' Beth said about half an hour later once Libby had outlined her plans and shown them the file she'd pulled together for her appointment with the broker. 'You don't even know who the buyer for this place is. What if they're not willing to let your dad out of the deal?'

Libby shrugged. 'They can't have exchanged on it, because we wouldn't be allowed to keep running the business, never mind live here if the ownership had legally changed hands. And if I'm only looking for a loan for half of what the place is worth, then surely that's got to be a halfway decent risk for the bank or whatever? Even if I ended up having to sell the place, I'd still make enough to cover what I owed them.'

Beth nodded, though she didn't look all together sure. 'I suppose so. It's just a lot to take on, what with the baby and everything.' Beth cringed. 'Oh, God, I can't believe I just said that. Even after all these years sometimes I open my mouth and my mother comes out. Ignore me. I think it's a brilliant idea and I'm sure you'll make a fantastic success of it.' She leaned in for another quick hug.

'What about Owen?'

Eliza's softly spoken question pulled Libby up short. 'What about him? We already talked about that, and I made my position clear. You might not agree with it, but I'd ask you to respect it.'

Eliza pulled a face. 'I'm not talking about the baby, although you know what I think about that. I'm talking about asking him if he'll help you with this place.'

Was she serious? Libby gawped at her. 'And say what? "Hi, I know I said I didn't expect anything from you but how about buying me and our baby the building my dad already owns?"' She shook her head at the mere suggestion of it.

'No, not like that.' Eliza folded her arms. 'He originally came to the bay looking for investment opportunities. He missed out on the emporium, and the restaurant is only a partial investment and nothing on the scale of what the emporium was on the market for. You could offer it to him as a proper business deal. His investment in return for a percentage of the profits. You'd save on interest payments, and you wouldn't have the risk of the bank changing their mind when they realise you're pregnant.'

She waved her off when Libby huffed, refusing to be distracted from hammering home her point. 'Be realistic. Sexist or not, by the time you come to sign on the dotted line in a couple more months, you won't be able to hide your condition. A single woman, starting a brand-new business and expecting a baby? Oh, they won't couch it in those terms, they'll give you some rubbish about change in market conditions, or blame it on Brexit like everyone seems to do with everything these days. But you have to face up to that being a real possibility.'

Eliza was right, but it was all too much to think about right then. Maybe she should just come clean with her dad and see if the news about the baby didn't change his mind about the whole thing. She shrugged the thought away almost as soon as she'd finished it. Her dad had given up so much for her already. He deserved the chance to retire, and if Spain was his destination of choice, then she would respect that. He needed to make that decision unencumbered by any sense of guilt or responsibility towards her. If she wasn't prepared to let the baby keep Owen in Lavender Bay, then she definitely wasn't going to use her dad as a way to make all her problems go away.

'I'll think about it,' she said, more to keep Eliza off her back for a bit whilst she sorted everything through rather than with any deeper intention. 'But let's talk about something else for a while.' Bending over, she retrieved her bag from the floor and fished out her scan. She placed the black-and-white image on the blanket between the three of them. 'Meet Baby Stone.'

Chapter 20

'Answer the phone, please just answer the phone,' Owen muttered to himself as Libby's number cut to voicemail for the umpteenth time that day. Not that he could blame her for not answering. He'd left the bay while she was still in the hospital, summoned by an urgent phone call from Alex about a serious incident on one of their sites. She could've probably handled the crisis on her own, but he'd jumped straight into work mode, grateful for the distraction and to be back in an environment where he felt in control. Every time he thought about the baby, his heart started racing like he was having a panic attack. He knew nothing about being a father—nothing good anyway. He hadn't told Libby any of that, though, had he? As far as she was concerned, he'd done a runner. She'd likely never speak to him again. Desperate to know she was okay, he'd called Sam, who'd assured him Libby was fine and being taken care of. The accusation in his tone had made it clear to Owen he should be the one looking after her. And he would, as soon as he'd sorted things out here. If he hadn't blown it, and that was a very big if.

A knock on his office door had him tossing his mobile on the desk behind him and standing up to greet the visitor Alex was ushering into the room. 'Hiya, Tom. Take a seat, mate.' He gestured to the little meeting table in the corner. 'Can I get you a coffee?'

The site foreman sank into one of the chairs and shook his head. 'No, ta, Boss. Alex already offered.' He scrubbed a hand over his thinning hair. 'I'm really sorry about all this mess.' The poor bloke looked devastated, and Owen's heart went out to him. He'd spent the journey up and most of the night going through the reports as they trickled in from different sources about the accident on one of their construction sites. A load had slipped from one of their scaffolds. Thankfully without causing any injuries, but the consequences could've been disastrous. It wasn't a reportable incident to the Health and Safety Executive, but Owen took his responsibilities seriously and had instructed a full-scale investigation to be carried out by their in-house safety team the moment Alex had called to notify him about the accident.

'Why don't you tell me in your own words what you remember about the other day. No pressure, I'm not going to take any notes and no one's trying to catch you out. I just want to hear it straight from you.'

Tom placed his arms on the table and sat up a little straighter. 'I was in the office when it happened, reviewing the lifting plan for that gazebo thing.' Owen nodded. Their client was having a large townhouse refurbished from top to bottom, including the installation of a rooftop garden, the central feature of which was a bespoke wrought-iron gazebo. Both the client and the designer had insisted it needed to be manufactured and constructed offsite and installed as a single piece. They were paying for it, so the project manager had found a way to make it work and hired a specialist lifting company to carry out that part of the works.

'Go on.'

'We'd just about finished when I heard this almighty bloody crash. We shot out the office and around the building to find an upturned barrow and a pile of smashed bricks scattered all over the ground.' He pulled out his phone to show Owen a photo he'd already seen several versions of.

'And do you know how it happened?'

Tom shook his head. 'There was a lump of dried render on the scaffold boards that no one had reported. Seems like the front wheel of the barrow hit that, knocking it off balance. The lad tried to hang on to it, but it slipped from his grasp and went straight through the edge protection.' He closed his eyes for a second then stared straight at Owen. 'Kid said the boards fell the moment the barrow touched them and when I inspected the area, the bolts were just lying loose on the ground.'

That caught Owen's attention, and he sat a little straighter. 'There's no sign of any sheering or buckling of the fastenings?'

'None at all. It's like they were deliberately removed.' That's what his H&S guy had said too.

Owen glanced from Alex to Tom. 'So, what are we thinking, some kind of sabotage? But what would be the motive? Not one of the neighbours, surely?' They'd had a couple of noise complaints as invariably happened on sites like that, but Tom had gone out of his way to keep in contact with the neighbours, even sending them little notes about any particularly disruptive works so they could tackle any problems before they arose.

Tom shook his head. 'Absolutely not.' His tone was vehement. 'That site is fully enclosed and secured, and the scaffold's alarmed. There's no way anyone could get near that scaffolding unless they were supposed to be up there.' Which narrowed the pool of potential suspects considerably. 'And I'd trust Pete's lads with my life. They've worked on a dozen or more jobs with me over the years and they're never anything less than careful.' He removed a folder from the rucksack at his feet. 'Here's the inspection logs for the scaffold.'

Owen flicked through them, knowing in his gut they'd all be in order. Tom was one of his very best guys, had been with him since not long after he'd started the business and Owen held him in very high regard. 'I just don't get it,' he said, sliding the folder across the table to Alex.

Tom's phone started to ring, and he cast an apologetic look at it. 'Answer it, it's fine,' Owen said. He listened with half an ear as he watched Alex peruse the folder with much greater attention than he'd given it. If it hadn't been such a serious matter, he might have smiled at her intense concentration. She was like a bloodhound with the scent, determined to hunt down her quarry.

'I'm here with him now, lad.' Hearing Tom's comment, Owen pointed at the phone with a questioning frown. Grabbing a piece of paper, Tom jotted down the name of one of the young apprentices they'd taken on a few months back. 'Why didn't you say anything to me about this before?' Tom asked with a shake of his head. 'No, no, you're not in any trouble, son, but you should've reported this straight away. No, it's not like being a grass. Not when it comes to dangerous or stupid behaviour. All right, we'll talk about this in the morning. You did the right thing by calling me. Goodnight, lad.'

Tom chucked his phone on the table as he ended the call. 'Bollocks.'

'You know what's happened?'

He nodded. 'Pavel's just told me a couple of the agency lads have been ignoring the rules about smoking on site. There's a balcony underneath that section of the scaffolding. Apparently, these boys removed the bolts so they can swing down onto it and have a crafty fag. Pavel saw them at it the other day and they told him to piss off and mind his own business, so he did.'

'Shit. Well, all right then, looks like we've got our answers.' He looked from Tom to Alex. 'You two happy to handle what needs to be done?'

'Yes, Boss.'

'Absolutely.'

'Great. I know I can count on you.' Owen stood and offered his hand to Tom who rose after him. 'Get on home, it's been a long day. And thanks for all your hard work as always.'

Tom shook his hand. 'I can't help but feel like I've let you down.'

'Nah, mate. We can only do so much. If people are determined to act like bloody fools, it's almost impossible to stop them.'

With a nod Tom left and Owen flopped down into his chair. 'What a mess.'

'I know, but we'll get it sorted. At least no one was hurt.' Alex's reassurance didn't make him feel any better.

'I feel like I've dropped the ball. Left you stranded while I swan off to the coast and play happy families.' A harsh bark of laughter escaped his throat. Talk about an unfortunate choice of phrase.

Alex walked over to perch on the edge of his desk, legs outstretched and crossed at the ankles. 'If you're worried you've put too much responsibility on me, please don't. Everything's been running like clockwork until this, and it's like you said—we can't do much if people are going to be idiots.'

He nodded. 'I don't want you to think I'm not impressed with how quickly you've grasped the nettle here. My head's just not in the game anymore.'

She stared down at her shoes and then up again. 'What are you saying?'

'I'm not sure.' He'd lain awake half the night thinking about it. 'I...I've been seeing this woman whilst I've been down in the bay—Libby. Anyway, I just found out she's pregnant.'

'Oh. Oh, wow! That's great...I mean, is it?' Alex looked so flustered he felt quite sorry for her. He'd never been one for personal stuff and then he'd just dumped that in her lap.

'I've no idea. I've only known for a couple of days and I'm really struggling to get my head around it. Kids were never on the cards for me.' He rocked back in his chair. 'Not that it makes much difference either way, because she's decided to go it alone.'

Alex frowned. 'She doesn't want you to be involved with the baby? But, surely you've got rights?'

Legally, perhaps, but morally? She was doing them all a big favour, especially the baby. Even so, he had a responsibility towards Libby, and he wouldn't leave her completely high and dry.

Whatever else happened, she would need his full financial support. Things were going to have to change. 'She's only doing what she thinks is for the best. My biggest issue is what to do about this place. I can't keep splitting myself between two different locations.'

Her face fell. 'You want to sell the business?'

He shook his head. 'Not really, but I'm not sure I can handle it on top of everything else. If I do decide to move to the bay, there's no way I can keep trying to run everything from there.'

Alex tapped her lip. 'I know we've been humming and aahing about it, but I think Nick's just about ready to come on board full-time here. His main worry was there'd be too many cooks and the three of us would end up butting heads. If he and I took over up here, you could look at opening up a new branch of the company down there. I don't mean necessarily in the bay itself, but somewhere close enough for you and Libby to give things a go if that's what you decide to do. It'd be extra income all round and you'll need all the money you can get now you're going to have a family to support.'

'I hadn't even considered that.' The breathless feeling in his chest started to ease. It would be a way to consolidate his business down in the bay, and Alex was right; if he was going to let Libby have the shop then he would need to replace that expected income stream with something else. He didn't have to do things exactly the same way as they were in London, he could focus on smaller jobs like the work he'd done to help Jack and his mum with planning the conversion of the old farm cottage into a glamorous granny flat for her.

Sure, there was a limit to the amount of business he could drum up in the immediate area, but Truro was within an hour's reach and the whole area around the bay was popular with the second-homes crowd. Working on the restaurant had really given him a taste for being on the front line of a project. It'd be like starting over again, but with the backstop of the London business behind him. He'd be on hand to continue helping Sam with the restaurant too, at least until it was fully up and running. He smiled at Alex. 'You're not just a pretty face.'

She laughed. 'That's because you're the pretty face, and I'm the brains of this outfit.'

'Cheeky mare.' It was full of affection, though. 'Are you sure you two can handle this place on your own?'

'Do you even have to ask?' She laughed at her own question. 'Of course you do, or you wouldn't be the control freak I know so well.' Growing serious, she held out a hand to him which he took. 'I wouldn't say it if I didn't believe it, Owen. You've built a remarkable team here, so we have everything we already need to continue your success. We can put whatever kind of transition arrangement in place that you want, but we *can* make this work.'

He squeezed her hand, then let it go. 'We damn well can.' And he wasn't just talking about the business side of things either.

Chapter 21

It had taken Owen longer than he'd anticipated to get his affairs in London in order, so he didn't make it back to Lavender Bay until the day before the Subterranean launch. Sam had assured him they were coping fine without him, which he tried to take in the spirit in which it was meant. Surprisingly, both Eliza and Beth seemed to be in his corner when it came to Libby, and although neither had spoken against her decision to split with him, they'd kept him up to date about her health which had been his primary worry.

He'd found an agent for his flat, and after several trips to the local tip the remains of his worldly goods were stuffed into every available space in his car. The furniture he'd left behind was mostly generic Ikea stuff and he'd never learned to attach much personal significance to his possessions.

He still didn't know what he was going to do about things with Libby, but his gut kept telling him he needed to be here in the bay to keep an eye on her, and his gut was rarely wrong. Head more focused on her than what he was doing, he almost missed the lights changing on the pedestrian crossing and had to jam on the brakes to avoid a woman who'd stepped out onto it.

A familiar face glared at him from beneath the brim of a black furry hat, and Owen quickly wound down his window. 'Sorry, Doris! Are you okay?'

'Lord, Owen, you did give me a fright! And where have you been? You were supposed to come to tea with me.'

Oh, hell, he'd forgotten all about it. 'I'm sorry, I had to go back to London to sort out some business. Can we make it another day?'

Her face split into a broad grin, and to his horror she marched around to the passenger side and stared at him expectantly. Leaning across the seat he popped open the door and she pulled it open. 'No time like the present! You can give me a lift back to Baycrest. I baked a Dundee cake this morning, so we can have a slice of that with our tea.' When he didn't move, she turned her head to stare at him. 'Well, what are you waiting for?'

Five minutes later they were pulling up outside the retirement home, with Owen none the wiser as to how he'd let her steamroll him into this. 'I really should be getting on, Doris. I've a lot to sort out.'

'Surely, you can spare half an hour? If you've driven all the way from London, you must be starving.' She placed a hand on his arm. 'I won't keep you long.'

Christ, she was probably lonely. This time of year did funny things to people, brought all sorts of stuff they tried to keep buried up to the surface. What would half an hour cost him in the big scheme of things? 'It'd be my pleasure, thanks, Doris.'

Pocketing his keys, he followed her along a wide hallway decorated with a hard-wearing, but nicely patterned green carpet then turned left. She stopped outside one of the white doors spaced out along the corridor and unlocked it. 'Come on in. Wipe your feet, please.'

She didn't say to, but he saw the neat row of shoes beside the door and quickly slipped his off, grateful he'd found a pair of socks without a hole in the toe. He swore the mice broke into his dresser drawers at night and gnawed through them.

Careful of her hair, Doris removed her hat and hung it on one of the hooks beside the door. As she struggled with the buttons of her coat with fingers no longer nimble, he helped her ease it off then hung it beside her hat. 'Thank you, dear. I'll just pop the kettle on, won't be a moment. Go in and make yourself at home.' Doris waved towards an open door as she passed by it on her way to the little open-plan kitchenette at the end of the short hallway.

Stepping inside, Owen did a quick scan of the room before deciding where to sit. There wasn't a lot of choice, although she'd managed to fit an armchair, a two-seater sofa as well as a gateleg table into the small room. A basket stuffed with skeins of wool and knitting needles rested beside the armchair, and it was also the closest one to the small gas fire on the wall, so he deduced that was Doris's favourite spot and opted for the sofa. The velvet blue seat was deeper than he expected, and he had to tuck a couple of the many scatter cushions behind him in order to sit up straight.

Photographs covered every inch of the wall facing him, from black-and-white shots, through the garish shades of early polaroid film through to newer ones which had been printed onto paper and secured in modern clip frames. As his eyes scanned from left to right, he was able to follow the story of Doris's life from early childhood right through to the present day where she sat, pride of place, surrounded by a group of grinning children, a fat baby nestled in her lap. 'My grandchildren,' she said with a proud smile as she entered the room carrying a tray laden with cups, plates and a huge china teapot hidden beneath a knitted cosy.

Jumping up, Owen took the tray so she didn't have to bend too far to place it on the coffee table. 'Thank you, dear.' She took a seat in the armchair, her gaze straying back to the photo he'd been studying. 'We took that just before last Christmas.'

'It's lovely. I didn't realise you had family.' From their first

191

conversation about hating living alone after her husband died, he'd assumed her childless.

Her smile softened. 'My Sheila lives up in Scotland with her husband and the kids. That's them in the photo. Marcus is over in New Zealand.' Her finger pointed to a smiling couple, a small boy perched on the man's shoulders. 'I haven't seen little Nicholas since he was a baby, but I'm going over there for a month in February. I'll soon have lots of new photos for my wall.'

She made herself busy, pouring the tea and doling out thick slices of cake for them both before settling back into her chair. 'You don't look at all well, my boy. What's the matter?'

Owen sipped his tea, wondering what he could say without getting involved in a discussion about his situation with Libby. Or without her, as it were. He hadn't told her about his plans to return, terrified she'd tell him not to bother. 'Bit of woman trouble, that's all.' The outrageousness of the understatement almost curled his tongue.

'These things happen, dear. Try not to fret.' Apparently content to leave it at that, Doris continued to sip her tea. 'As I said when I saw you the other day, I knew you reminded me of someone.' She gave him a rueful smile. 'I'm afraid inviting you to tea comes with something of an ulterior motive. When we talked, you said you were looking for a distant relative, but that's not quite right is it?'

Caught off guard by her bluntness, Owen almost sputtered on his mouthful of tea. 'My mother,' he admitted after swallowing.

'Ah. I did wonder. You have a look of the family about you, particularly around the eyes.'

Stunned, Owen put his cup down, trying to ignore the way it rattled against the saucer. His hands *never* shook. 'You've remembered something about the Blackmores?'

Doris smiled. 'I know them very well. I know I should've told you so at the time, but my first thought was to protect a very close friend of mine. If you'll let me, I'll try and explain everything.' Speechless at her admission, he jerked his head in a nod. 'They lived next door to me when I was a child; remember I mentioned living next door to the chapel?'

He didn't but nodded again anyway. *Just get on with it.*

'Gideon Blackmore was the minister there. And a more miserable, evil man I've yet to meet, God forgive me for saying so.' Doris wrung a lacy handkerchief between her gnarled fingers. 'He lived there with his wife and two children, Margery and Gerald. Margery was a great friend of mine, but Gerald was his father's son to the bone. He followed in his father's footsteps and took over as minister when Gideon dropped dead in the street of a heart attack. My mother always said it was the bitterness he held inside that killed him.' She nodded as though agreeing with her mother's opinion and Owen bit his lip, so he didn't scream at her to get to the bloody point.

'Ned and I had married and moved out, but Margery stayed at home, even after Gerald married and had a family of his own. She was devoted to the chapel, and kept house for them all. Gerald's wife was always a sickly, wisp of a woman and didn't stand a chance with a bully like that for a husband.'

Owen began to feel vaguely sick. The more Doris unveiled her tale of woe, the less he wanted to know about it. The cake he'd eaten sat in his stomach like a dead weight. 'And you think I'm somehow related to them?'

Doris nodded. 'Gerald's younger girl got herself in a bit of bother, so to speak, and just upped and vanished one day. The word went around that she'd been sent to London to nurse an elderly aunt of her mother's but even thirty years ago, we knew what it meant when a young woman left the community so suddenly.'

She extended a sympathetic hand towards him. 'Time moves slowly in little towns like this, even more so in traditional households like ours and the Blackmore's. A child out of wedlock was a thing to be ashamed of still. Even in the late Eighties. Sure

193

enough, young Deborah returned home about seven months later, a bit plumper and an awful lot sadder than when she'd left.'

Deborah. Well, if he'd need any more proof, that name was enough. He'd never given Doris anything more than the surname. 'Wh...what happened to her?'

Doris shrugged. 'The rumours got too much for Gerald, I think, because a few months later he moved the whole family up north to Lancashire. I can't say I was sorry to see the back of them, though I did miss Margery. We got a new minister—a lovely man. He's still with us today.'

'The pieces certainly seem to fit,' Owen admitted. 'You said this Margery was a friend of yours? And she was Deborah's aunt, have I got that right?'

'That's right.' Doris nodded.

'I don't suppose you're still in touch with her? Do you know what happened to Deborah?'

'Margery and I are still very much in touch, but I'm afraid the news about Deborah isn't good. She passed away a few years ago, some kind of cancer.' She shuddered. 'Terrible bloody disease.'

Dead. His mother was dead. He'd ripped open his oldest and darkest wound, and for what? Numb, Owen could only stare at the patch of carpet between his feet, his eyes tracing the rosette pattern over and over as he tried to process his feelings. Beneath the usual anger and resentment was something new and unwelcome—grief. He dug his fingers into his thighs; he wouldn't cry for her. He. Would. Not.

Doris shuffled in her fluffy slippers to the far end of the wall where the black-and-white photos hung. She removed one and held it out and he found himself taking it on reflex. A scowling man stood in the centre of a group of solemn-faced children dressed in their Sunday best in front of a plain brick edifice. Each child clutched a book in their hands. 'That was our confirmation day.' Doris tapped the photo with one gnarled finger. 'That's me on the left, and Gerald and Margery are standing in the middle on either side of their father.'

Lifting the photo closer, Owen squinted at the blurred image. Perhaps there was something of him about the man; the jawline looked enough like his own, and as Doris had said there was something around the eyes, too. His eyes strayed lower to a small bear dangling from the girl's hand. A row of buttons marched neatly down the toy's chest. *Mr Buttons*. 'Bloody hell,' he whispered.

She patted his shoulder. 'I know this is a lot for you to take in, but we weren't sure the best way to go about it.'

'We?' Owen had to swallow around the lump in his throat before he could get the word out.

'After Gerald—your grandfather, I suppose I should say. After he died, Margery moved back down to the bay.'

'She's here?'

Doris nodded. 'She lives a few doors down from me. She knows about your visit, but she didn't want to presume anything. If you want to meet her now, I can go and fetch her, or you can wait and think about it a bit, if you'd rather?'

Owen stared down at the photo in his hands, searching for any kind of a connection to the people staring back at him. Not just people—his great-grandfather, grandfather and great-aunt. Surreal didn't even begin to describe that notion. He'd never really thought beyond looking for his mum, hadn't dared let himself think of a wider family. Were there others, or had Deborah been an only child? Did he have any cousins? Did he *want* cousins? The only way to find out would be to meet Margery, his great-aunt Margery. 'I don't know what to say to her.'

'You could start with "hello"?'

Owen nodded. 'I can manage that, I think.' It felt like he sat alone for hours with nothing but the blank faces from an old photograph and the ticking of the clock on the mantle for company, before a knock came from the open living-room door.

He glanced up, and felt the world sliding away from him. The years hadn't been kind to her, but there was no mistaking the woman standing in the doorway as anyone other than the one in the picture he was clutching. 'Margery?'

Her hand fluttered up to her mouth, tears shining in her eyes. 'Oh, it really is you. When Doris came to me the other week, I couldn't dare hope it was true. But, I'd know you anywhere. I wanted to look for you so many times, but Gerald refused to tell me where he'd sent Deborah to have the baby, and she wouldn't talk about it.'

'You wanted to try and find me?' It was the strangled tones of a desperate child.

Margery hurried across to him, then seemed to freeze with a hand outstretched as though not sure she should try and touch him. 'So very much. I didn't do enough to help your poor mother. I was still too afraid of Gerald, but after she…' Her eyes widened in horror.

'It's all right,' he said with more gentleness than he knew he had in him. 'Doris told me she's dead.'

Crumpling onto the cushion beside him, Margery fumbled a tissue from the sleeve of her cardigan and dabbed at her eyes. 'After I lost my poor Deborah, I was determined to try and find you, but I didn't know where to start. I'm so sorry.' She choked off into sobs.

It was too much. He couldn't deal with her emotions right now, not when he had no idea how he was supposed to feel about it. Did she think an apology would make up for all those years he'd been left alone? He stood, desperate to get away before the ugliness boiling inside of him spewed out. 'I can't do this.' Christ, was that to be his default response to everything?

He was halfway out the room when Margery called out, stopping him in his tracks. 'Wait, I brought something for you, it's in the bag beside the front door. It might give you some of the answers you're looking for. I…I'm so sorry, Owen.'

'Me too. I just need some time to think.'

Margery swallowed hard, but thankfully there were no more tears. 'Take as much time as you need. I'll be here whenever you're ready.'

'Thanks.' The way he was feeling right then, he wasn't sure if he'd ever be ready. Barely pausing to snatch up the carrier bag by the door, he fled the confines of the flat.

He didn't know how long he sat there in the little car park outside Baycrest, but it was dark when he finally came back to himself enough to notice how cold it was. Condensation from his breath covered the inside of the windows. Turning on the engine, he shoved the temperature up to full blast and tilted the vents towards the water-beaded glass. His hand brushed the carrier bag still sitting in his lap, and he shoved it off. A scattering of envelopes spilled out into the footwell, and he flipped on the internal light with a curse before bending to retrieve them.

He glanced at the top one. And unable to resist the stab of curiosity, he slid open the flap. Toy soldiers spelled out the words Happy Birthday on the front of the card. Heart racing, he slowly opened it up and scanned the words inside. A tear plopped onto the card, smudging the ink. More filled his eyes, blurring the innocent words of love shaped by an almost childish hand.

Scrubbing his face, he placed the card carefully to one side then opened the next envelope, then the next one, and the next one. For an hour, he did nothing but read, not stopping until the bag was empty and a stack of empty envelopes littered the footwell beneath the passenger seat. Whatever her faults, whatever her failures and weaknesses, Deborah Mary Blackmore had loved her lost little boy.

Owen pulled on his seat belt and backed the car out of the car park. Turning away from the sea front, he steered the vehicle through the quiet streets of Lavender Bay. There was only one place he wanted to be right then.

A couple of minutes later he pulled his car into the free space beside the little white van behind the chip shop. Taking a deep breath, he told himself he was doing the right thing. 'I can't do this' would not be the motto by which he lived the rest of his life. Not giving himself a chance to talk himself out of it, he grabbed a loaded carrier bag from the passenger seat, hopped out and pressed his thumb to the doorbell. A loud buzzing echoed from the other side of the obscured window glass. He counted to five, then pressed again.

'All right, all right.' The irritated shout was followed soon after by a blurred outline visible through the glass. When the door swung open it was all he could do not to grab Libby up in his arms and squeeze her tight.

She looked more than tired, she looked drained of all the sparkle and verve he loved so much about her. Her signature hair hung limp and greasy around her face, at least an inch of mousy-brown roots showing at the top of the faded yellow and pink strands. Sallow was a word he'd often read but never applied to someone's skin before, and the dark smudges beneath her eyes seemed to stretch almost down to her delicate cheek bones. Even for her usual baggy style, her dirty T-shirt hung off her too-thin body.

He swallowed down a bite of anger at himself for the terrible state she was in and forced himself to relax against the doorframe. 'Hello.'

A brief flash of fire showed in her eyes, giving him hope. '"Hello"? Is that all you've got?'

Only a bite to the inside of his cheek stopped the smile threatening to quirk his mouth. She'd lost none of her fire. 'I tried to call you.'

She folded her arms across her body, tugging the shirt tight. His anger roared back as one of her collar bones showed stark against the thin cotton. He'd done this to her, left her alone to try and cope when he should've been glued to her side making she was taken proper care of. He'd have to make a start on the stack of baby books weighing down the rucksack still in his car.

'I said what I needed to say to you.' She sounded tired, and utterly defeated.

Unable to stop himself, he wiped a dirty smudge off her cheek. 'You look like you've been up the chimney.'

Ducking away from his touch, she lifted a hand towards her greasy hair then caught herself and dropped her clenched fist and began to bump it against her outer thigh. So, she still cared enough about her appearance even if she didn't want him to know. It was another tiny thread of hope and he wove it quickly around the first. He'd keep tugging and pulling until he had enough threads to build an unbreakable bond between them. 'I was cleaning the oven.' She glanced past him, spotted his car then eyed him with a deep suspicion. 'What do you want?'

'To take care of you.' It was the unvarnished truth.

'Just like that?'

He shook his head. 'I found out what happened to my mum. And just like with you and the baby, my first instinct was to run away from it.' Reaching out, he cupped her cheek. 'I need to stop doing that.'

Her lashes fluttered a mile a minute and when she spoke, there was a huskiness to her voice. 'I can take care of myself.' The words might have been a rejection had she not leaned into his palm resting against her cheek.

'I know you can, you're bloody amazing, but take pity on a man. Can't you at least let me pretend I'm of some use to you? Don't you have a jar that needs reaching from a high shelf, or something?'

The tiniest of smiles twitched her lips and he gathered the thread. 'The fryers need degreasing.'

It sounded like the worst job she could possibly think of, and he snatched at it like she'd offered him the Crown jewels. 'Deal.' Give a man an inch... 'So where can I put my stuff?'

199

'Your stuff?' The whites of her eyes shone bright against her dull complexion.

He gestured to his car. 'The Barneses are already packed to the rafters, and I can't take care of you from the pub now, can I? Spare room's on the second floor?'

'You think I'm going to let you move in here?'

'Until I can find a more permanent solution, yes. Like it or not, Libs, that's my baby, too. I might not have a clue what I'm doing, and I'm sorry it's taken this long for me to step up, but I take my responsibilities seriously. And right now, my first, last and only responsibility is the pair of you.' He reached for her hand, and when she didn't pull away he added that thread to the others. 'No pressure, no expectations, just a friend who cares very much for you who's trying to do his best.'

'Oh, you don't play fair at all.' Still holding his hand, she turned her head to swipe a tear from her cheek onto the shoulder of her T-shirt. 'Damn hormones.' Eyes dry once more, she fixed him with a gimlet stare. 'You can come in and clean the fryers, and then we're going to sit down and you're going to tell me everything about your mum, your time in care. Every ugly little bit of it, and then we'll see. Your stuff stays in the car for now.'

It was more than he might have hoped for, and a damn sight more than he deserved in the circumstances. 'Okay.'

As he took a step closer, the carrier bag in his hand swung forward and she pointed at it. 'What've you got in there?'

Owen smiled as he held open the top to show her the contents. 'A few things for you. Ginger ale, digestive biscuits, some Granny Smiths and a bit of strong cheddar.' An eclectic collection, but he'd surveyed a couple of the women at work who'd had children and asked them what had made them feel better during the early months of their pregnancies.

Taking the bag, she turned on her heel and walked inside, leaving the door open behind her. *Another thread.*

Chapter 22

Three hours later, Libby found herself sitting at the little down-stairs kitchen table with a plate of sliced apple, cheese and biscuits before her. Everything she'd put even near her mouth over the previous week had set her stomach heaving. Panicked about not getting enough nutrition inside her for the baby, she'd forced herself to eat then instantly regretted it. Before long, it had become a spiral of panic, sickness, tears and more panic. Desperate for a distraction, she'd thrown herself into clearing and cleaning the large kitchen behind the shop. They'd used it mostly for prepara-tion, storage and baking the pies they served alongside the fish and chips.

The oven sparkled like new, and the cupboards had been ruth-lessly stripped of their contents and restocked thanks to a supermarket online delivery service. Her eyes strayed to the plate in front of her, and miracle of miracles, her tummy gave a little rumble of pleasure rather than warning. Snapping off a tiny piece of biscuit, she nibbled at it then washed it down with a gulp of ice-cold ginger ale. Her lashes fluttered down in bliss. Had anything ever tasted so good?

Before she knew it, the plate was empty, and she was eyeing the beaded curtain separating the kitchen from the front-of-house area. Owen Coburn was some kind of bloody wizard. A loud thump and a curse stirred her from her seat and she swept through the curtain to find Owen bent over the counter clutching the top of his head. 'Are you all right?'

Turning, he favoured her with a rueful grin. The front of his pale grey T-shirt was covered in grease stains, and further streaks decorated his arms. 'I was trying to get into the back of the fryer and managed to catch my head on the edge of the warming cabinet. I'll live.'

'Let me see.' When he ducked his head low enough for her to check, she ran careful fingers over his scalp. There was a thin line of red visible through his close-cropped dark hair, but no blood, thank goodness. 'You might have a bit of a bump. Do you feel okay? Not dizzy or anything?'

Tilting up to meet her eyes, he grinned. 'No matching concussion, I don't think.' He straightened up. 'I reckon another half-hour and I'll be finished here. How are you doing?'

'Oven's done.' Feeling a little bit shy, she glanced away. 'Thank you for the food, it was exactly what I needed.'

Gentle fingers touched her chin. 'You've got a bit more colour in your cheeks, which is a good thing. I'm going to check out the restaurant once I'm finished here. Why don't you have a shower and a nap whilst I'm out?'

Her first instinct was to bristle against the suggestion. If she let him, he'd keep pushing and worming his way in beneath her defences. But she was tired, and filthy having fallen out of bed and straight into her work clothes with little more than a brush of her teeth. 'We still need to talk.'

Face solemn, he nodded. 'We will, I promise, but you look half dead on your feet, and it won't be a five-minute conversation.'

As it turned out, the shower and the nap were exactly what she wanted, and she didn't stir until she heard a gentle knock on her bedroom door. Struggling to sit up, she was surprised to see Eliza peering in. 'Hello, how are you feeling?'

Libby pushed back her quilt and swung herself out of bed. 'Better than I have in ages.' A soft orange glow spilled in from behind her bedroom curtains and she then realised just how dark her room was. 'What time is it?'

'Just after six. Owen asked me to pop over because he's caught up with some crisis at Subterranean. Something to do with the lighting.' She shrugged. 'It all got a bit complicated, so I left him, Jack and Sam crawling around under the seating units with the electrician.' Holding the door wide, she held her arm out towards the landing. 'Why don't you come downstairs? Mum sent over a pot of her chicken soup and Beth's just heating it up.'

The creamy, rich, familiar smell of Annie's homemade soup wafted up the stairs towards her as Libby padded down still in her pyjamas. 'Gosh, that smells good.'

'Doesn't it? I've been freezing my bum off in the shed all day so I'm in dire need of thawing out.'

They were soon settled around the upstairs kitchen table with steaming bowls and hunks of freshly baked bread before them. Libby took a couple of cautious spoonfuls, then sat back to nibble on a bit of bread. 'This is yummy.'

Eliza grinned. 'Sally's contribution to the cause. She's been trying to teach me to bake bread, but I think I'll stick to making soap.'

'I'd love the recipe.' Nutty, with just the right hint of malt, the brown bread would be perfect for the Ploughman's style basket lunches she had in mind for the teashop. Filing the thought away for later, she turned her attention to Eliza's other comment. 'How's the soap coming along. Do you think you'll be ready in time?'

Her friend nodded. 'I think so. Sally's been an absolute star. I've had her on potpourri mixing duties. I've found some fantastic net bags covered in silver snowflakes and stars to fill with it. I think they'll make perfect stocking filler gifts.' The Christmas market weekend festival was fast approaching. The wooden huts were booked and each business along the promenade had agreed to take one, together with lots of individual local artists and a few local charities.

The shop windows would all be decorated, and the promenade Christmas lights would be switched on to mark the start of the festival on the Friday evening. Beth was planning to fill her hut with a selection of wares from the emporium, while Annie and Paul would be serving mulled wine and hot spiced cider from their hut outside The Siren.

Libby's original plan had been to hire her own hut to run alongside the one her dad should've taken to serve their usual fish and chips, but now he was away she'd decided to concentrate on testing the water with things she planned to sell if she managed to get the teashop up and running.

Her meeting with the mortgage broker had been non-committal. He couldn't give her any real reassurances until the mystery surrounding the buyer of the chip shop had come to light, or until Libby could persuade her dad to change his mind. Things with him were still a bit delicate, and their regular Skype chats had been kept to general pleasantries and frantic reassurances on both sides that everything was fine. As frustrated as she was with him, nothing was worth losing him over and if the worst came to the worst, she'd look for another premises to fulfil her dream.

'Downstairs is all ready to go, so I plan to start baking tomorrow.' A bit of food and a decent nap had done wonders for her general mood, and she was feeling a lot more positive about everything. She refused to listen to the little voice whispering in her head that some of her relief might have anything to do with Owen's return to town.

'I'm glad you're feeling a bit better, Libs, and I really like your idea for the mince pies,' Beth said as she wiped the bottom of her bowl with a chunk of bread. In addition to selling mince pies on the day, Libby planned to batch bake a load and freeze them so people could order and collect them at any point running up to Christmas.

She nodded. 'It feels like a good way to trial the idea I had for doing special order bakes alongside the day-to-day stuff in the teashop.'

'So.' Eliza set her spoon down beside her empty bowl. 'Are we going to talk about Owen showing up and you letting him move in here?'

Libby ducked her head. 'He's not moving in. I haven't agreed to anything until we sit down and have a talk. If I do decide to let him stay, he'll be sleeping in the spare room for a few days at the most until he can find a better solution.'

Beth raised her brows. 'You know he's put his flat on the market? I overheard him chatting to Sam about it earlier.'

'He didn't say as much, but I did wonder when he turned up with a car full of his possessions. He told me he wants to take care of me.' Her hand fluttered over her middle. 'Of us.' Glancing between her two best friends she knew she could tell them anything and they'd understand. 'I was just so relieved to see him, I didn't really care why he was on the doorstep.' She'd told him they needed to talk, and she was determined to get him to open up, but there was no denying the way her heart had soared at the sight of him on her back step.

'Ah, Libs.' Eliza reached out to cover her hand. 'This is a proper tangle you've got yourself into, isn't it?'

Cursing herself for getting all teary—bloody hormones!— Libby shrugged. 'He deserves to be a part of the baby's life, and whatever else happens, I need him as my friend. As for the rest...' She'd like to believe it was true, that she could rely on Owen and he'd not let her down, but something was holding her back. There was still time for him to change his mind, especially once the baby actually arrived and he had to deal with the reality of it. At least he'd have that option should he choose it. The prospect of being responsible for something so delicate and vulnerable was terrifying right now.

'All right, I won't push. I will say I feel better that you've got someone here with you.' Eliza raised her hands when she glared at her. 'Not because I think you're helpless, but I'm still not quite over the fright you gave us when you fainted.'

Mollified, Libby gave her a weak smile. 'I must admit I scared myself, too. It'll be good to have someone around while Dad's away. I just hope it isn't too awkward.'

'Speaking of which…' Beth folded her arms and rested them on the table before her. 'Are you still coming to the opening for Subterranean tomorrow?'

'Oh.' It had entirely slipped her mind that the six of them had planned to celebrate the first night of the restaurant together. She was so proud of all the hard work both Sam and Owen had put into the place, and had been really looking forward to seeing it all come to fruition. 'Do you think I should? I mean, I want to, but I suppose it's up to them.' Another thought occurred to her and she lifted a strand of her limp, faded hair. 'I look an absolute fright.'

'We can help you with that,' Eliza said. 'The guys will probably be stressing like mad tomorrow and be glad to have us out of the way. Why don't we have a bit of a pampering session and all get ready together?'

'Count me in!' Beth agreed. 'I haven't even had a chance to paint my nails lately, never mind anything else.'

'I've been really worried about dyeing my hair, in case it does something bad to the baby,' Libby admitted.

'Is that a thing?' Eliza reached for her phone and started tapping away. 'Hmm, it says here on the NHS website that although some women choose to avoid it for the first twelve weeks, there's no evidence of a risk given the small amount of chemicals in a single batch of hair dye.' Two spots of colour highlighted her cheeks. 'Has it been twelve weeks since you and Owen started…you know?'

Libby bit her lip and nodded. 'Remember that first night we all came to the pub to check Jack out?' The midwife had told her at the scan that from the baby's rate of development it was likely she'd fallen pregnant during one of her earliest encounters with Owen.

Eliza's mouth formed a perfect 'O'. 'Blimey, Libs, I didn't think you were even talking to Owen back then.'

She covered her face with her hands. 'It was a heat of the moment thing. And then we had lots of other moments, and... oh, shut up!' she finished as the other two burst out laughing. 'It's not funny.'

'It kind of is,' Beth managed between giggles. 'Lord, you made such a hoo-ha about how much you couldn't stand him, and all that time you were sneaking around together!'

'All right, all right, don't rub it in!' Libby gave in and started to chuckle.

'That's what he said!' Eliza chimed in and it was enough to finish them all off.

'Everything okay?' Owen's deep voice stopped them all in their tracks, and as one they turned towards the door where he stood with his hands on his hips staring at them all in bemusement.

Don't look, don't look, don't look. Biting her lip, Libby made the mistake of catching Beth's eye and the three of them burst into a screaming fit of laughter. With an affronted shake of his head, he turned on his heel muttering something about 'mad bloody women'.

'Oh, oh, poor Owen,' Eliza said as she flapped a hand in front of her face to fan herself.

'Poor Owen, my arse. It's at least fifty per cent his fault I'm in this mess to begin with!'

Feeling better than she had since her accident, Libby waved goodbye to the girls about half an hour later then headed to the downstairs kitchen which was where Owen had retreated to. She found him bent over his laptop, a cup of coffee in one hand. Glancing up, he gave her a smile. 'Well, you're in better spirits.'

Cheeks heating, she returned his smile. 'Sorry about that, we weren't really laughing at you, it was just a bit of bad timing.'

'My ego will just about survive, I reckon. It was good to see you enjoying yourself.'

Feeling a bit awkward, she twisted her hand in the bottom of her baggy top. 'We were talking about the restaurant opening tomorrow night. The girls want to come around and get ready here…assuming you still wanted me to come along.' She studied her toes, noting the chipped nail polish was something else she needed to sort out. God, she'd really let herself go.

A whisper of sound and he was at her side, taking her hand in his. 'I'd love for you to be there. It wouldn't be the same without you after all those hours you listened to me moaning on about it.' His words cast her back to those nights curled up side by side in the little beach hut. Everything had seemed so simple then.

'Well, you spent plenty of time listening to me talking about my plans for this place.'

He was silent for a few moments. 'How are you getting on with those? Any further forward?'

Here it was, the chance to tell him about what her dad had done, to ask his advice on what she should do, maybe even see if he'd be willing to help. She swallowed the temptation down. It wouldn't be fair on him, not now with the baby and everything. He'd feel obliged to do something. Feeling torn, she traced a pattern through the thick pile of the carpet with her toe. 'I'm doing a bit of a test run for the Christmas market, just to see what people think about a change in direction.' It wasn't a lie, but it wasn't close to an honest answer to his question.

'Well, that sounds like a good idea. I'm glad you're making some progress with it.' He stepped away, stealing his warmth as he went. When she glanced up, his back was turned to her and the set of his shoulders screamed with tension. Did he know something? Had Eliza or Beth let something slip which had found its way back to Owen? They'd promised not to breathe a word to anyone, and they'd never betrayed a confidence before. She gave herself a shake. She was just being paranoid, reading too much into everything.

'Are you ready for that talk now?'

Hands on his hips, he huffed out a breath. 'Not really, but let's do it.' Once she'd slid into a chair, he resumed his seat then reached down for something by his feet. 'You'd better start with these,' he said, offering her a carrier bag.

Peering inside, she saw a stack of handwritten letters mixed in with a few cards. 'Where did you get these?' Haltingly at first, Owen told her about meeting Doris and how that had led to meeting Margery. 'Your great-aunt? And she's been here all this time?'

'They left town when it all happened. Couldn't handle the shame apparently.'

Unable to bear the bitterness in his voice, she clasped his hand and squeezed it tight. 'That's their pride talking, nothing to do with you. There's nothing shameful about you.'

He gave her a nod, but she wasn't sure he believed her. 'Margery's the only one of them left now, so it's not like it matters anyway. She moved back to the bay a few years ago. I don't have all the ins and outs of it; it was all a bit much to take in at once.' Leaning back in his chair, he stared up at the ceiling. 'I kind of ran out on her. I need to stop doing that.'

It was the same thing he'd said to her earlier. 'You're here now.'

'I didn't know where else to go.' Sitting up, he tightened his grip on her hand. 'No. That's not right. This was the only place I wanted to be—with you. I feel like I'm at home with you, Libby, and that's something I've never had before.'

The tears stinging her eyes had nothing to do with hormones this time. 'Oh, Owen.'

'There's a lot of stuff I need to deal with, I know that, but it's hard for me because I've always just shoved it all down inside and ignored it. The people who were supposed to take care of

209

me never did, so I don't have any kind of example to follow. I'm so scared that I'll get it wrong. That I'll mess up and hurt you, or the baby.'

'You don't have to be perfect, Owen. No one is. I'm scared to death about the baby, too, and I'm sure I'll make mistakes—we both will. But that's not why I didn't want you to be involved. I was scared you'd feel trapped or obligated to do the right thing.'

He nodded. 'I want to tell you that I don't, but I also don't want to be saying that because I'm so used to pushing my emotions to one side and getting on with things.'

Not exactly a declaration of undying love, but that was a good thing. Her head knew it, even if her heart felt as fragile as a piece of blown glass. 'So, we'll take our time. You can stay here in the spare room for now and we can see how things go.'

Taking a deep breath, Libby glanced between Beth and Eliza as they waited at the top of the stairs. Sam had asked them to come early so they'd have a chance to look around in peace before the first of the official guests arrived. The door swung open, and Libby was sure she wasn't the only one who gasped at the sight of Sam in all his splendour. Gone were his casual T-shirts and jeans, the tumbling curls and laughing eyes. Clad in a crisp white chef's jacket with a row of black buttons up the right-hand side and a pair of smart black slacks, he looked the epitome of a professional chef. His hair had been tamed with a handful of gel, and there was an air of authority about him she'd never seen before.

'Wow, Sam, you look the bee's knees!' She popped up on tiptoes to brush a kiss to his cheek and a glimpse of the cheeky guy she knew and adored showed in a flash of white teeth.

'You don't look so bad yourself.' Taking her hand, he twirled her in a slow circle. 'You've got legs!'

Blushing, Libby dropped a hand to smooth the soft jersey of the navy dress she'd fished from the back of her wardrobe. The material draped gently from nape to just below the knee, clinging just a little to the beginning swell over her stomach. Not quite willing to give up her usual style, she'd teamed it with thick dark tights and a pair of black ankle boots covered in studs. She watched as Sam greeted his sister with a quick kiss, and Beth with a more lingering one. He whispered something which turned her cheeks a delicate rose pink and she ducked her face into his shoulder. 'Behave,' Libby heard her murmur, and felt a pang of wistfulness strike her heart.

Letting his fiancée go, Sam faced the three of them with open arms. 'Welcome to Subterranean. Please follow me.'

Whatever regrets she might have about her own situation vanished beneath a sense of wonderment the moment they started down the steps. Low-level lighting cast shafts of light up the dark walls, picking out bright rainbow specks in the smooth surface. 'What is this?' she asked as she trailed a hand over the hard surface. It felt almost like plastic, yet shimmered with the colours of a rich black opal.

Sam paused below her to glance back. 'Isn't it fab? Owen recommended it. The company that makes it usually supplies schools, and hospitals. High traffic areas which need to be kept clean. It's really hard-wearing and easy to wipe down as well as coming in a whole range of incredible designs and patterns.'

Owen again. He'd really made his mark on the place, for all it had been Sam's dream. She never got the sense from Sam he was anything less than grateful for Owen stepping in to assist him with the project. His experience had enhanced Sam's vision, without altering it from the original theme. 'I love it.'

Her appreciation only grew as they entered the main dining area. There was so much to look at, she didn't know where to start. The ethereal glow of the fish tank was the first thing to catch her eye, its occupants swimming gracefully through their own little world. Lights glittered everywhere, from the fake gems studded into the rough stone-effect walls to the embedded fairy lights in the smoked Perspex backs of the seating units. It really was like entering another world—a dragon's treasure trove, or a deep mine the dwarves from *Snow White* might spend their days working in. Soft music drifted from hidden speakers, just low enough she couldn't quite focus on the tune carried by the heavenly choir. It added to the otherworldly experience.

'Come and see.' Like a kid in a candy shop, Sam led them over to one of the custom-made booths. 'Look, there's a control panel here so you can adjust the lighting and the volume of the music.' He pressed a couple of buttons and the embedded lights switched from a rainbow to emerald green. The music was a little louder, but still not enough to distract from conversation or to disturb diners at the surrounding tables. The booths had also been offset to afford each grouping with a sense of privacy. It really was brilliantly thought out.

A hidden door swung open, spilling a bright shaft of light into the far end of the room as Jack and Owen entered from the kitchen area. 'What do you think?' Owen asked as he approached them.

'Isn't it fantastic?' Jack said to Eliza as he bent to kiss her cheek.

'I can't believe it. I mean we've seen it in all its different stages, but I still couldn't imagine how breathtaking the whole effect is.' She held out a hand to her brother, tears glistening on her lashes. 'I'm *so* proud of you.'

Blushing, Sam grinned at her. 'You haven't tasted the food yet.'

Owen clapped him on the shoulder. 'I've been tasting it all day, and you've got nothing to worry about.' Catching Libby's eye, he moved towards her. 'You look lovely.' He teased one of the curls Beth had set into her hair with a hot wand. 'I love this.'

Not knowing what else to do to cover the mess left thanks to her previous pink-yellow dye job, she'd opted for a single colour. It looked black at first glance, until the light caught it and showed it to be a deep, sapphire blue. Even with the reassurance from the NHS website, she'd been nervous about getting any of the dye upon her skin, so Eliza and Beth had coloured it for her, making sure to wipe away as much of the dye from her scalp as possible once they'd coated her hair. She felt enough like herself while retaining the ability to blend in. Tonight wasn't about her, it was about the man in front of her and one of her oldest friends. It would be their triumph on everyone's lips, not the weird girl with the rainbow hair.

'You look nice, too.' His black-on-black look drew all attention to the sharp lines and plains of his face. He looked hard, uncompromising and completely in control of his environment. All that brash confidence which had first turned her head was oozing from every pore. His heart could be racing a mile a minute, his back damp with a nervous sweat, but nobody would see that.

His eyes strayed down her body, and in a moment he'd twirled her away from the others so they were half-hidden behind one of the seating units. Clutching his arm to steady herself, she followed his gaze down to where it was locked on the little curve outlined by her dress. 'It's really real.' His voice was hushed, tone almost reverent.

She nodded. 'Really, really real. I was in the shower last week and all of sudden it was there. I've got a scan at home.'

His head shot up. 'Can I see it?' He sounded so excited, she felt awful for not showing it to him the night before.

'Of course. They did it at the hospital so it's a couple of weeks out of date.' His gaze flicked down again and something softened and flowered inside her at the sheer fascination written large upon his face. Reaching for his hand, she placed it gently on her belly. 'It'll be a while before we can feel anything.'

He nodded. 'I was reading a book about it last night.'

'You were?' She didn't know why that would surprise her; he was the kind of man who'd do all the research he could.

'Yeah.' His hand pressed gently before he let it fall away. 'I've bought every title I could find in the book shop. The cashier said they regularly get that happen. Called it new dad panic buying.'

213

She laughed softly. 'You're going to be better prepared than me. I'll have to borrow some.' She gave a little shudder. 'Nothing with any gory photos, though. I'm not quite ready to face *that* reality.'

'I'll vet them for you, first.' He touched a finger to her cheek, the merest breath of a caress. 'Thank you for letting me be a part of this.'

'Thank you for wanting to be. I feel a bit less scared now I know you're around.' The concession was worth it for the look of sheer delight he gave her. 'Come on, let's celebrate. I've got a bottle of ginger ale on ice with your name on it.'

Chapter 23

The evening was an unqualified success. Sam had outdone himself in the kitchen, and although they'd both spent more time away from their friends than they would've liked, the response from the guests at every table Owen had visited had been enthusiastic to say the least. He'd been a tad sceptical about Sam's plans to try and create an immersive sensory experience—fearing it would distract from the food and turn the place into a one-off gimmick rather than somewhere people would wish to return to again and again—but he was delighted to be proven wrong.

Even the mystery boxes created by an artist in London at Sam's request worked a treat judging by the oohs and giggles they'd elicited as guests explored their hidden contents with tentative fingers. They'd been a real talking point, too, with more than one diner assuming he knew the secrets they contained. He wasn't sure they believed him when he swore he didn't know, but both he and Sam had agreed to be kept in the dark. They'd tested them out, of course, to double-check there were no unpleasant surprises, and he had his own ideas what each one contained, but that wasn't really the point. The whole enjoyment was in stimulating a single sense without the others tainting one's judgement. From cool, silken ribbons of fabric, to smooth spheres which warmed on contact with the skin, he'd found they questioned his basic understanding of what reality meant to him and left him determined to expand his sensual relationship with the everyday world.

Speaking of which…Owen's gaze strayed once more to the booth in the corner occupied by his friends. *Friends*. He still had to pinch himself over that one. Now the final course had been cleared and almost everyone was relaxing over cups of coffee and considering whether they could possibly manage one more handmade chocolate truffle, Sam had finally emerged from the kitchen to slump next to Beth. His arms were draped across the back of the booth, and his face bore the look of an exhausted, but very contented man. Although his fingers were playing lazily through Beth's hair, his attention was focused on Libby who was using her hands as much as her words to describe something to Sam. Her whole being vibrated with the urgency of whatever it was she was trying to convey.

God, how he loved her.

Stunned by a depth of feeling he'd never believed himself capable of, Owen turned away from the group before any of them saw him, sure the naked truth would be spelled out on his forehead in flashing neon lights. An unnoticed napkin lay on the floor nearby and he busied himself with picking it up and placing it neatly on the edge of one of the booths where a member of the waiting staff would spot it. So caught up in his compelling need to do the right thing, to be the stand-up guy and accept his responsibilities towards her, he'd singularly failed to notice how she'd slipped beneath every single one of his carefully erected barriers against the world. He'd liked her well enough, found her spark and bite irresistible, her body a sensuous delight, but not once had the word love entered into his consciousness. Everything about his current campaign to win her back had centred around the fact of her pregnancy, but that had been an excuse, he realised now, to give him the thing he craved above all else. Baby or no baby, Libby was the family he'd always longed for.

The couple in the booth beside him began to stand, and he found himself caught up in a round of handshakes, farewells and promises to return again soon. Like a pebble dropped into a pond, that first movement created a ripple effect around the room until the rest of the invited guests had taken their leave. Within quarter of an hour, only their personal party in the corner remained and he had no more excuses to avoid them. Tucking his hands in his pockets, he affected his best devil-may-care attitude and propped one shoulder against the edge of the booth. 'Well, that went well.'

Jack raised a brandy glass containing an inch of deep-amber liquid in his direction. 'That might be the understatement of the century. The whole evening was a triumph.' He sipped the brandy with the air of a man well fed and watered.

'We did it. We only bloody did it.' Sam sounded drunker than Jack, though Owen knew it to be from the same euphoria and relief fizzing through his own bloodstream rather than the contents of a glass.

Extending his hand across the table, he grinned as Sam shook it. 'We certainly bloody did.'

Gentle laughter rose from the rest of the group followed by a huge yawn from Libby. Waving her hand in front of her face, she apologised. 'Sorry, sorry.'

As though they'd been looking for the merest excuse, his eyes locked on her. Beneath the carefully applied make-up which ringed her blue eyes, making them shine like the jewelled high-lights in her hair, he could see signs of strain. The tangle of his own emotions forgotten beneath concern for her, Owen shifted until he was crouching beside her seat. 'Are you all right, would you like to go home?'

She started to shake her head, before changing her mind with a rueful shrug. 'It's all caught up with me suddenly. I can hardly keep my eyes open.'

'Come on then.' With a hand, he helped her up then tugged

off his suit jacket to drape it over her shoulders before she could protest. 'Let's get you home.' He turned to the others. 'Thanks for making tonight even more special. Sorry to duck out. I'll pop back and give you a hand once I've got Libs settled.' The last he addressed to Sam, who waved him away.

'Nah, mate. I'm going to send the kids home and we can sort everything else out in the morning. The dishwasher's been on twice already so it's only the dessert plates and glasses.'

'If you're sure?' When Sam nodded, he acquiesced. 'I'll be back for about 9 a.m. See you tomorrow.'

Libby gave them all a sleepy wave and seemed content to allow him to steer her towards the stairs and outside with a hand to her back. The bitter winter wind cut through his cotton evening shirt the moment he stepped onto the promenade making him grateful he'd already given Libby his jacket because the odds on her being willing to accept it from him once she'd realised how cold it was were slim to none. Stubborn little thing.

She shivered. 'Wow, that's a wake-up call and a half.'

'Refreshing,' Owen said, hoping his teeth weren't chattering too badly.

Her laugh told him she'd seen through him. 'I forgot you've not experienced a proper Lavender Bay winter, yet. Wait until the wind's howling in from the sea adding a lovely sting of salt water to its bite. This is balmy in comparison.'

'Can't wait.' Reaching for her hand was as automatic as breathing, and he cursed himself when she didn't respond to his touch. Shoving the offending hand in his pocket, he settled for a little nudge to her shoulder. 'Last one home has to make the hot chocolate.' Clutching the lapels of his jacket close, she darted ahead of him, her laughter floating back to him on the chilly wind. Content to watch her blue-black hair flashing under the street lights, he hurried in her wake, but not quite fast enough to catch her up, of course.

Cheeks glowing from the wind and her exertions, Libby

218

unlocked the front door to the shop and they hurried inside the blessed warmth. Taking the keys, Owen pointed in the direction of the stairs. 'Right, up you go and into your pyjamas. I'll check down here and then get the kettle on.'

She wrinkled her nose at him. 'You're so damn bossy.'

'Deal with it.'

Her eye-rolling response might have been more effective had a huge yawn not overcome her. 'Well don't think I'm going to let you get away with it too often,' she grumped but didn't stay to argue further.

The kettle was just clicking off when she wandered into the kitchen clad in the same pyjama bottoms he'd seen the day before and a thick hooded sweatshirt decorated with an incongruous mixture of fluffy kittens and grinning skulls. The curls in her hair had begun to droop from their earlier neat cloud and all traces of make-up had been washed from her face. She looked tiny and tired and he wanted nothing more than to scoop her up and into his bed. Instead, he turned his back and concentrated on fixing their drinks. 'Sugar?'

'No thanks. That instant mix is sweet enough as it is.'

When he carried the mugs over to the table, she had her hands tucked into the sleeves of her sweatshirt, her bottom lip caught between her teeth. Her attention was fixed on a black-and-white image lying in the centre of the table.

Oh.

Like a marionette with its strings suddenly cut, he dropped into the nearest chair, spilling hot chocolate on the back of one of his hands in the process. He didn't even notice the mugs were tipping until she reached over to steady and guide them down. Uncurling his fingers from the handles, he flexed then opened them, his palms itching with the need to touch the photo. He remained frozen in place, knowing the moment he slid it closer, his life would change forever.

'It's okay.' Libby's gentle tone told him she'd experienced something similar to the terror-joy flooding him like the strongest shot of adrenaline.

'Fuck.' Not the most profound of statements, but it was about all he could manage. He'd thought the sight of her body beginning to reshape itself to accommodate their child had been shock enough, but this was something else again.

Libby slid the photo closer and he finally girded himself enough to turn it around. Puzzled, he turned it again. And again. Was it like one of those magic eye things, perhaps? He tried squinting, but that didn't make it any better. It was just an amorphous mass of fuzzy grey and white shadows. A nail tipped with sparkly blue polish appeared in his line of vision to trace the outline of something in the centre of the image. Oh. Okay. Now he had it. Maybe? 'It looks like a kidney bean.'

She laughed. 'I know. It was easier to see on the screen once the nurse pointed it out, but even so, I was very confused.' She touched a tiny black dot. 'That's the heart.'

A heart. Christ. For a second, he thought his own might stop beating at the sheer wonder of it. 'We're having a baby.' It came out wet; choked.

'We really are.' Her own voice didn't sound any steadier than his, and when he glanced up her image wavered through a shimmer of tears. He'd never been a crier. Libby sniffled and dabbed the sleeve of her sweatshirt to her eyes. 'At least I can blame my hormones every time I start watering like a pot.'

Owen scrubbed a hand across a knot in the back of his neck. 'I'm not sure I'm ready for this.'

A shadow crossed her face and she hunched a little closer around her bent knees. 'Too late now.'

Oh, hell. 'I didn't mean it like that. Please, Libs, you're going to have to give me a tiny bit of leeway here because I'm making this shit up as I go along. I'm doing my best, and I won't ever leave you stranded, I swear.'

She nodded, her chin resting on her knees. 'Okay. Okay. We'll figure this all out somehow.'

'We will.' All of it. 'Here, take your chocolate and go snuggle down in bed before you fall asleep at the table.'

Stifling another yawn, she nodded. 'I will, goodnight.'

'Goodnight. And thanks for showing me this.' He tapped the edge of the photo.

'Of course. I've got the date for the next scan in my diary. Remind me tomorrow and I'll let you have it.' She hesitated. 'Assuming you want to come along.'

He nodded. 'Wouldn't miss it for the world. Anything like that, please, I'd like to be part of it.'

Her expression softened. 'You're going to be a good dad, Owen.'

Touched to the core, he could only smile in response. Libby believed in him, he just had to start believing in himself.

The next few weeks were a never-ending misery of storms. From hail to horizontal rain, the sky threw everything at their little town bar actual snow. Being cooped up didn't suit Libby one bit, as he found to his cost every time she snapped and snarled at him over the simplest things. With his own temper decidedly frayed, Owen opted for discretion over valour and kept out of her way as much as possible. The scents from the downstairs kitchen were as heavenly as the words from her lips were foul, and he found his stomach rumbling every time he set foot inside the door. The one time he'd tried to pilfer a hot sausage roll fresh from the oven after a cold, muddy day up at the farm helping Jack review the works on his mum's cottage and the new workshop for Eliza, she'd smacked his knuckles with the back of a wooden spoon and sent him upstairs with a flea in his ear.

Thankfully, things were calmer at the restaurant. Their soft launch continued to be a success, and whilst they weren't booked out every night, word was spreading, and they were gratified at the steady flow of new and returning diners through their door.

The team had settled beneath Sam's calm, confident guidance and one of the lads they'd taken on as part of the waiting team had already expressed an interest in transferring his college course to focus on cooking. Even when he wasn't on shift, he could be found more often than not helping Sam with the daily prep, bending his ear with a million eager questions.

The obvious satisfaction Sam drew from mentoring the kid had given Owen an idea of his own, and he'd already reached out to the college to see what kind of construction courses they ran. There was another unexpected bonus coming through his involvement with the restaurant: people were curious about Owen's background and once he started talking about his other business interests, a number expressed an interest in speaking to him about works they wanted doing. His notebook was filling up with new contacts, and when he wasn't either at the restaurant or the farm, he was tucked away in his room—sitting at the desk and old captain's chair he'd retrieved from the beach hut—sketching out plans and pulling together quotes for kitchen extensions, loft conversions and the like. It was a far stretch from the complex jobs he'd been handling through his firm in London, but it took him back to his roots, reigniting his passion for the work all over again. He'd have to take on some administrative support soon, and he had the perfect person in mind. A meeting had taken place, and Owen was hopeful the contract he'd offered would be signed and returned to him any day now.

It wasn't the only bit of paperwork he was waiting for, nor the most important.

When his alarm went off, the first thing Owen noticed was the silence. He'd become so used to the sound of rain drumming on the roof over his head, that the absence of it threw him for a moment. Trying not to feel too hopeful, he climbed out of bed and tweaked up the edge of the blackout curtains he'd hung to block out the glare of the security lights which lined the rear alley which his room overlooked. So sensitive were some of them, that the merest puff of wind seemed to set them off. His first few nights, he'd been startled awake more times than he cared to count. Having thrown himself on Eliza's mercy, she'd presented him with the thickly lined dark drapes a couple of days later, and he'd slept like a baby ever since.

The view which greeted him brought a broad smile to his lips. Pale pink and red streaks of the passing dawn were giving way to an icy-blue sky dotted with white fluffy clouds. The never-ending storm had blown itself out overnight, just as the forecasters had predicted. Whistling to himself, he wandered towards the bathroom to grab a quick shower.

Up and down the various businesses along the promenade and all around the town, others did the same. The morning of the Christmas market weekend had arrived, and it would need every-one's input to ensure its success.

With his background, Owen had been assigned to the team over-seeing the installation of the wooden chalets lining the length of the promenade. Installing them over three filthy days had been hellish, but as they made their way from one to the next, checking for any residual damage, there was a real sense of camaraderie and achievement among them.

'Oh, here, the felt's come loose on this one. Give us a hand.' Following the gruff voiced request from Will, who was a carpenter by trade, Owen braced his foot at the bottom of the ladder, then handed up tools and nails from the belt slung around his waist as Will requested them.

'It's not bad, all things considered,' he observed as Will clam-bered back down. Apart from the torn felt on this hut, a loose front shutter on another, and one which had lost a plank from the side wall, they'd come through pretty well unscathed. As each hut was given the all clear, traders and their friends swooped in behind them to begin decorating and filling their assigned huts with produce and wares they hoped to sell to the expected crowds.

Another team worked the opposite side of the prom, checking the decorations that had been affixed to each of the street lamps and at intervals along the iron railings. Everywhere Owen looked, people were busy, the entire seafront teaming with life, laughter and friendly banter.

A nudge at his elbow drew his attention, and Owen glanced over his shoulder to find Doris from up at Baycrest beaming up at him with a steaming mug in her hands. 'You look like you could do with a hot drink, dear.'

'Ah, thanks, that's lovely.' Accepting it, he took a quick gulp, enjoying the burn of the hot coffee through his belly. It might be bright and clear, but there was little warmth coming from the pale, winter sun. 'I'm sorry I ran out on you and Margery the other week. How is she?' Guilt sat heavy on his shoulders. He felt awful for not being in touch with Margery, especially after the gift she'd given him of Deborah's letters, but he was still not sure what to say to her. He'd reconciled with the past, but whether he wanted her to be a part of his future was another thing.

She patted his arm with a gnarled hand. 'Don't you worry about it. I shouldn't have sprung it all on you like that. As for Margery, she's still feeling very guilty about everything.'

'She's not the only one,' Owen admitted.

'It'll all come out in the wash, as my mother used to say. Give yourself a bit of time. We're neither of us going anywhere for the foreseeable future.'

'Are you coming to the grand switch-on later?' he asked, having drained his coffee.

'Oh, yes, I'm very much looking forward to it.' She gave his arm another pat. 'Margery will be coming down with me.'

Owen drained his mug, then handed it back to her with a

smile. 'Perhaps I'll see the two of you later then.' It didn't have to be a big deal, he told himself as he walked away. A quick "hello, how are you?" to get the ball rolling and see how they both felt. He owed her a thank-you for the letters, if nothing more.

Chapter 24

'Wow, look at you! Don't you look fantastic?' Leaning on the counter of her hut, Libby couldn't help but smile at the adorable scene before her. From the antlers adorning his dark hair, to the little fuzzy tail sewn onto the seat of his brown trousers, Michael's costume was fantastic.

Clutching the hand of his little sister who was clad in a fetching fluffy red bobble hat, navy down coat and shiny red wellingtons on her feet, the little boy who was Noah's best friend beamed up at her. 'I'm a reindeer! I'm going to be in the parade later! Will you watch?'

'I sure will! I love your costume.'

A smiling woman came to stand behind Michael, a rosy-cheeked baby in her arms. 'Eliza made them, she's an absolute whizz with that sewing machine of hers.'

Libby nodded in agreement. 'She always has been. They're around here somewhere. I think her hut's between the ones for the pub and the emporium.' She pulled a mock-glum face. 'They've all deserted me. Even Owen's up there helping Sam with some taster treats from the restaurant.'

Michael's mother wrinkled her nose. 'I've heard lots of great things about Subterranean, but I'm not sure it's our kind of thing.'

She surveyed the array of goods Libby had on display. 'This all looks so delicious. We saw someone earlier with a sausage roll and I've been trying to find out where they got it from for the past half an hour. I must say, I never thought to try your hut because I assumed you'd be doing fish and chips.'

'I fancied a bit of a change.' It had been the stock response she'd given all afternoon to variations of the same comments from people. She'd been tempted to tell people about her plans, then decided against it. With her dad still away, time was running out and the prospects for her little teashop were slipping ever further from her grasp. Without the prime seafront location the chip shop occupied, it would be a struggle to tempt visitors to stray from the beach into one of the streets further up the hill upon which the town was laid out. Perhaps she could speak to the council about a permit to trade upon the beach, instead. She just didn't know. But those were problems for another day, and she was determined to make the best of the festive weekend. If she could impress enough people with her pies, pasties and pastries then word of mouth would soon spread once she got herself up and running.

'Well, I for one, am delighted you did. We'll take three sausage rolls, and…' She glanced over her shoulder to her husband. 'You wanted a pasty, didn't you, love?'

Coming to stand at her side, he slipped an arm around her waist, the other balancing a smiling baby—the twin to the one in his wife's arms. 'Yes, please, and maybe a Bakewell tart for afters?' He grinned up at Libby. 'Everything looks smashing, I could eat the lot.'

Blushing from the compliment, she made herself busy wrapping the ends of the sausage rolls and the pasty in thick paper napkins. 'There you go. Mind your fingers, Michael, they're still quite hot.'

With a serious nod which made the antlers on his head bobble about, Michael took a sausage roll and handed it carefully to his sister. 'Careful, April.' Only once he was sure she wasn't going to drop it, did he reach for his own. 'Thank you, Libby!'

'You're most welcome. I think Noah is up by the pub helping Eliza.'

'We're going there next! Daddy wants some molly wine.'

After perching the baby on the edge of the hut's counter and bracing her in place, Michael's dad dropped his other hand to his son's head, careful not to dislodge his antlers. 'He certainly does!' Turning back to Libby, he reached inside his jacket and pulled out an envelope which he offered to her. 'I don't suppose there's any chance I could leave this for Owen?'

With a lift of one shoulder, she took it from him. 'Sure. I'll stick it inside. I'm going back to get some more stuff out of the warmers anyway.' Curious, she couldn't help but run her fingers along the sides of the A4 envelope to trace the stack of papers inside it.

'Thanks. I was going to post it, but then I wanted to make sure it got to him so decided to hand deliver it instead. Though I suppose I could've just hung onto it as I'll be the one sorting out all that kind of stuff for him soon enough once I'm his office manager.'

The announcement rocked her back on her heels. Owen had recruited an office manager? She knew he'd taken on a few building commissions, though he'd kept the details to himself. An office manager implied something bigger than she'd been envisaging. Something more permanent... 'Really? Oh, wow, that's great news.' Her heart did a funny little flip in her chest. Owen sure was doing a good impression of a man planning on sticking around for the long term.

Beaming, his wife shifted the baby into the crook of her other arm as she reached for her sausage roll. 'It really is. He'll finally be able to give up his taxi job, and I won't have to worry about him out on the roads in the awful weather we've been having. When I see Owen, I'm going to give him a big sloppy kiss. He's not just Michael's hero anymore.' A sheen of moisture glittered in her eyes. 'You've landed yourself a keeper there, Libby, and no mistaking.'

Her husband nudged her hip with his, then gathered their other baby up in his arms. 'If I have to watch you mooning over my new boss all evening, I'll definitely need a glass of molly wine!' He was grinning from ear to ear as he said it. 'Now come on, we've taken up enough of Libby's time.'

'Bye, you guys.' Libby waved as they moved away.

The rest of the afternoon flew past, and the stall was so busy Libby didn't even have time to notice the cold. Even if the work hadn't kept her warm, Owen had made sure she was okay, popping by frequently to bring her one kind of hot drink or another he'd picked up for her and checking the cardboard he'd lined the floor of the hut with was still in place to keep her feet insulated from the cold ground. When she'd told him about the envelope from Michael's dad, he'd shrugged it off like it was no big deal, as though giving an entire family grounds for hope was something he did every day. Maybe it was, for all she knew.

A wave of laughter, cheering and applause rippled its way along the promenade, and Libby slipped from the back door of her hut to worm her way into the crowds gathering along the railing facing the beach. When she caught a glimpse of the little tractor chugging towards them, she too began to laugh and wave. Behind the tractor was a trailer decorated to look like Santa's sleigh, with huge sacks of presents piled around the bearded, red-suited figure of Father Christmas sitting pride of place. Six little brown-clad figures with antlers on their heads waved from the front of the trailer, their bodies linked with a bright red harness. And as for the driver of the tractor…Libby did a double-take then gave a scream of laughter because it was none other than Jack, dressed in an adult-sized version of the kids' costumes and with a bright red flashing stick-on nose. Oh, Lord, how Eliza had talked him into doing that, she'd never know!

Behind the tractor, a crowd of green and red clad pixies shook jingle bells in one hand, while carrying yellow collection buckets in the other. The local Lions club always did something for the local community in the run up to Christmas. The presents in the sacks would be delivered to children stuck in the local hospitals over the holiday period, as well as being donated to refuges and hostels in the area.

The tractor and trailer chugged on towards the far end of the beach, did a slow, wide turn and began to make its way back. Each time it passed a set of steps leading to the promenade, a pair of the pixies peeled off from the group to make their way into the gathered crowd to collect donations. Like the other adults around her, Libby delved into her pocket for a handful of coins to drop into a bucket and received a bright smile and a 'Merry Christmas!' in return.

With a smile on her face, Libby returned to the chip shop and opened the door. It would be dark soon, and the grand switch-on of the lights would begin. With Owen's help—and by help she meant his insistence on doing all the work under her direction—she'd covered the windows and door of the shop with a waterfall cascade of white lights. By blocking any view of the counter, she'd hoped to distract people enough to deter them from thinking the chippy would be opening for business. She crossed her fingers, then flipped the switches on the plug sockets. The inside of the shop glowed from the stunning display in the window.

As she let herself back out, securing the door behind her, she could see lights blinking on up and down the promenade as the other business owners and traders turned on their own window displays. All the colours of the rainbow glittered and flashed for as far as she could see on either side. Oohs and aahs rose from the crowd as they began to stroll once more, pointing and nudging each other as a particular display caught their attention.

Libby resumed her position in her hut just in time to greet an older man and his wife. 'Hello, Mr Wallis, Mrs Wallis. What can

I tempt you with this fine evening?' Mr Wallis had been a fixture on the local council for as many years as Libby could remember, and his wife a stalwart in the WI. They were what her dad had always called properly civic-minded people.

Mr Wallis rubbed his hands together as he surveyed the display. 'Well this all looks very tempting.' His eyes lit up as he spotted one of her handwritten plastic signs. 'Curried chicken? I'll have to give that a go.'

She wrapped the pasty for him then turned to his wife. 'And for you?'

'Oh, one of those lovely looking mince pies, I think.'

Libby handed it over, accepting a handful of change in return. 'There you go. If you like it, I'm taking orders for Christmas.'

Mrs Wallis widened her eyes. 'Are you really? How fantastic. I do prefer homemade, but who has the time these days?' She bit into the pie, and her lashes fluttered for a second. 'My word, that's delicious. Put me down for two dozen. Can I come in and see you next week to sort out the particulars?'

'Absolutely.' Libby scribbled a quick note on the pad under the counter. There was already a gratifyingly long list of names and orders on it.

'Well,' said Mr Wallis with a grin, 'I think it's safe to say that based on this, your new venture will be a roaring success. I must say I wasn't sure when your young man first submitted his planning application, because we've always loved the chip shop. But times move on, and if you're going to be serving delicious fare like this, I know where I'll be coming for my lunch. Merry Christmas to you, Libby!'

Open-mouthed, she watched the Wallises stroll away arm in arm. *Her young man...planning application...* Heedless of the other customers waiting, she dashed out of the back door of the hut, through the chip shop and upstairs to the second floor. Without hesitating, she began to rifle through the folders and documents on Owen's desk. Unfurling and abandoning several

231

sets of plans, she finally found what she was looking for and sank down on the edge of his bed.

There in black and white was a three-storey plan of the building she knew every inch of. Only it looked nothing like the layout she knew like the back of her hand. The ground floor had been opened up into one large space, the kitchen and seating areas divided by a right-angled counter. It was everything she'd imagined, and more besides, as though Owen had somehow reached into her brain and translated her dream into a 3D sketch.

Gone was the higgledy-piggledy jumble of rooms on the first floor, and in their place a sleek, sophisticated layout which flowed seamlessly from living/dining to kitchen and sleeping 'zones'. There was even a tiny rendering of a teddy bear in the smallest of the two bedrooms. Her heart began to pound harder. The second floor had been equally transformed. In place of her own cosy bedroom and the spare room she was currently sitting in was an open-plan one-bed apartment with a short staircase leading up to a roof terrace covered in raised bedding areas and even a soft-play zone.

'Libs? Libby, where are you? Is everything okay?' Owen's shout from below was followed by the thunder of his feet on the stairs. 'What are you doing in here? I came to give you a break, but when the stall was empty I panicked.'

Unable to speak, she simply thrust the plans in her lap towards him. He tilted his head to study them for a moment, the colour draining from his flushed face as he realised what she held. 'I…I can explain.'

'Explain what? How you and Dad have been lying to me for months? How you thought it was okay to leave me in the dark, while I worried and fretted over my future?'

'It's not like that, I swear.' Sinking to his knees beside her, he tried to reach for her hand, but she tugged it out of reach. A weary sigh escaped his lips. 'Look, I promised your dad I wouldn't say anything, and then it all became such a bloody tangle I didn't know what to do for the best. I thought if I could get everything squared away, show you I had it all in hand, then you wouldn't be quite so mad at me.'

He was in for a disappointment then, because she'd never been so angry in all her life. Of all the high-handed, bloody arrogant things he could've possibly done, this had to be the worst. 'What did you think you were doing, Owen? Just because your own family was a disaster, did you think that gave you the right to buy mine lock, stock and fucking barrel? I'm not a toy you can manipulate to fit into this perfect world you've created on a piece of paper. I'm not for bloody sale!' Her hand convulsed, crumpling the plans as she began to sob.

All day long she'd been thinking about him, about the conversation she'd had with Michael's parents and what it had revealed about Owen. She'd even entertained the idea of giving him a second chance, if he'd wanted one after she'd pushed him away. She had imagined them at the Christmas market next year, Owen carrying their own rosy-cheeked baby as they strolled hand in hand between the stalls. She'd thought he'd been sincere about giving her space and time to sort things out, when all the time he'd been going behind her back to lay the trap before her. To put her in a position where she had everything she wanted, but only because he'd made it so.

God, he'd taken it all away from her. All her power and self-determination to build a future for herself robbed with a few strokes of a pen and the money in his pocket. What he'd laid out on the plans clenched in her hands wasn't a partnership, it was a contract of ownership.

Dashing the tears from her eyes, she let the plans fall to the floor at her feet and forced herself to look at Owen. How would he explain it? How did he think he could possibly justify his actions?

He stared back, his dark eyes wide with shock, disbelief and more than a hint of pain. He had a bloody nerve to feel hurt over this when she was the wronged party, but as usual everything was about him. 'Well?' she demanded. 'What have you got to say for yourself?'

'Do you really think I'm trying to buy my way in here?' A shutter fell, blanking his expression as he pushed to his feet. 'If that's what you honestly think of me, there's nothing more I can say to you.' And with that, he turned on his heel and walked out of the room.

The sky outside darkened, cheers rose and faded—marking, she assumed, the grand switch-on of the promenade Christmas lights—and still she sat there on the end of Owen's bed. Her initial anger had faded to disappointment, and then sadness that she'd been proven right in the end not to trust to him. A creak sounded on the steps followed by a gentle tap on the open door. Hating herself for the surge of hope that it might be him creeping back with his tail between his legs, she glanced up to find Eliza watching her from the doorway. 'Owen's up at the farm. He asked me to fetch a few of his clothes and his laptop, that kind of stuff.' She edged into the room. 'Oh, Libs, what happened?'

Pointing the plans on the floor, Libby swallowed down her disappointment. 'That happened.'

Kneeling, Eliza studied the drawings for a few moments before glancing up at her. 'I don't understand.'

A bitter laugh escaped Libby's throat. 'Neither do I as he didn't bother to stay long enough to explain himself, but Owen's the one who's bought this place from my dad.'

'*Owen*? But how? You didn't even tell him it was for sale, so how did he find out? Did he gazump the original buyer, or what?'

All the same questions had been ricocheting around in her brain for the past few hours, none of which she had an answer to. 'You tell me.'

Eliza dropped her eyes back to the plans. 'It looks wonderful. Is...is the upstairs flat supposed to be for your dad?'

Tears filled Libby's eyes. 'I suppose so, not that he'd want to live in it. That's why he's gone to Spain, to find himself somewhere to live.'

'Oh, darling.' Rising on her knees, Eliza wrapped her arms around Libby and held her as she sobbed out all her pain and grief over the loss of what might have been. When she finally quietened, Eliza sat back to regard her. 'You'll have to forgive me for being stupid, but I don't understand why this has caused such a rift between you and Owen. Anyone can see he's absolutely mad for you, and if you didn't already know that yourself, then this surely proves it.' Her hand waved towards the plans. 'Look what he wants for you, Libs. Look how hard he's trying to give you everything you've ever wanted.'

Libby could only shake her head, gobsmacked at her friend's blindness. 'It's not for him to give it to me, don't you see that? I should've been able to do this for myself. I *was* doing it for myself, and he's just swanned in and taken it all over.'

Eliza frowned. 'That doesn't make sense, at all. He's not taking anything from you, he's helping you to achieve your dream.' Her arms came across her chest in a defensive motion. 'Do you think less of me because Jack's building a workshop at the farm for my soap-making and stuff? That I should've waited and struggled on my own rather than adapt my original plans to encompass a better life we can have together? Does it offend your feminist sensibilities that Sam now lives with Beth and their combined income will allow her to expand and experiment the ranges she carries in the emporium because he's now shouldering half the rent and bills?'

Libby stared. 'That's not what I said, not at all. And it's different for you two, you're in love.'

'And you're not?' Eliza snorted. 'Honestly, Libby, you talk nonsense at times. Do you know what I think this is all about? I think you're terrified that Owen will let you down somehow and that's why you broke up with him in the first place. Ever since he moved in here with you, you've been looking for another excuse to push him away, to slam the final nail into the coffin of a relationship you've always assumed was going to fail anyway.'

Anger flared, and beneath it a flash of shame which Libby stuffed back down immediately. 'That's not true! I've bent over backwards to accommodate Owen, to let him be a part of the baby without feeling like I've been trying to trap him into anything. I didn't ask him to do this, I didn't ask for any of this!'

'Ask for what? For a decent, honest, generous man to fall in love with and embrace your accidental pregnancy while barely batting an eyelash? God, Libby, you're so right. Why on earth would you ask for something like that?'

'Shut up! You're twisting my words.' Feeling sick and sad and sorry for herself, Libby stormed out. Shaking, she threw herself down on her own bed. She couldn't bear it. Eliza had never so much as raised her voice at Libby in all the long years they'd known each other, never mind spoken to her in such harsh tones. She didn't understand. Nobody, it seemed, would understand. The tears came, and she let them pull her under.

She didn't know how much time had passed, when Eliza knocked once more. 'I've got Owen's stuff, and I'm going now. I'll lock up and push the key back through the door behind me.'

Too afraid to speak in case either of them said something that might rend the very fabric of their friendship apart, Libby lay silently on her side. A soft sigh reached her ears, then Eliza spoke once more. 'We all love you, Libby, so much. I just wish you could learn to love yourself even half as much as we do.'

Chapter 25

He'd considered leaving town a thousand times in the past few days, and only Eliza's pleading for him to be patient had kept him in the bay at all. Needing something to keep himself from going mad, or from storming down into the town to camp outside Libby's door and beg her to give him another chance, Owen threw himself into the final decoration and renovation works on Sally's cottage. Jack and Eliza were busy with preparations for their first Christmas together, and he hated being the spectre at their otherwise happy feast. When he couldn't stand to be cooped up inside, he took Bastian for long walks over the windswept hills and cliffs surrounding the bay. The Labrador seemed ecstatic at all the attention, and Jack expressed his thanks on more than one occasion for keeping the big dog out from under everyone's feet.

Jack, Eliza and Sally had gone off to Truro in the family Land Rover after lunch for another endless round of Christmas shopping, leaving Owen and the dog to fend for themselves. Not being able to bear being cooped up inside, he clipped on Bastian's lead, shrugged on a thick jacket and headed for yet another walk.

Still feeling a little hollowed out, but better for some fresh air, Owen let himself in through the front door of the farmhouse.

Laughter and chatter echoed down the stone corridor from the kitchen, loud enough, he hoped, to cover his entrance. Not in the mood for conversation, he'd made it a couple of treads upstairs when a voice piping high with excitement froze him mid-step. 'Owen! There you are, you've been gone ages!'

Plastering a smile to his lips, Owen turned to stare down at Noah who was practically vibrating with excitement. 'Hey, Noah. Sorry, I went for a walk and lost track of time. What's all the ruckus?'

Noah clapped his hands together as he did a little dance on the spot. 'Uncle Jack says we can decorate the tree tonight. We were going to start straight after tea, but I wanted to wait for you. Come on!'

Unable to think of a way to refuse without bruising this sweet little boy's ego, Owen took his outstretched hand and allowed Noah to tug him towards the sitting room. Chairs scraped back on the kitchen tiles and Eliza, Jack and his mum followed them into the main family room. A huge pine tree dominated the corner between the window and the Inglenook fireplace, the top branches almost touching the ceiling. 'That's a tree and a half,' Owen said, unable to keep the admiration out of his voice.

'You're telling me,' Jack responded with a cuff to his shoulder. 'Imagine how much fun I had wrestling the bloody thing into place without you here to help me.'

'Sorry, I lost track of time...'

Jack waved his excuse off with a casual gesture. 'Don't sweat it, mate. You've got a lot on your plate, I was only teasing.' Leaning closer, he lowered his voice to make sure he couldn't be overheard. 'Look, I know Noah's keen to have you involved, but don't feel like you have to stay.'

The sympathy in his gaze told Owen some of the bleakness inside him had leached out onto his features. He glanced across at Noah who was kneeling before the tree in a jumble of bright tinsel and felt a glimmer of something good stirring. Perhaps an evening of innocent fun might be just the distraction he needed. 'Thanks, but I'm good,' he said quietly to Jack before raising his voice. 'I've never decorated a Christmas tree before, Noah, so you'll have to tell me what to do.'

Eyes like saucers, Noah stared up at him. 'Not ever? Not even once?'

Owen shook his head. 'Nope. We weren't big on Christmas when I was a kid.'

'Oh, that's very sad.' Noah patted the rug beside him. 'You can sit here with me.'

Ten minutes later, Owen was almost wishing he'd snuck upstairs after all. The string of lights in his lap were even more tangled than when he'd first taken them from the cardboard box of decorations—though how that was even possible, he had no idea.

'Here, I'll swap you.' He looked up to see Eliza extending a bottle of beer in his direction.

'Thank you, God,' he muttered to her laughter. Checking behind him to make sure none of the five hundred baubles Noah had tipped from the box was at risk of getting smashed, Owen scooted back until his shoulders rested against the edge of the sofa. Plonking down next to him, Eliza crossed her legs then tugged the tangled mass from his lap into hers.

He watched for a few moments as her clever, nimble fingers tugged and teased the first section of lights into a neat, straight row. 'How do you do that?'

With a glint in her eye, she grinned at him. 'Magic.' She pointed to a section of the wire. 'Hold it there so that bit doesn't get snarled up again.'

Her bossy tone amused him no end. 'Yes, ma'am.' She flashed him a quick look then bent her head back to her task.

Sally switched on the television and scrolled through the music stations until she found one playing non-stop Christmas videos.

Grabbing Noah by the hand she boogied on the spot to 'Rockin' Around the Christmas Tree'.

'You've been hiding those moves from us, Mum,' Jack said with a grin as he attempted to herd the baubles into a neat pile before they fell victim to some very enthusiastic jiving.

'You don't know the half of it!'

The little glimmer inside Owen continued to grow as he watched their antics and a strong sense of rightness settled in his heart. He didn't need the Blackmores and all their darkness and unhappy secrets, he needed this. To be surrounded by good friends who might one day become more to him than that. He'd have to find a way to heal the rift between him and Libby to do so, and he still wasn't sure he could forgive her.

As though reading his thoughts, Eliza gave his elbow a nudge. 'Have you seen her?'

He shook his head. 'Didn't seem to be much point.'

Shoving the tangle of lights aside, Eliza curled her knees up under her chin and his heart lurched at the familiarity of the pose. 'I know she hurt you, but you should try and see things from her point of view.'

Biting his lip against the urge to demand why it shouldn't be Libby trying to see things from his side, he settled for a grunt which was clearly enough of a cue for Eliza to continue. 'Libby's never had anything of her own—not really. Though she'll tell you until she's blue in the face it was her choice to stay in the bay, there was never any way she was going to leave her dad. They grew so close after her mum died, and I know the thought of leaving him alone was impossible for her to comprehend, so she convinced herself that everything was of her choosing.

'I don't think she'd ever allowed herself ambitions of her own, not that she was willing to admit, at least, and then she saw Beth making a go of things with the emporium and I think it stirred up a need in her. The teashop would be her *thing*, a way to prove to herself, and everybody else, that there was more about her than mad hair and an ability to sling chips into hot fat six nights a week.'

'She's much more than that.' Owen was unable to hold back the protestation from spilling forth.

Eliza patted his knee. 'I know that, and you know that, but Libby's always allowed other people to define her by the image she projects. If she looks like a misfit, and acts like a misfit then nobody can see the little girl inside still lost and broken after all these years. With this new dream of hers, she was taking her first steps out from beneath the shadows of the past…'

Realisation dawned. 'And I took it from her, just like she said. She let me see behind the mask, and I betrayed her trust by lying to her from the start. I thought if I gave her everything she wanted, she'd see I was in it for the long haul, but instead I ruined it because now she thinks I think she couldn't manage to get it for herself.' Owen's head dropped back against the sofa cushion. 'I've been such a bloody fool.'

Chapter 26

The wind howled under the eaves of her bedroom window, sending Libby burrowing deeper beneath the layers of quilts and blankets piled upon her bed. She couldn't seem to get warm, despite her fleecy pyjamas and a thick pair of her dad's old walking socks which came to her knees. Every time she got close to dropping off, the wind would rattle her window, or a creak would sound from somewhere inside the house, sending her ears straining. The familiar noises had never bothered her before, nor had sleeping alone in the house, but it wasn't fear that kept her tossing and turning—it was hope. Hope that the next creak would be the pressure of a footfall on the steps rather than the beams shifting and settling in the storm.

Idiot.

Bashing her pillow into some semblance of comfort, Libby turned on her side and curled her legs up tight, trying to keep within the little cocoon of warmth her body had created beneath the sheets. She lay there unblinking for five more minutes before throwing off her covers with a sigh. Perhaps some hot chocolate would warm her up enough to sleep. Having settled the quilts back down to try and keep the heat trapped beneath them, she shoved her arms into the sleeves of her black fuzzy dressing gown and padded from the room. She only made it as far as the landing before stopping, her eyes drawn to the half-open door of what had been Owen's room like iron filings to a magnet.

Forget about him. Unheeding of her brain's silent demand, Libby pushed open the door and switched on the light. She hadn't been in here since the night of her row with Eliza and there were still clothes spilling out from the chest of drawers, still papers scattered over the old desk in the corner from her friend's hurried attempts at packing. After two weeks of stubborn silence, it was clear to Libby that Owen would not be returning. She should sort out the rest of his stuff and arrange for it to be dropped at the farm. Thanks to her insomnia, now seemed a good a time as any.

Refusing to question her motives, she spent the next fifteen or twenty minutes emptying the drawers and folding his remaining clothes into neat piles. She refused to think about how good he'd looked in the navy T-shirt she was refolding for the fourth time, how the stark lines of his tattoo had poked from beneath the edge of the sleeve, revealing that little hint of the dark, rough youth who lurked under the shiny veneer of arrogance Owen wore like a second skin. The old grey jumper beneath her fingers was just a lump of wool, not a heated reminder of the last time they'd been together in the hut. She didn't long to go back to that afternoon, when they'd been nothing more than carefree lovers without a clue of how fate would turn their lives upside down.

Abandoning the clothes—and the bittersweet memories trapped between their folds—she moved towards the bed. The covers still sat in a rumpled heap at the bottom, where he'd kicked them away on the morning of the Christmas market, she supposed, and one of the pillows remained on the floor knocked there in his haste to be up and about. Bending, she picked up the pillow and spotted a notepad lying half-hidden beneath the edge of the bed. Thinking to place it on the desk with his other paperwork, she picked it up and the words on the page caught her eye.

Dear K.B.

It's the start of the Christmas market today, and there's so much to do. Your mum will be selling her stuff for the first time, and I know it's going to be a huge success. I'll have to keep an eye on her, make sure she doesn't do too much, you know how stubborn she can be! I wonder what it'll be like to show you all the Christmas lights and decorations for the first time. I can't wait to find out what makes you smile.

Love, Daddy x

Choked, Libby read the note through twice more, then began leafing back through the pages. The first half of the notebook was filled with similar little letters, and she had to blink back her tears to be able to scan through this secret world filled with Owen's observations and wishes for their baby. Half in a dream, she wandered back towards her room and settled herself on the window seat beneath the old blanket her mum had knitted whilst carrying Libby. With trembling fingers, she turned to the very first entry.

Dear K.B.

I saw you for the first time today. Not that I could make head or tail of you until your mum showed me. You looked like a kidney bean all curled up around yourself, so that's what I'm going to call you until we meet properly—K.B.

You should've seen your mum tonight, she looked magnificent. I've always loved her hair, even when it was bright bloody pink, but there was something sophisticated about her tonight, like a glimpse of the woman who's been hiding beneath the girl. If she ever lets the rest of the world see her the way I do, she'll conquer it the way she's conquered me.

244

I can't wait for you to meet her, I know you're going to love her just as much as she will you, and that won't even come close to how much I love both of you. I'm lying here in bed, wondering how I ended up this lucky.

I'm going to give you everything you need, no matter how worried I am right now of mucking things up—of mucking you up. I'd pull down the moon if you asked me to, and all the stars too. It scares me to think there's no ends I won't go to to make sure you're happy. You're only a shadowy image in a photo, a little ripple under your mum's skin, and already I'd burn the world to keep you safe.

You're everything to me, and so is she. I'll <u>always</u> keep you safe.

Love, Daddy x

A tear plopped onto the page, and Libby quickly brushed it away, catching her nail in the tiny hole Owen had scored through the page from repeatedly underlining the word 'always'. Holding the notepad close to her chest, she rested her forehead on the ice-cold pane of the window. 'Oh, bloody hell, Owen. Now what am I supposed to do about you?' The wind had dropped, bathing the empty promenade in an eerie silence, and to her astonishment a snowflake fluttered past the window. It almost never snowed in Lavender Bay; they weren't on the right latitude for something like that, or so her dad tried to explain to her once when she'd bemoaned the lack as a child. Another flake drifted past, and then a third until soon the world beyond her window was obscured by a thick floating curtain of white.

Hours later, she was still locked in the same position, eyes fixed on the excited children running up and down the promenade, laughing parents following in their wake. The snow hadn't lasted long and had left barely enough of a covering for them to scrounge up more than a snowball or two, but they didn't seem to care. The image should've given her joy, but all it did was drive home what might never be for her and Owen, and their own little one.

A creak upon the stairs disturbed her. She was ready to dismiss it as one more phantom shift of the old building, when it came again, and she was up off the window seat like a jack springing from his box. Heedless of the pins and needles, she ran on numb feet out onto the landing and stopped short.

'Hello, Libby-girl. Aren't you a sight for sore eyes?'

'Dad? What are you doing here? I thought you were planning on staying with Aunty Val until after Christmas.' He looked leaner than when she'd seen him last, and not just from the deep tan toning his skin to a golden brown. The softening line of his jaw from the beginnings of a double-chin had smoothed out, and the thick jumper didn't cling quite so much around the middle.

Looking shame-faced and thoroughly miserable, Mick Stone shook his head. 'I couldn't stand it there another minute more. I tried, lovey, Lord knows I tried, but I hated every minute of it.'

'What? But I thought Spain was what you wanted?'

He sighed and shook his head again. 'So did I, but it turns out being away from the places that remind me of your mum was worse than being close to them. And, apart from all that, I missed my girl so hard it nearly broke my heart. Can you forgive me for making such a hash of everything?'

'Oh, Dad.' Libby flung herself into his arms, clinging like a limpet to the familiar rock of his sturdy frame. Glancing up at him through her lashes, she managed to laugh through her tears. 'Why didn't you come home straight away, if you hated it so much?'

The tips of his ears turned pink. 'After making such a bloody song and dance about it, it didn't seem right to come slinking home with my tail between my legs.' He sighed. 'Blame the stubborn, foolish pride of a silly old man.'

'Well, I'm glad you came back. Hopefully, we can put all this nonsense behind us for now, as long as you stop trying to force me to leave here, that is.'

Mick's brow creased into a deep frown. 'It won't be me forcing you from here, lovey, but it might be beyond my powers to let you stay.' He bit his lip and she could tell he was wondering how to tell her the truth.

'It's all right, Dad. I know about your deal with Owen.'

'You do? Well that's a relief, I must say, as I was dreading how I was going to tell you.' With gentle fingers he tipped up her chin. 'Oh, dear. It's not all right, is it?'

She closed her eyes against the sting of yet more tears. 'Not even close. You're not the only one in this family to let their stubborn pride get in the way.' Moisture spilled over her closed lashes and down her cheeks.

'Come here, lovey,' her dad said, pulling her tight against him once more. 'Come on now, we'll sort it all out somehow, I promise.'

Clinging to him, Libby prayed it would be true.

Chapter 27

'I'll get it,' Owen yelled towards the sitting room as he reached the bottom of the stairs just as the front doorbell rang. Balancing the small stack of presents he'd just been up to retrieve in one arm, he tugged open the front door with the other. 'You're just in time,' he said, expecting it to be Beth, Sam and his folks come to join the gift unwrapping.

'Hello, Owen, Merry Christmas.' Looking like a candy cane in a red and white striped tunic-dress over bright green leggings tucked into a pair of scruffy-looking Ugg boots, the love of his absolute life gave him a sweet smile.

His heart turned over, and he might not have kept hold of the presents under his arm had Mick not reached past his daughter to steady them with a beefy hand. 'All right, son? Do you need a hand with those?'

'No, no, I've got them. When did you get back, Mick?'

'A few days ago. Got sick of paella and sunshine, but I wasn't expecting this to be waiting for me.' He gestured over his shoulder at the white fields beyond. It had been snowing on and off for the past forty-eight hours, sending Noah into paroxysms of joy over his first white Christmas.

'That wasn't all you weren't expecting, was it, Dad?' Libby said with a chuckle as she laid a tender hand on the roundness beneath her dress.

'Indeed.' Mick shot Owen a gimlet stare which told him there was much more to be said on the subject at a later time.

'Well, you'd better come in, then.' He stepped back to let them in, and they'd just crossed the threshold when a car horn announced the arrival of the Barnes family together with Beth. Soon the hallway was a roiling chaos of hugs and kisses as Jack, Eliza and Sally came out to greet everyone.

Noah bounced from group to group, peering inside carrier bags, excitement growing to fever pitch as he received assurance after assurance that yes, there were presents for him, too. Making his escape, Owen headed for the sitting room to deposit his own stack beneath the already impressive pile beneath the tree.

Everyone filed in, the older members of the group finding seats on the sofa and chairs whilst the rest of them made do with any old space they could find on the floor. Sam and Jack positioned themselves beneath the tree and began to pass out gifts.

To no one's surprise, and everyone's delight, the majority of the presents were for Noah. Owen hadn't been the only one conscious of it being the boy's first Christmas without his dad and had gone out of their way to find him things to keep his mind on happier thoughts. The pile of discarded wrapping paper grew and grew until Eliza excused herself to return with a black rubbish bag.

Pleased with his own little stack of toiletries, a new laptop bag from Sam and Beth who'd noted the fraying strap on his old one, and—Hallelujah!—socks, Owen gave Eliza a smile as he shoved the wrapping paper from them into the bag as she held it out to him.

'Not a bad haul,' she said. 'And thank you for the ribbons, I'll be able to put them to good use.' Uncertain what to get for her, he'd found a craft shop in town and purchased a selection of wide metallic ribbons in various shades of purple.

'I thought they'd be handy for decorating your little bags of lavender, and whatnot.'

'They're perfect,' she assured him, before moving on.

As she stepped to one side, his eyes caught a flash of red and white as Libby turned to laugh at something her dad had said. She was curled up at his feet, her knees tucked beneath her chin, the dress stretched over them and almost down to her ankles. He flicked his gaze to the pile of presents beside her. There were no gifts from him, as there were no gifts from her in the stack next to his knee. He hadn't known to expect her, had assumed she was coming only for lunch as previously agreed so he'd left the things he'd bought for her upstairs. She'd known he would be here, though, so what did it mean that she'd missed him out? He rubbed at the sudden pain over his heart. Nothing good, he warranted.

'How about coffee and mince pies?' Sally announced as she stood.

'What a good idea, I'll lend you a hand.' Annie jumped up next. 'Come on, Paul.'

'All right, love, I'm coming.' Her husband heaved himself to his feet. 'Pops, you want to stretch your legs for a bit?'

'That's a good idea, son. This cold weather does my joints no good at all.'

'I'll give you a hand, Pops.' Sam was on his feet in an instant. 'Hey, Noah, why don't you bring your helicopter outside and we can give it a test flight without risking your Nanna's china?'

'Can we, Uncle Jack?'

'Don't see why not. But put your wellies and your coat on first.'

Before Owen's eyes, the room emptied as one after another everyone left with seemingly plausible excuses for their departure. Soon the only people left were him and Libby. 'Well, that was subtle,' she said with a sigh.

'You arranged that?'

She rolled her eyes heavenward. 'I didn't expect them all to tumble out on top of each other, though. I'd hoped they'd space it out a bit so it didn't look quite so obvious.' With a ruffle of her fingers through her thick fringe, she flicked her eyes towards the tree and then back to him. 'There's something left.'

Following where she'd looked, Owen spotted a large red envelope propped up beneath the lowest branches of the tree. His heart might have stopped beating for a moment or two. 'For me?' She nodded, and a hint of scarlet glowed on her cheeks.

On hands and knees, he scooted across and retrieved the envelope. With one more quick glance at Libby, he slit the flap open with a finger and pulled out a thick white card. Turning it over, he found his hands were shaking as he studied the riot of glittering teddy bears romping over the front of the Christmas card. The words *Daddy's First Christmas* were inscribed across a winding ribbon held up in the bears' paws.

Swallowing a lump the size of a rock, he flipped the card open and started to read.

Dear Daddy,

I know it's not officially our first Christmas together, but I couldn't wait to tell you how much Mummy and I love you. We're so excited for all the lovely plans you've got in store for us. I'm especially excited about seeing all the pretty fairy lights with you, and to sleep in my new bedroom knowing you and Mummy will be next door to keep me safe.

I can't wait to meet you, either. I just know you'll be the best Daddy in the whole wide world.

Love,

K.B. x

'Oh, shit,' Owen croaked through the tears coursing down his face, before he clamped a hand over his mouth. 'I shouldn't swear anymore, should I?'

Laughing through her own tears, Libby crawled over to his side. 'You've got a few months yet before you have to worry about tiny ears hearing you. And I'm sure getting all those conversion works done in time will make us both swear a time or two before we're finished.'

He grabbed her shoulders, terrified he was dreaming, that he would wake up any second and find himself alone and staring at the ceiling as he had on far too many recent mornings. 'Don't say it unless you mean it, Libs. If this is some kind of joke, it'll break my heart.'

Twining her arms around his neck, she crawled up into his lap. 'No joke, Owen. Not about something as important as the rest of our lives together.'

'Together?' He could hardly bring himself to breathe the word against her lips.

'Forever.' She kissed him. 'You.' Kiss. 'Me.' Kiss. 'And K.B.' Kiss.

'Oh, and me and all,' came Mick's deep voice from the doorway followed by roars of laughter.

Holding Libby firmly in place, Owen turned to look at the group of once strangers who'd first become friends and then his family beaming back. 'There's always a downside to everything,' he said, to another round of hoots and hollers.

Epilogue

Five women stood side by side leaning on the iron railing that ran along the edge of the prom. 'Look at the bloody state of them,' Annie Barnes said with a shake of her head.

'I've never seen anything like it,' Sally replied from the opposite end of their little row.

'We could pretend we don't know them,' Beth offered.

'I think Jack looks rather fetching, actually.' They all turned to stare at Eliza, making her snort with laughter. 'Had you going there for a moment. He looks even more ridiculous than the rest of them.'

Their eyes returned to the spectacle before them. As far as the eye could see, the sand was covered in fairies. Short ones, tall ones, fat ones, thin ones. Even Libby squinted at Pops, one in thermal long johns and a flat cap. One of the fairies, taller than most and dressed in nothing more than a pink tutu over black swimming trunks and a pair of iridescent wings strapped to his back, waved and blew her a kiss before adjusting the sparkling pink tiara perched proudly on the top of his close-cropped hair. 'What's to be done with them?' she sighed.

'There's nothing to be done, love. You're going to have to accept you've hitched your wagon to an absolute lunatic like the rest of us,' was Annie's sage advice.

'So it would seem.'

A whistle blew on the beach below drawing the chattering, shivering fairies into closer order. 'Are you ready?' a voice bellowed through a megaphone to a roar of cheers.

'Five...four...'

'Three...two...one.' The five women joined all the other spectators lining the prom in the countdown before 200 fairies—and one barking chocolate Labrador with a tutu of his own wrapped around his middle—ran whooping and shrieking into the sea. The Lavender Bay Annual Boxing Day charity swim was well and truly underway.

Some barely made it into the shallows before they dashed back up the beach to find their towels and warm clothes, but others, hardier—or just plain foolish—went all the way in and began to swim. Eyes fixed on a bobbing pink tiara, Libby lowered her hand to cover the little bump hidden beneath the layers of jumpers and coats Owen had bundled her into that morning. 'That's your Daddy, that is,' she whispered.

Cosy and warm inside her, a little flutter of movement responded.

Acknowledgements

So here we are on our final visit to Lavender Bay, and it's an emotional one. It's hard to express how much these wonderful characters all mean to me, and it means the world to me when people take the time to let me know how much they've enjoyed reading about them. From her very first appearance in *Spring at Lavender Bay*, Libby stole my heart and quickly became a favourite of many readers. The pressure was on when writing *Snowflakes* to give her a hero worthy of her huge heart, and I hope you agree that Owen fits the bill.

To my husband. This book would literally not have been finished without you. Thank you for taking care of me during those final frantic days as I tried to pull this book together. Love you, bun x

The other person who always goes above and beyond for me is my lovely editor, Charlotte Mursell. Your boundless enthusiasm and support are appreciated more than I can say. I'm so excited that we can continue to work together – *Bluebell Castle*, here we come!

Everyone at HQ Digital who helps behind the scenes, from designing my beautiful covers to production, publicity, distribution and beyond – thank you all x

To Rachel Burton for reading all my manic messages, random texts and muppet flails. Thanks for not blocking me! x

And, finally, to all my wonderful readers. You make this possible, and I am living my best life because of your support. Thank you xx

Dear Reader,

Thank you so much for taking the time to read this book – we hope you enjoyed it! If you did, we'd be so appreciative if you left a review.

Here at HQ Digital we are dedicated to publishing fiction that will keep you turning the pages into the early hours. We publish a variety of genres, from heartwarming romance, to thrilling crime and sweeping historical fiction.

To find out more about our books, enter competitions and discover exclusive content, please join our community of readers by following us at:

🐦 *@HQDigitalUK*

🇫 *facebook.com/HQDigitalUK*

Are you a budding writer? We're also looking for authors to join the HQ Digital family! Please submit your manuscript to:

HQDigital@harpercollins.co.uk.

Hope to hear from you soon!

Turn the page for an exclusive extract from *Sunrise at Butterfly Cove*, the first novel in the enchanting Butterfly Cove series…

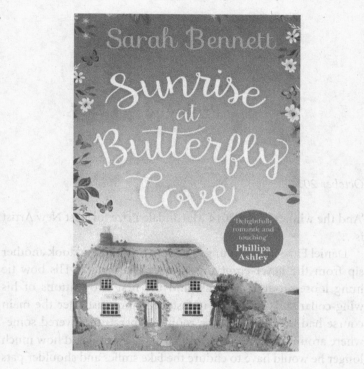

Prologue

October 2014

'And the winner of the 2014 Martindale Prize for Best New Artist is…'

Daniel Fitzwilliams lounged back in his chair and took another sip from the never-emptying glass of champagne. His bow tie hung loose around his neck, and the first two buttons of his wing-collar shirt had been unfastened since just after the main course had been served. The room temperature hovered somewhere around the fifth circle of hell and he wondered how much longer he would have to endure the fake smiles and shoulder pats from strangers passing his table.

The MC made a big performance of rustling the large silver envelope in his hand. 'Get on with it, mate,' Daniel muttered. His agent, Nigel, gave him a smile and gulped at the contents of his own glass. His nomination had been a huge surprise and no one expected him to win, Daniel least of all.

'Well, well.' The MC adjusted his glasses and peered at the card he'd finally wrestled free. 'I am delighted to announce that the winner of the Martindale Prize is Fitz, for his series "Interactions".'

A roar of noise from the rest of his tablemates covered the

choking sounds of Nigel inhaling half a glass of champagne. Daniel's own glass slipped from his limp fingers and rolled harmlessly under the table. 'Bugger me.'

'Go on, mate. Get up there!' His best friend, Aaron, rounded the table and tugged Daniel to his feet. 'I told you, I bloody told you, but you wouldn't believe me.'

Daniel wove his way through the other tables towards the stage, accepting handshakes and kisses from all sides. Will Spector, the bookies' favourite and the art crowd's latest darling, raised a glass in toast and Daniel nodded to acknowledge his gracious gesture. Flashbulbs popped from all sides as he mounted the stairs to shake hands with the MC. He raised the sinuous glass trophy and blinked out at the clapping, cheering crowd of his peers.

The great and the good were out in force. The Martindale attracted a lot of press coverage and the red-carpet winners and losers would be paraded across the inside pages for people to gawk at over their morning cereal. His mum had always loved to see the celebrities in their posh frocks. He just wished she'd survived long enough to see her boy come good. Daniel swallowed around the lump in his throat. *Fuck cancer.* Dad had at least made it to Daniel's first exhibition, before his heart failed and he'd followed his beloved Nancy to the grave.

Daniel adjusted the microphone in front of him and waited for the cheers to subside. The biggest night of his life, and he'd never felt lonelier.

Mia Sutherland resisted the urge to check her watch and tried to focus on the flickering television screen. The latest episode of *The Watcher* would normally have no trouble in holding her attention—it was her and Jamie's new favourite show. She glanced at the empty space on the sofa beside her. Even with the filthy weather outside, he should have been home before now. Winter had hit earlier than usual, and she'd found herself turning the lights on mid-afternoon to try and dispel the gloom caused by the raging storm outside.

The ad break flashed upon the screen and she popped into the kitchen to give the pot of stew a quick stir. She'd given up waiting, and eaten her portion at 8.30, but there was plenty left for Jamie. He always said she cooked for an army rather than just the two of them.

A rattle of sleet struck the kitchen window and Mia peered through the Venetian blind covering it; he'd be glad of a hot meal after being stuck in the traffic for so long. A quick tap of the wooden spoon against the side of the pot, and then she slipped the cast-iron lid back on. The pot was part of the *Le Creuset* set Jamie's parents had given them as a wedding gift and the matching pans hung from a wooden rack above the centre of the kitchen worktop. She slid the pot back into the oven and adjusted the temperature down a notch.

Ding-dong.

At last! Mia hurried down the hall to the front door and tugged it open with a laugh. 'Did you forget your keys—' A shiver of fear ran down her back at the sight of the stern-looking policemen standing on the step. Rain dripped from the brims of their caps and darkened the shoulders of their waterproof jackets.

'Mrs Sutherland?'

No, no, no, no. Mia looked away from the sympathetic expressions and into the darkness beyond them for the familiar flash of Jamie's headlights turning onto their small driveway.

'Perhaps we could come in, Mrs Sutherland?' The younger of the pair spoke this time.

Go away. Go away. She'd seen this scene played out enough on the television to know what was coming next. 'Please, come in.' Her voice sounded strange, high-pitched and brittle to her ears. She stepped back to let the two men enter. 'Would you like a cup of tea?'

The younger officer took off his cap and shrugged out of his jacket. 'Why don't you point me in the direction of the kettle and you and Sergeant Stone can make yourselves comfortable in the front room?'

Mia stared at the Sergeant's grim-set features. *What a horrible job he has, poor man.* 'Yes, of course. Come on through.'

She stared at the skin forming on the surface of her now-cold tea. She hadn't dared to lift the cup for fear they would see how badly she was shaking. 'Is there someone you'd like us to call?' PC Taylor asked, startling her. The way he phrased the question made her wonder how many times he'd asked before she'd heard him. *I'd like you to call my husband.*

Mia bit her lip against the pointless words, and ran through a quick inventory in her head. Her parents would be useless; it was too far past cocktail hour for her mother to be coherent and her dad didn't do emotions well at the best of times.

Her middle sister, Kiki, had enough on her hands with the new baby and Matty determined to live up to every horror story ever told about the terrible twos. Had it only been last week she and Jamie had babysat Matty because the baby had been sick? An image of Jamie holding their sleeping nephew in his lap rose unbidden and she shook her head sharply to dispel it. She couldn't think about things like that. Not right then.

The youngest of her siblings, Nee, was neck-deep in her final year at art school in London. Too young and too far away to be shouldering the burden of her eldest sister's grief. The only person she wanted to talk to was Jamie and that would never happen again. Bile burned in her throat and a whooping sob escaped before she could swallow it back.

'S-sorry.' She screwed her eyes tight and stuffed everything down as far as she could. There would be time enough for tears. Opening her stinging eyes, she looked at Sergeant Stone. 'Do Bill and Pat know?'

'Your in-laws? They're next on our list. I'm so very sorry, pet. Would you like us to take you over there?'

Unable to speak past the knot in her throat, Mia nodded.

Chapter 1

February 2016

Daniel rested his head on the dirty train window and stared unseeing at the landscape as it flashed past. He didn't know where he was going. Away. That was the word that rattled around his head. Anywhere, nowhere. Just away from London. Away from the booze, birds and fakery of his so-called celebrity lifestyle. Twenty-nine felt too young to be a has-been.

He'd hit town with a portfolio, a bundle of glowing recommendations and an ill-placed confidence in his own ability to keep his feet on the ground. Within eighteen months, he was *the next big thing* in photography and everyone who was anyone clamoured for an original Fitz image on their wall. Well-received exhibitions had led to private commissions and more money than he knew what to do with. And if it hadn't been for Aaron's investment advice, his bank account would be as drained as his artistic talent.

The parties had been fun at first, and he couldn't put his finger on when the booze had stopped being a buzz and started being a crutch. Girls had come and gone. Pretty, cynical women who liked being seen on his arm in the gossip columns, and didn't seem to mind being in his bed.

Giselle had been one such girl, and without any active consent on his part, she'd installed herself as a permanent fixture. The bitter smell of the French cigarettes she lived on in lieu of a decent meal filled his memory, forcing Daniel to swallow convulsively against the bile in his throat. That smell signified everything he hated about his life, about himself. Curls of rank smoke had hung like fog over the sprawled bodies, spilled bottles and overflowing ashtrays littering his flat when he'd woven a path through them that morning.

The cold glass of the train window eased the worst of his thumping hangover, although no amount of water seemed able to ease the parched feeling in his throat. The carriage had filled, emptied and filled again, the ebb and flow of humanity reaching their individual destinations.

Daniel envied their purpose. He swigged again from the large bottle of water he'd paid a small fortune for at Paddington Station as he'd perused the departures board. The taxi driver he'd flagged down near his flat had told him Paddington would take him west, a part of England that he knew very little about, which suited him perfectly.

His first instinct had been to head for King's Cross, but that would have taken him north. Too many memories, too tempting to visit old haunts his mam and dad had taken him to. It would be sacrilege to their memory to tread on the pebbled beaches of his youth, knowing how far he'd fallen from being the man his father had dreamed he would become.

He'd settled upon Exeter as a first destination. Bristol and Swindon seemed too industrial, too much like the urban sprawl he wanted to escape. And now he was on a local branch line train to Orcombe Sands. Sands meant the sea. The moment he'd seen the name, he knew it was where he needed to be. Air he could breathe, the wind on his face, nothing on the horizon but white-caps and seagulls.

The train slowed and drew to a stop as it had done numerous

264

times previously. Daniel didn't stir; the cold window felt too good against his clammy forehead. He was half aware of a small woman rustling an enormous collection of department store carrier bags as she carted her shopping haul past his seat, heading towards the exit. She took a couple of steps past him before she paused and spoke.

'This is the end of the line, you know?' Her voice carried a warm undertone of concern and Daniel roused. The thump in his head increased, making him frown as he regarded the speaker. She was an older lady, around the age his mam would've been had she still been alive.

Her grey hair was styled in a short, modern crop and she was dressed in that effortlessly casual, yet stylish look some women had. A soft camel jumper over dark indigo jeans with funky bright red trainers on her feet. A padded pea jacket and a large handbag worn cross body, keeping her hands free to manage her shopping bags. She smiled brightly at Daniel and tilted her head towards the carriage doors, which were standing stubbornly open.

'This is Orcombe Sands. Pensioner jail. Do not pass go, do not collect two hundred pounds.' She laughed at her own joke and Daniel finally realised what she was telling him. He had to get off the train; this was his destination. She was still watching him expectantly, so he cleared his throat.

'Oh, thanks. Sorry I was miles away.' He rose as he spoke, unfurling his full height as the small woman stepped back to give him room to stand and tug his large duffel bag from the rack above his seat. Seemingly content that Daniel was on the move, the woman gave him a cheery farewell and disappeared off the train.

Adjusting the bag on his shoulder as he looked around, Daniel perused the layout of the station for the first time. The panoramic sweep of his surroundings didn't take long. The tiny waiting room needed a lick of paint, but the platform was clean of the rubbish and detritus that had littered the Central London station he'd started his journey at several hours previously. A hand-painted, slightly lopsided *Exit* sign pointed his way and Daniel moved in the only direction available to him, hoping to find some signs of life and a taxi rank.

He stopped short in what he supposed was the main street and regarded the handful of houses and a pub, which was closed up tight on the other side of the road. He looked to his right and regarded a small area of hardstanding with a handful of cars strewn haphazardly around.

The February wind tugged hard at his coat and he flipped the collar up, hunching slightly to keep his ears warm.

Daniel started to regret his spur-of-the-moment decision to leave town. He'd been feeling stale for a while, completely lacking in inspiration. Every image he framed in his mind's eye seemed either trite or derivative. All he'd ever wanted to do was take photographs. From the moment his parents had given him his first disposable camera to capture his holiday snaps, Daniel had wanted to capture the world he saw through his viewfinder.

An engine grumbled to life and the noise turned Daniel's thoughts outwards again as a dirty estate car crawled out of the car park and stopped in front of him. The side window lowered and the woman from the train leaned across from the driver's side to speak to him.

'You all right there? Is someone coming to pick you up?' Daniel shuffled his feet slightly under the blatantly interested gaze of the older woman.

His face warmed as he realised he would have to confess his predicament to the woman. He had no idea where he was or what his next move should be. He could tell from the way she was regarding him that she would not leave until she knew he was going to be all right.

'My trip was a bit spur-of-the-moment. Do you happen to know if there is a B&B nearby?' he said, trying to keep his voice light, as though heading off into the middle of nowhere on a freezing winter's day was a completely rational, normal thing to do.

The older woman widened her eyes slightly. 'Not much call for that this time of year. Just about everywhere that offers accommodation is seasonal and won't be open until Easter time.'

Daniel started to feel like an even bigger fool as the older woman continued to ponder his problem, her index finger tapping against her lip. The finger paused as a sly smile curled one corner of her lip and Daniel wondered if he should be afraid of whatever thought had occurred to cause that expression.

He took a backwards step as the woman suddenly released her seat belt and climbed out of the car in a determined manner. He was not intimidated by someone a foot shorter than him. *He wasn't.*

'What's your name?' she asked as she flipped open the boot of the car and started transferring her shopping bags onto the back seat.

'Fitz…' He paused. That name belonged in London, along with everything else he wanted to leave behind. 'Daniel. Daniel Fitzwilliams.'

'Pleased to meet you. I'm Madeline although my friends call me Mads and I have a feeling we will be great friends. Stick your bag in the boot, there's a good lad. I know the perfect place. Run by a friend of mine. I'm sure you'll be very happy there.'

Daniel did as bid, his eyes widening in shock as *unbelievable!* Madeline propelled him in the right direction with a slap on the arse and a loud laugh.

'Bounce a coin on those cheeks, Daniel! I do so like a man who takes care of himself.' With another laugh, Madeline disappeared into the front seat of the car and the engine gave a slightly startled whine as she turned the key.

Gritting his teeth, he placed his bag in the boot before moving around to the front of the car and eyeing the grubby interior of the estate, which appeared to be mainly held together with mud and rust. He folded his frame into the seat, which had been hiked forward almost as far as it could. With his knees up around his ears, Daniel fumbled under the front of the seat until he found the adjuster and carefully edged the seat back until he felt less like a sardine.

'Belt up, there's a good boy,' Madeline trilled as she patted his knee and threw the old car into first. They lurched away from the kerb. Deciding that a death grip was the only way to survive, Daniel quickly snapped his seat belt closed, scrabbled for the aptly named *oh shit!* handle above the window and tried to decide whether the journey would be worse with his eyes open or closed.

Madeline barrelled the car blithely around the narrow country lanes, barely glancing at the road as far as Daniel could tell as she sang along to the latest pop tunes pouring from the car radio. He tried not to whimper at the thought of where he was going to end up. What the hell was this place going to be like if it was run by a friend of Madeline's? If there was a woman in a rocking chair at the window, he'd be in deep shit.

The car abruptly swung off to the left and continued along what appeared to be a footpath rather than any kind of road. A huge building loomed to the left and Daniel caught his breath. Rather than the Bates Motel, it was more of a Grand Lady in her declining years. In its heyday, it must have been a magnificent structure. The peeling paint, filthy windows and rotting porch did their best to hide the beauty, together with the overgrown gardens.

His palms itched and for the first time in forever, Daniel felt excited. He wanted his camera. Head twisting and turning, he tried to take everything in. A group of outbuildings and a large barn lay to the right of where Madeline pulled to a stop on the gravel driveway.

Giving a jaunty toot on the car's horn, she wound down her window to wave and call across the yard to what appeared to be a midget yeti in the most moth-eaten dressing gown Daniel had ever seen. *Not good, not good, oh so not good…*

Don't miss *Spring Skies over Bluebell Castle*, the next book from Sarah Bennett, coming in March 2019!

If you enjoyed *Snowflakes at Lavender Bay*, then why not try another delightfully uplifting romance from HQ Digital?